Out of Time Series

Gabrielle

Debra Rard Ledford

Re-edited First Edition

The characters and events in this book are fictional and purely a work of the author's imagination. Any resemblance to actual persons or events is unintentional.

Depending on the time period, scripture quotations are taken from either the New International Version or the King James Version of the Bible.

Cover Design by Selfpubbookcovers.com/RLSather

Copyright 2016
Debra Rard Ledford
Ledford Publishing
ISBN: 978-0-9840777-7-9

Acknowledgments

Many thanks to the following people, who have been invaluable in the writing of this book.

Laura Ledford, my beta reader, for your many ideas and inspirations.

The members of our writers' critique group:
Dr. Ellouise Carroll, Jayme Walter, Anna Flynn, V.Ann Mandeville.

Suzie Biggs, for your encouragement.

And most of all, my husband, Bob Ledford, who encourages and supports my writing as well as all aspects of my life.

Out of Time Series

(Can be read in any order)

Gabrielle

Sage

Emily

Other Books by Debra Rard Ledford

Fructose Malabsorption: The Survival Guide

Fructose Malabsorption: The Shopping Guide

Oregon Brew Tour: Craft Beers…Microbrews, Nanobrews, Festivals, & Homebrew Info

Also Available from Ledford Publishing

Slowman Snowman
Written By Philip Egleston
Illustrated by Jayme Walter

1

Gabrielle slipped from the bed while the night's blackness still engulfed her world. Not wishing to provoke her husband, she breathed an anxious sigh of relief and stole her way out of the bedroom. If she could finish packing the car and make breakfast before he awoke and showered, maybe the day would go smoothly.

The toothbrush kept in the children's bath for just such times seemed to have spouted legs, so settling for a swish, she washed her face before hurrying to the kitchen for a cup of tea. Gabrielle knew she could ill-afford the luxury of relaxing with it, so she sipped between tasks.

Despite spending all evening after dinner–not going to bed until well after midnight–preparing for the day's outing, many finishing touches still required attention. Around this, she must cook, serve, and clean after the family's breakfast. To keep it simple, she settled on scrambled eggs, bacon, and toast, before deciding to add fried potatoes. An acceptable meal might determine the mood of the day. One bad decision could ruin the entire day.

With breakfast prepped for cooking, Gabrielle headed to the garage and grabbed the ice chest and ice packs from the freezer. After arranging the picnic items in the chest in a precise manner, while taking pains to be quiet, Gabrielle remembered lemonade and hurried back to the garage, only to discover a dusty jug in need of washing.

Back in the kitchen, she listened for sounds from the bedroom or bathroom. Relieved by the silence, she hurried her task. A quick check on the potatoes and she added the garlic and onions, rinsed the cutting board and knife, and arranged them in the dishwasher with precision. After scrubbing the jug, she dumped in the ice, cringing and closing her eyes at the explosive sound in the quiet house. She listened. Then she heard it. He was awake and up.

She rushed to each child's room, advising them to hurry and get dressed, breakfast would soon be ready. At the stove, she turned on the burner under the bacon and grabbed a skillet from the cupboard, poured in olive oil before dumping the veggies, immediately rinsing, and quietly placing the bowl in the dishwasher. She mustn't create noise when working with dishes. Stirring the veggies until tender-crisp, she broke ten eggs into the skillet. Then she played it safe and added two more. Better to have leftovers than to upset breakfast. Just as the eggs finished cooking, she paused. The shower had started.

Not yet dressed, she wondered how she could get done in time. She moved the eggs from the stove to a plate, covered them, then checked and lowered the temperature under the potatoes before removing the bacon from the skillet and placing it on a paper towel covered plate.

She glanced at the dirty cookware a moment before rushing to the bedroom to dress in a pale blue, light cotton skirt, which hit her mid-calf, and a cream colored peasant blouse, coupled with a pink and green flannel shirt, for warmth until the day's temperature increased. Thankfully, he liked to primp after his shower, so if she dressed quickly, she should have time to get back to the kitchen and begin washing pots and pans before he came out. She might even get the table set for breakfast.

Spying the unmade bed, she glanced at the bathroom door as she hastened to make it with precision, forming meticulous hospital corners before arranging the decorative pillows in the exact, approved manner. Hearing the shower stop, she dashed back to the kitchen.

Seeing eight-year-old Nicholas, her speedy-child, dressed and waiting in the kitchen, eating a piece of bacon, she gave thanks. "Nick, could you please be a big help and set the table for breakfast?" He headed for the plates. "Please remember to wash your hands first." The look of alarm on his face pained her.

By the time she finished washing the pans and putting them away, Nicholas almost had the table set.

"Mmmm, bacon." Her husband, Kyle, strode into the kitchen, fresh and stylish. "Nicholas, did you wash your hands before doing that?" The stern tone of his voice gave evidence of the seriousness of his question.

Nicholas responded with a proud smile and an enthusiastic nod.

"Why didn't you wake me? We're already late." Kyle glared at his wife.

"But Dad, it's not even light yet," Nicholas said as he peered out the window.

"Yes, but by the time I get things ready, the car loaded, and drive there, we'll miss the fish. You want to try out that new fly rod, don't you?" Nicholas enthusiastically agreed as he ran to get his sisters for breakfast. Of its own volition,

Gabrielle's eyebrow lifted at his use of the word "I" regarding preparations and loading the car.

"Why didn't you wake me?" Kyle asked again, his tone accusing and barely contained, before sitting at his place at the table.

"I'm sorry; you were sleeping so soundly, I figured if I got breakfast ready and you weren't up yet, I would wake you."

"And just when would I have showered and dressed?"

With the children's arrival, talk turned to plans for the day. They were anxious to know how long before they would arrive, if others would be there, if they could swim, or fish, or take any of a dozen toys with them.

As they passed plates of food around the table, Kyle glared at Gabrielle, "Why didn't you make the eggs over-easy? You know I prefer over-easy. Why do you always take the easy way?"

Gabrielle smiled and replied that she had hoped to get some vegetables into their breakfast, since there weren't many included in their picnic.

"Then you should have made omelets. You know I don't care for scrambled eggs."

"I like them, Dad," said Alyson.

"That's because you are such a positive person, just like your grandma." Kyle smiled at Alyson as he compared her to his sainted mother.

Finished with his breakfast, Kyle left the table and headed to his fishing equipment. Despite having checked it last night, he would need to double-check everything before they could leave.

Assured that all was immaculate, Gabrielle started the dishwasher before carrying the full ice chest to the car. Straining under its weight, she loaded it in the space left among the multitude of items a family of five requires for a "proper" picnic, which she'd had the foresight to load the previous night. With the car loaded, she hurried to the master bath, brushed her teeth and hair, and plaited her hair into a waist-length braid. With no time for makeup, a touch of gloss over her lips would have to do.

After informing Kyle they were ready and waiting in the car, the family waited another twenty minutes before he put his fishing gear in the back, readjusting items so his equipment had the best, most secure space. Despite Gabrielle's attempts to provide the perfect spot for his things, she always failed. Fifteen minutes later, he joined the family, and they were off for a day of family fun.

"You could have made sure we were ready to leave on time." The quiet reprimand encouraged Gabrielle to apologize.

She luxuriated in a deep breath, releasing it slowly and quietly, not wishing anyone to hear. Thoughts of a hot shower crept in, but she pushed them aside and focused on the countryside as they hurried toward the "ideal" picnic site.

The three children were quiet in the back seat, looking out the windows, hoping to see something exciting to point out to the family, perhaps a fox or a beautiful bird that would give them hero status for such a valuable sighting. As Gabrielle glanced back at them, so quiet and still for children, an involuntary sigh escaped.

"Great! Now what?" Kyle snapped. "Don't tell me you're tired already. Can't we ever have an enjoyable outing without you trying to ruin it?" When he stopped talking, the movements of strain in his jaw gave him the appearance of chewing.

Gabrielle thought fast and gave a light laugh. "I was just thinking how fortunate we are to have such wonderful, well-behaved children. Don't you agree?" While her statement was true, from a point of view, she felt guilty, knowing it was a stretch of the truth.

"Of course they are! As I keep explaining, it's all about being a good parent, and I had excellent examples of parenting. It's all about family."

"Are we almost there yet?" Nicholas asked miles later, proving himself a typical eight-year-old, rather than the angelic example of boyhood his father expected.

"How many times have I told you, kids, we will get there when we get there? Why can't you just enjoy the ride? There is so much beauty to see; I am just in awe of it. I can just drink in its glorious majesty. All your whining and complaining makes it hard to enjoy." Kyle's face contorted into something ugly as he barked at all the children for Nicholas's innocent child's statement.

Glancing out the window for something amazing to distract and calm, Gabrielle gave thanks for twin fawns lying under a fir tree. "Look! Twin fawns, by that tree across the stream."

6

"Good spotting! Mom wins the first sighting." Kyle's enthusiasm contrasted with his anger only seconds before did not go unnoticed but was the welcomed response for which Gabrielle had been hoping.

The responsive cheers from the back seat brought a smile to Kyle's face. He liked that his family was together and supportive of one another. He seemed to think they were the ideal family—or would be if Gabrielle were more cooperative. Of course, they would never be the family he had growing up; Gabrielle would never measure up to the example set by his mother.

Nature talk was always safe, so Gabrielle mentioned anything she saw along the road. Montana's beautiful Rocky Mountains provided an abundance of subject matter, but to avoid sounding like a tedious child, she peppered her observations with questions, knowing Kyle considered himself a nature expert. The rapt attention she showed was not lost on Kyle, whose concept of conversation was limited to his interests only.

At the picnic spot, the excited children jumped out of the car and ran toward the water but stopped short at the sound of Kyle's sharp reprimand. "Run to the water, and you'll scare the fish away, then none of us will catch fish. Show some consideration!"

They're just children! Gabrielle chastised herself for disrespectful thoughts toward her husband. She prayed a short prayer, asked forgiveness, and then added a request to help her remember the phrase that had become her mantra: *You do your part, let God and Kyle do theirs.*

While reading Ephesians 5:25-33, it occurred to her the only message to the wife in this entire paragraph was "and the wife must respect her husband." While these verses speak at length of the necessity of the husband loving his wife, the word for the wife was simply to respect her husband. Preceding this paragraph, wives are admonished to "submit to your husbands as to the Lord...in everything." While at times Gabrielle struggled a great deal with acceptance and implementation of both respect and submission, it had become much easier since the Lord had given her this mantra.

Calling the children to her, she asked them to help lay out the picnic while Kyle grabbed his fishing gear and found his way to the river. After washing the table, Gabrielle unfolded the tablecloth, careful not to allow the top of it to touch the table. Though she had wiped the table with a bleach-water cloth, it was impossible to sanitize. She mustn't contaminate the tablecloth. After clipping it to the table, to be sure, Gabrielle washed the tablecloth with a second bleach-water cloth she had placed in a plastic container for this purpose.

"Mom, shall we unload the cooler?" Francis, their oldest daughter, asked.

"No, let's wait until it's time to eat, so the food stays fresh. But we should move the cooler from the car so it will be in the shade at the end of the table. Then it'll be handy when it's time to eat."

The children took the chairs and entertainment items out of the car, placing the chairs where they could see their father fishing. "Mom, can I go down by the river with Dad?" Nicholas asked.

"Let's let Dad have a little fishing time first, okay? In the meantime, how about a scavenger hunt?" Gabrielle must keep the children amused while Kyle fished. After lunch, he would take them fishing for a bit, but until lunchtime, he demanded solitude around the river. Gabrielle refused to think about the disparity of Kyle not allowing the children to fish at the time he felt the fishing was best.

The children's excitement for the scavenger hunt was infectious as Gabrielle handed out the prepared lists. "First one back with all the items wins a prize!" As the children checked their lists and ran off, Gabrielle reminded them to stay away from the water and limit their search to where they could see her.

The joy of her children enjoying themselves was tempered by the need to assure nothing of potential or imagined danger happened. She also needed to make sure they didn't get too dirty. Despite this being a picnic, Kyle would not tolerate dirty children or dirty clothes. Why couldn't they could just relax and be children?

When the children returned with their treasures, Gabrielle exclaimed over them, telling the children they all did such a good job, everyone would have a prize. Squeals of delight rang out as Gabrielle handed each child a small bag of organic gummy bears, made with real juice and no sweeteners. "Can we eat them now, Mom?" Francis wanted to know.

"Sure you can." She smoothed Francis's hair. "They'll be a nice snack while you wait for lunchtime. Be sure the wrappers land in the garbage, okay," Gabrielle reveled in the pleasure her children received from this rare treat.

When the children finished their snacks, jumps of delight surrounded her at the suggestion of going for a walk. According to the sign, they had a choice of four trails: a ten mile, a five-mile, a two-point-five-mile, and a one-fourth-mile circle. With three young children and limited time, Gabrielle chose the one-fourth-mile circle. Upon their return, it would be time to set up for lunch. Timing was everything to assure a good day.

As they started down the trail, Gabrielle spotted Kyle fishing. He was oblivious to the children walking by. He was in his world, his focus intense. Francis waved, ready to call out to him, but Gabrielle touched her arm and shook her head, putting her finger to her lips in a reminder to be quiet when Dad was fishing. Francis's eyes got big, and she covered her mouth with an expression that said she almost blew it. Gabrielle's heart ached that a nine-year-old should know such caution regarding her father, but she smiled to show her daughter how proud she was of her.

The children bounced along the trail, searching for unusual items to point out to the others. As Alyson pointed to a burl on the side of a fir tree, she tripped on a root in the trail and fell, with her knee landing on a finger of the same root. Her quiet cries seemed out of place in the forest. Gabrielle picked her up, cuddling her and inspecting the scraped knee. Gentle and soothing words helped to calm Alyson, who then wanted to examine her knee. Somehow a scraped knee carried with it a badge of honor.

Gabrielle struggled to carry her daughter back to the picnic area. Though Alyson was only six, Gabrielle was small, barely five feet tall herself. The distance made the small child seem heavy for a woman who topped the scale at a hundred pounds.

Setting Alyson down on the picnic bench, Gabrielle retrieved the first-aid kit from the car. After cleaning the wound, she poured hydrogen peroxide over it and dried it with one of the sterile gauze pads. Opening the bandage, she added antibiotic cream and affixed the bandage. "There! All better," she smiled at Alyson, who smiled back. "Would you like to help me get lunch?" Excited, Alyson jumped off the bench, but then, in the way of children everywhere, limped, knee bent, to the tub containing picnic supplies.

Just as Alyson returned with the paper plates, Kyle strode up from the river, spying Alyson's limp. "Oh no! What happened?" His voice sounded panicky as he hurried to Alyson, picking her up and setting her on the table to examine her knee. After looking under the bandage, he turned on Gabrielle, "How could you allow this to happen? Can't I trust you to watch my children? She depends on you!" His angry and sharp tones scared Alyson, who started crying again. Nicholas and Francis stood still in their tracks, looking wide-eyed at their father.

Gabrielle took a quick breath. "We took the short trail; there was a root in the trail she didn't see because she was looking at a burl on a tree."

"Watch for such things! What if it gets infected? Who knows what germs are eating at her, or do you even care?" As he yelled, his large eyes took on a gleam, darting to and fro, with his jaw working back and forth.

"We cleaned it with distilled water, then disinfected with hydrogen peroxide and antibiotic cream before bandaging." She spoke as though the day depended on it, because in a way, it did. Smiling at Alyson, she continued, "She was a very brave girl, one any dad would be very proud of."

As she hoped it would, the statement seemed to help calm Kyle, momentarily refocusing his attention on comforting and helping Alyson. He moved her onto the bench. He glared at Gabrielle again. "Why was she walking? Are you so lazy you will make an injured child do your work?"

"Kyle, she's fine. She enjoys helping."

"Fine!" He yelled. "You uncaring bitch! You've caused her body horrible scarring. We can only pray she doesn't get a massive infection!" Kyle continued his tirade as the other children ran to sit on the bench beside Alyson, hoping the explosion would end soon.

"I'm sorry, Kyle. You are right; I realize I should have watched the trail better. I promise I will keep a keen eye on her knee and at the first sign of infection I'll take her to the doctor."

Kyle had much more to say, which turned into a jumble of mush in Gabrielle's mind, despite her attempt to pay close attention. She never knew when he would stop and expect a response. Her heart ached for the children. Though she asked him many times, he refused to keep his anger and scolding for her away from the children.

Never taking her eyes from Kyle, for fear he would accuse her of not listening, Gabrielle continued setting the picnic supplies on the table, hoping that soon his hunger would calm him enough to cease the belittling rant. Finally, he seemed to wind down a bit, so she placed the cold fried chicken on the children's plates, knowing from experience that, while he would not forgive her, possibly for days—and would never forget—for now he should at least stop his diatribe.

Lunch was uncomfortable. Kyle said nothing to Gabrielle, making over the children as though he were the only good parent they had. He reminded the children to remember to come to him when Mom was bad or mean. Poor Alyson innocently spoke up, "Mom's never mean to us, Dad. She's nice."

A furious glare flashed across Kyle's face. Gabrielle wondered if she imagined it. "It's okay, Alyson, no need to protect her. I will always be here for you." Gabrielle knew the emphasis Kyle placed on "I" was meant for her. He felt she was not there for their children. Or in his words, his children.

The meal Gabrielle spent so many hours preparing was finally over. Kyle, with a tone that made it clear he was the superior parent, told the kids they had better come with him. When all three pairs of eyes just looked up at him, he said, "I thought you wanted to fish." With a chorus of cheers, the children ran to the river. With a glare at Gabrielle, Kyle grabbed the children's fly rods and headed for the water.

Gabrielle put away the leftovers, making sure there was still plenty of ice in the ice chest. After tossing the paper plates and other disposable picnic supplies into the trash, she washed the tablecloth, and then placed a cup of water in the center.

13

After picking a few nearby flowers, she arranged them in the cup, forming a pleasant centerpiece. While lunch may be over, the flowers would delight the children and Kyle's picture of a picnic meant everything needed to be perfect, both before and after eating.

Gabrielle then grabbed her reusable water bottle and the novel she kept hidden in the car, which filled time during the long waits when Kyle would be "just a minute." She then headed up the trail, thankful for a few moments to herself. She dare not stay gone too long, so she limited herself to reading one chapter. Experience taught her that each chapter in this book took about twelve minutes to read. While that long may push it, she hoped to skim a little and squeeze in a full chapter.

Hurrying down the trail, Gabrielle drank in the peace and beauty of the mountains. She wished she could make this a leisurely stroll, coupled with losing herself in the depths of her book, but she knew that was out of the question. For Kyle to take the children for even a few minutes was an extraordinary occurrence—to not be available upon their return would lead to certain disaster.

Seeing a smooth bolder jutting out over the river, Gabrielle smiled, thinking how wonderful the warmth of the rock, coupled with the warmth of the sun, would feel as she closeted herself to read. Oh, how she would love to read in the open, rather than in secret. Kyle thought novels to be an incredible waste of time and made life miserable if he suspected her of reading. But reading had been her passion since the age of four; she simply could not bring herself to obey her husband in this regard.

14

As she spotted an old fishing line dangling from a branch over the river, her thoughts slipped to comparing her hours wasted reading to the hours he spent arranging and rearranging his several, large, well-stocked tackle boxes. Despite large sums of money paid acquiring the extensive collection, except for a small, separate box, the tackle went unused. Fear of losing any of his collection precluded its use. Her thoughts raced unbidden to the ill-afforded money, which he spent on this treasure—money often budgeted for essentials or received as a gift to Gabrielle or one of the children.

Realizing where her thoughts had wandered, Gabrielle chided herself and then asked forgiveness. "You do your part, let God and your husband do theirs."

The warm rock felt good as Gabrielle settled on it and stole a moment to look into the swirling water below. Odd, the rest of the river was a beautiful, blue-green, so clear you could see individual rocks at the bottom of the deep water, but this particular hole was dark and foreboding, not clear at all; the swirls dizzying in their intensity. The contrast held Gabrielle's attention and curiosity momentarily, before she decadently opened her book, borrowed from the church library.

Despite Kyle's reservations regarding novels, Gabrielle found these stories of faith and love heartening. Although she had tried to explain this, Kyle comprehended neither her love of reading nor the inspiration she received from fictional stories.

The sun felt good as Gabrielle read, letting the peace of God and the beautiful setting flow through her. Though immersed in the coveted chapter, the breeze on her flesh, the distinct aroma of the forest, and the sounds of nature relaxed her. Drinking in the peace of the moment meant far more than just reading.

All too soon, Gabrielle finished the allotted chapter. After tucking the book into the pocket of her skirt, she stood while simultaneously reaching to retrieve her reusable water bottle. As she grasped the bottle and stood, she stepped on her skirt. The effect pulled her back down. With the upward momentum of standing in opposition to the sudden downward force caused by stepping on her skirt, Gabrielle lost her balance and fell. Dropping the bottle to catch herself was ineffective. Time seemed to convert to slow motion as she endeavored to grasp the edge of the rock. She watched as her fingers slid down the surface, unable to attain a grip.

Though the space from the rock to the water was not long, a multitude of thoughts ran through her mind. She hoped the water wasn't too cold, though she knew it would be. Kyle would be so angry! Her only dry clothing would be her swimsuit; Kyle would consider wearing it home inappropriate. Maybe if she wore it with a towel as a skirt while her clothes dried in the sun. She needed to return to care for the children…

As the dark, cold water surrounded her, she felt a tremendous pull. Swirling around and around, her skirt tangling around her legs, preventing their movement. *I'm trapped!* With the struggle to release herself from the powerful embrace of the vortex and her tangled skirt, awareness of each moment and detail assailed Gabrielle. Attempts to lift her skirt to free her legs accomplished nothing; the whirlpool kept the material glued in place. She fought to stroke with her arms and to kick her legs mermaid style, but the tumultuous swirl of the water held her body prisoner.

Oddly, it made her think of the *Round Up* ride at the carnival when she was a teen. It was a large circle with walls. The rider would stand against the wall in a three-sided cage with handles. The whole ride would then spin. As it attained speed, it would tilt until it was almost perpendicular to the ground. The centrifugal force kept the riders in place. Even lifting a foot away from the wall was next to impossible.

She sent a silent plea for help. Her children! What would happen to them without her? The calm she had exhibited threatened to desert her. Her soundless prayer was a plea which went beyond words.

Just as her lungs felt they would burst, she felt herself thrust outside the swirling prison of water into a speeding current, giving her a moment of hope. Then she realized she was being pulled deeper and deeper into blackness. The walls of an underwater cave scraped and scratched her as the high-velocity water shot her toward the unknown. Her oxygen-starved lungs burned as she lost consciousness.

2

Ah-h, the warmth feels good, Gabrielle stretched, wincing at sore muscles and scrapes. An attempt to open her eyes met with blinding brightness. As she relaxed to allow her eyes time to adjust to the light, the realization dawned that she was not in her bed, or any bed. She could feel the prickle and smell the aroma of long grass around her. An uncomfortable lump underneath her prompted a check. The book in her pocket!

The terror of the whirlpool came flooding back to her, prompting her to take slow, deep, calming breaths. She sent a prayer of thanks, knowing her survival was a miracle. How she had gotten out of that rushing cave, she could not remember, but thankfulness flooded her entire being as she thought of her children.

She must get back to the picnic site! Kyle would be furious with her for being gone when they returned. Perhaps after hearing her story, he would be thankful she was still alive. Sadness gripped her as she knew this would not be the case. He would only use the opportunity to chide her for being irresponsible and not listening to him about the evils of novels. He would tell her she should have stayed at the picnic site and prepared their dessert or some other productive, wifely duty. She would pay for this for a very, very long time.

Finally able to open her eyes, astonishment gripped her as she looked around. Where were the mountains? Where were the trees? In the distance, she could see mountains surrounding what seemed to be a broad valley. Also visible were scattered trees, but not the thick forest she had been in before falling in the river. Confusion at this turn of events held her still. Even the mountains in the distance seemed wrong. These were not the tall, jagged, wild mountains of Northwest Montana. These mountains were smoother, more rounded. While this area resembled her Flathead Valley, it was not. "But how did I get here? There's no river. Where am I?" Gabrielle's perplexing questions went unanswered.

Rising, Gabrielle felt the effects of the shock and torment her body had suffered through the whirlpool, cave, and whatever else had occurred. She stretched and moved her aching arms and legs, attempting to work the soreness out of them before beginning her journey to locate her family. After convincing her limbs they wanted to move in the directions she wished them to, Gabrielle pulled the hair band from her hair and finger-combed the long, curly hair. As her fingers caught and worked their way through the unruly mass, a thought occurred to her; it was dry. In fact, all of her was dry, her clothes, her shoes, even the book she had been reading. *Odd,* she thought, before realizing dryness was the least strange thing happening.

After plaiting a single braid down her back, she looked around, trying to decide which way to go. None of the advice about being lost seemed to apply. A scan of the valley revealed no apparent buildings or roads. While there were no bodies of water visible, there were a few groups of trees, indicating possible water sources or houses. Taking a deep breath and saying a quick prayer for guidance, Gabrielle walked toward the closest trees, toward the nearest hills.

As she walked, the long grasses scratched her legs and caught on the bottom of her skirt, making walking difficult and painful. In the warmth, she removed the flannel shirt she had used for covering and tied the sleeves around her waist. After some time, she realized the flatness of the valley was an illusion. Toward the horizon, the land looked flat, but in reality, it was rolling, just enough to hide whatever might lie in the next dip.

The heat of the sun took its toll on Gabrielle as she neared the group of trees. Awareness of a growing thirst and the need to find drinkable water spurred her on. Disappointment gnawed at her determination to keep a positive attitude when there was neither water nor buildings near the upcoming trees.

Thankful for all the hikes Kyle had insisted the family take in the mountains "to be close to nature," Gabrielle kept walking toward the next group of trees. The movement of the sun told her she was headed in a southeast direction.

To keep her mind in a positive place, Gabrielle sang. After singing the songs she knew so well from church, she dared to sing songs from her childhood and teen years. As she sang *500 Miles*, she pictured the camp she attended as a child, where she had learned the song, then smiled as she realized how appropriate the song was to her current situation. Surprised she could remember the words, she sang *Harper Valley PTA*, despite Kyle's warnings that singing such ungodly songs was inappropriate. At the moment, her concern was not Kyle's sense of propriety, but encouragement for self. Singing kept her mind busy, staving off the worry and stress produced by her current dilemma.

At the next grouping of nothing but trees, a brief stop against a tree allowed her respite and a prayer. Lifting her braid, she wiped at the sweat pouring down her back and then wiped her face on the flannel shirt hanging from her waist.

Determination spurred her on her way. With thirst making singing uncomfortable, she switched to prayer and set her sights and direction a bit more due east, toward a larger grouping of trees, hoping more trees meant water. As her parched throat became painful, her prayers became more fervent.

Topping the final rise before the group of trees, she breathed a sigh of thanks. There, next to the trees, ran a small, but blissfully wet creek. Though she ached to run, fatigue kept her walking. By this time, she had walked enough to know her oasis was much farther than it appeared.

At the creek, the thought of parasites and pathogens contaminating the water flitted through her mind. Thirst drove the thought away. If the water made her sick, she would deal with it. Right now Gabrielle knew her situation was dire; she was suffering from dehydration and needed water, regardless of what it might contain.

Gabrielle delighted in the miraculous experience of the cold water on her parched throat, enjoying the sensation as it continued down into her stomach. After drinking her fill, she removed her shoes and socks before wading into the creek. Deeper than it looked, she tied her skirt up to help keep it dry, then splashed water on her face, arms, and itchy legs. While enjoying the watery bliss, she sent prayers of thanks heavenward. Savoring the delight of being surrounded by the fresh, flowing goodness of the creek, Gabrielle drank a bit more and with longing, thought of the water bottle dropped on the rock at the river.

The river. By now, her family was undoubtedly searching for her. Kyle would be furious. With a deep intake of breath, Gabrielle dashed to her shoes, knowing she must get back. Experience had taught her when Kyle became angry about anything, everyone suffered. She needed to be there to protect the children.

As she had been taught to do when lost in the wilderness, she followed the creek, with its added benefit of available water. The cool air surrounding the creek made the long walk more bearable. The water had cooled her aching feet, giving Gabrielle renewed vigor as she hurried downstream. It occurred to her that with the way creeks meander, she was walking much farther than necessary. However, after becoming so dehydrated, it seemed a good choice not to lose sight of it. She did, however, straighten the trail as much as possible, while remaining in view of the water.

With the shade they provided, occasional groups of trees were a welcome addition. After the whirlpool and several hours passing since Gabrielle applied sunscreen to her fair skin, the painful effects of the inevitable burn forced her to drape the flannel over her shoulders.

Topping yet another rise, Gabrielle gasped at the sight of smoke rising in the distance. Though unable to see the source, it gave hope. Hurrying, she ventured forth, hoping to arrive before the fading light became darkness.

"Wow!" A tiny cabin with smoke curling from the chimney despite the heat showed through the growing darkness. Right out of *Little House on the Prairie*, though smaller, much smaller, the tiny cabin, a small barn with a corral, what looked like a large garden, and a man leading a horse from the field, all worked to complete the effect.

Approaching the house just as darkness set in, no light graced the exterior. Relief overcame nerves as she knocked next to the open cabin door. A sturdy, work-worn woman turned at the sound. Seeing Gabrielle, the surprise on her face soon switched to a welcoming smile.

"Oh my, please, come on in." The woman, even shorter than Gabrielle and quite rotund, seemed overwrought by Gabrielle's appearance at her door.

Having schooled her children in all the cautionary rules regarding strangers, Gabrielle was reluctant to enter the cabin. "Oh, thank you, but if I could just use your phone, I had a bit of an accident." Though most people carried cell phones, Kyle thought they were dangerous and that her place was at home where a land-line served all her needs. No consideration was given to the fact that they lived in the woods, a forty-five-minute drive from town.

"An accident, oh no," she said with a mixture of sympathy and an odd look at Gabrielle's clothes. "I'm so sorry, but since I don't know what a phone is, I'm assumin' we don't have one. Why don't you just come on in and join us for supper? The mister will be in shortly an after we eat, maybe he can find somethin' to help you."

The warmth in the woman's words and manner gave Gabrielle the feeling she had just arrived at Grandma's house, despite her shocked puzzlement over the woman's lack of familiarity with telephones. She endeavored to ignore the hunger pains encouraged by the enticing aromas from the stove. Entering the hot cabin, Gabrielle asked "Would it be possible to get a ride to town? I need to find a phone."

"Town? Hmm, I don't expect Marvin has a trip to town planned for at least another month, but I suppose he might be able to go sometime within the week. We'll have to check with him. Whatever this phone thing is must be pretty important to you."

Hearing the woman talk about going in a month, or even a week, left Gabrielle weak with trepidation. "Might there be a neighbor with a phone?"

"Oh-h-h, I doubt that, if it ain't needed for farmin' or livin', folks around here won't have it. Any luxuries got left behind. Besides, the nearest neighbor is halfway to town."

Puzzled, it occurred to Gabrielle that she could walk to town, once it got light again. "How far is it to town?"

"Near ten mile."

Gabrielle wanted to groan at the idea of walking another ten miles. She thought of those who ran over twenty-six miles in one day doing a marathon and felt like a wimp. Common sense told her she would need to wait until morning to resume her journey; it was too dark, and she was tired from the day's long walk.

"Where are my manners? Please come on in and take a seat. I'm Wilma Hargrove. My husband, Marvin will be in shortly. Have you eaten? We're just about to sit down to supper. We don't get many visitors; it sure is nice to see another woman." As Wilma spoke, it occurred to Gabrielle that she had no opportunity to answer any of the questions. Fanning herself, Wilma continued, "My, it sure got hot today. Makes chores rough, needin' to heat the water and all. What did you say your name is?"

"Gabrielle Fallon, it's nice to meet you. And thank you so much for the offer of supper; if you have enough, yes, I would be happy to join you." The woman's prattle had calmed her enough to realize there were no electric lights in the cabin. It also appeared Wilma prepared food on a small, old-fashioned, but simple, two-burner, wood cook stove. No wonder there was a fire on such a hot day.

"Well, have a seat, Mrs. Fallon. There's plenty; Mr. Hargrove likes me to always be sure there's plenty on the table. Says he works hard in the fields and wants to partake of his hard work."

Noticing the use of the formal mister and missus, Gabrielle followed suit, "Is there anything I can do to help, Mrs. Hargrove?"

"Oh, my goodness no. There's hardly enough room in here for one to work; you just sit there and rest. I'll have it on the table in no time." Bustling around the cabin, Wilma continued, "Since you're needin' a ride, I'm guessin' you walked. Where'd you come from? Wouldn't it be nice to have a new neighbor!"

Gabrielle sat at the tiny handcrafted table. It felt good after the long day of walking. Though the single room cabin was small, it was neat and possessed a warmth that went beyond temperature: the patchwork quilt on the bed, the pitcher and washbasin, a hand-braided rug on the floor, and even the clothes hanging from pegs on the wall.

"Whitefish," Gabrielle answered. "I love your stove!"

"Why thank you." Wilma laughed. "When Mr. Hargrove wanted to come here, I said I'd be happy to, as long as we took my stove. I didn't want to cook over a fireplace. Course, we didn't bring *my* stove, it was much too big and heavy–never would have made the trip. He traded it for this little one. Even this one Mr. Hargrove threatened to dump every time we climbed a mountain. I don't mind though, that big ol' thing woulda taken half this room. Took time to get used to the temperature difference of this one, but I'm sure pleased to have it."

As Wilma set a cast iron skillet of cornbread on the table, movement at the doorway drew Gabrielle's attention. Marvin Hargrove seemed to fill the room. "Well my, I didn't realize we had company." The man was large, both wide and tall, though he wasn't at all fat. He removed his hat, hanging it on a peg by the door. His odd hairstyle glistened with the sweat of a hard day's work. His large, brown eyes had a tired look to them.

Gabrielle stood. "Mr. Hargrove, so nice to meet you, I'm Gabrielle Fallon. Your wife was good enough to invite me to stay for supper when I stopped to ask to use the phone."

"Phone? Whatever it is, we don't have it. Is there something that would work instead?"

Gabrielle didn't even bother to ask if they had a computer. "No, I don't think so. I'll just walk to town and see if I can find one there. Maybe you could point me in the right direction after dinner."

Wilma spoke up. "Now Mrs. Fallon, it's so dark out there tonight, you'd not see a thing. You just wait 'til mornin'.

In the meantime, Mr. Hargrove will sleep in the barn, and you can bunk with me."

With an intake of breath, Gabrielle said, "Oh no, I'm sorry, but I can't take Mr. Hargrove's bed. I'll sleep in the barn." She hoped there were no rodents or snakes.

Marvin Hargrove bristled. "I can't allow a woman to sleep in the barn. If'n I sleep on the floor in here, would that help you feel better? Mrs. Hargrove's made sure we have plenty of quilts, so it would be down-right comfy."

"The floor sounds great, but only if I sleep on it. I'm sure with quilts it will be quite nice. After the day I've had, I think I could sleep sitting on this stool!"

Wilma spoke up as she set a large pot of beans on the table. "Now that we've settled the sleepin' arrangements, how 'bout we sit down to dinner? Mr. Hargrove, if you could grab a chunk of wood to sit on, I'll get us some coffee." She sighed. "Where are my manners! All this time and I haven't offered you a cup of coffee. It's just been too long since I entertained."

They continued to chat as they ate, with Wilma doing most of the talking. All the while, Gabrielle wondered at their lifestyle. The dress wasn't right for Amish, but perhaps they were an off-shoot of the Amish. If only she could think of a polite way of asking.

While Gabrielle was wondering about the Hargroves, she could tell they were curious also. Finally, the gregarious Wilma broke the ice. "Mrs. Fallon, I believe I have a bit of material that would match your skirt if you would like me to lengthen it before you go into town. May be a small town, but I'm sure you don't wish to create scandal. I've always thought it would be convenient to have a shorter skirt for certain work–

my, wouldn't it be nice in the garden! What happened that you would wear it away from home?"

Marvin, being used to his wife's expressive nature and seeing the perplexed look on their guest's face, smiled and added the comment, "My wife has quite a talent with the needle. I think the only thing she likes more'n sewin' is helpin' others. So if you let her help you out, you'll be makin' her a happy woman."

While she didn't understand the situation, she had no wish to show a lack of respect for them or their community with her "short" mid-calf length skirt. "That would be wonderful! I'd appreciate it, Mrs. Hargrove. I'm not very good with a needle myself. Hopefully, some of your talent will come with the extension."

"Oh, good! We'll get started right after I get the supper dishes done."

Gabrielle looked around. Seeing no indoor plumbing meant they probably didn't have a bathroom in the small cabin. "I'm sorry, but where would your restroom be?"

Wilma puzzled over this one. "Restroom?"

"I need to pee," Gabrielle whispered, due to the delicacy of the subject.

Wilma smiled in recognition. "Behind the house. Mr. Hargrove, could you take Mrs. Fallon to the outhouse. In the dark, it will be difficult for you to see without knowing where it is."

Outhouse. While she had no problem with rustic, she was not an outhouse fan. But necessity dictated that she go, now.

Mr. Hargrove held the lantern as he led her to the outhouse. "You go on in, and I'll hold the lantern up to the moon to light the way."

Perplexed, Gabrielle looked up and noticed the crescent cut from the outhouse door, to look like a moon. She smiled. "Thank you." Pleased to find it clean in appearance and smell, Gabrielle lifted her skirt. When done, she looked for a roll of toilet paper. Instead, a pile of rags lay on the board seat and a bucket on the floor. Not confident of their intended use, she squeezed several times to drip dry, before standing. Feeling a bit uncomfortable, she held her legs tightly together for a moment before stepping outside.

Back at the house, Mrs. Hargrove dumped the dishpan of water on the plants just outside the front door. "Oh good, let's get to work on that skirt." She said upon seeing Gabrielle. Pulling three different pieces of material from a trunk at the end of the bed, one blue-green, one navy, and one floral, she held them next to Gabrielle's skirt. "What do you think? I kind of like the floral."

At a loss, and not wishing to offend, Gabrielle smiled. "Exactly what I was thinking!"

"If you'll take that skirt off, we'll get to work."

Mr. Hargrove remained outside when they returned from the outhouse, so Gabrielle assumed it would be okay, though she was uncomfortable. As she removed the skirt, Mrs. Hargrove handed her a small, light-weight blanket, which Gabrielle used to wrap around herself as a skirt.

As she worked, Wilma described all she did, taking her role as instructor seriously. She would make an excellent teacher.

"Have you ever been a teacher, Mrs. Hargrove?" She couldn't resist asking.

"Oh, no. I married Mr. Hargrove when I was fifteen. Thought at first we'd have us a passel of babies I could teach, but it never happened. Then we came here, and there's been so much work to get this place going, and neighbors so far away."

Gabrielle tried not to express surprise regarding the young age she had married. She wondered how old Mr. Hargrove had been. Instead, she asked, "How long have you lived here?"

"Be two years this fall. Hasn't been easy startin' fresh, from nothin', but the soil's fertile, the seasons are mild, and it sure is peaceful. Been frightenin' at times, but we still like it."

Gabrielle wondered at the term "frightening," but left it alone for now. Who knows, she thought, maybe this strange story will keep Kyle entertained, and avoid an explosion.

Mrs. Hargrove sewed with astonishing speed and soon converted Gabrielle's "scandalous" skirt to a respectable floor length. *Maybe it will prevent the grasses from tearing my legs to shreds.*

She had always heard farm families went to bed early but was still surprised when Mrs. Hargrove handed her a nightgown, saying, "You can use my spare. Mama always insisted a woman needed two nightgowns, said you just never know when an extra might come in handy. Never understood it myself. Well, I guess this is one of those occasions. We'll go ahead and change before Mr. Hargrove gets in from beddin' down the stock."

As Gabrielle saw that Mrs. Hargrove turned her back to change, she did the same. The nightgown was floor length, flannel, and rather warm for a hot summer night with a cookstove burning, but she was grateful. She couldn't help wondering if Mrs. Hargrove always changed while Mr. Hargrove bedded down the stock, then suppress a giggle at the thought. *I must be getting punchy.*

By the time Gabrielle finished changing, Mrs. Hargrove had two quilts out and folded on the dirt floor. Gabrielle hated the thought of the beautiful patchwork quilts on the floor. Although the dirt was kept as clean as possible, she still cringed.

"Mrs. Fallon, are you sure you wouldn't rather sleep in the bed with me. It may sag a bit, but it's a sight more comfortable than the floor."

"I appreciate it Mrs. Hargrove, but I'm so tired after the day I've had, I think I could sleep standing up. The floor won't bother me."

As Gabrielle lay down, she thanked the Lord for leading her to this safe and friendly place. Even as she prayed, she couldn't help worrying about Kyle with the children. What must they think? Were they scared? Was Kyle angry? Before she could get further in her wonderings and prayers, exhaustion won, and sleep overcame her.

The next morning, when Gabrielle woke to hushed movements, she panicked. She had overslept and needed to fix Kyle's breakfast and lunch. When the smell of coffee reached her, she remembered, and it was more than a nightmare.

Opening her eyes, it was still dark, except for the candle burning on the table. As she rose, Gabrielle found aches in places she didn't know could hurt. Besides the scrapes and bruises from the water cave, she was sore from hours spent walking the day before. Her slashed calves both itched and burned from the incessant grass beatings they had received. Add sleeping on a hard-pack dirt floor to a sunburn, and it was all she could do not to groan as she arose. She scolded herself for complaining and gave thanks for provision.

"Mornin', Mrs. Fallon. Sure hope you had a good night's sleep. Mr. Hargrove's out doin' mornin' chores, so if'n you want to change, I'll just keep working on breakfast with my back to you, and you don't have to worry none."

"Thank you." What Gabrielle wanted was to brush her teeth. Not brushing them the previous night had left her whole mouth feeling like a sticky coating of mud. After changing, she folded and laid the borrowed nightgown on the bed, undid her braid, and finger-combed her hair again. After rebraiding it, she stepped to the washbasin and splashed water on her face. Not seeing anything else, she used the towel hanging on the nail above. Catching water with her hand as it poured from the pitcher, she captured the water in her mouth and swished hard, before spitting it into the bowl. Repeating the procedure, she tried using her tongue to clean her teeth. After spitting, this time she rubbed her teeth with her finger, then with more water, tried swishing again. Though it would not meet Dental Association recommendations, it felt better.

"Mrs. Hargrove, what can I do to help?"

"You just have a seat an' breakfast will be on the table shortly. I know you're wantin' to get started to town, so I've been tryin' to rush so you can leave with first light. While Mr. Hargrove would love to help you out by takin' you, he just can't take a couple of days off right now. But you'll make it there almost as fast on foot as you would with the team and wagon."

"You have been more than helpful, and I appreciate it." Then a thought came to Gabrielle. "What is the name of the town?" She knew the state of Montana well, so if she could place the town, she might feel less lost.

"Calapooia."

"Hmm, Calapooia, Montana." She shook her head. "I don't believe I'm familiar with the town."

"Montana?" Mrs. Hargrove laughed. "Why honey, you passed it a while back, this is Oregon!"

"Oregon..." The word came out sounding foreign, startled, and questioning all at once. "Oh, my."

As Gabrielle pondered the word, Oregon, she willed herself to wake up. *This must be a dream.* But the smells of coffee and ham suggested otherwise. Looking at the dirt floor, the room seemed to spin. Breathing deeply. Gabrielle gripped the stool. *Oregon.*

"Mrs. Fallon, coffee's ready, if you'd like a cup."

"Please," Gabrielle replied automatically, not thinking for a moment she didn't drink coffee–she didn't like coffee. She couldn't think. Words would not form. *Oregon.* Her whole vocabulary seemed to have condensed into one word, *Oregon. Oregon. Oregon.* Like a skipping record, the word played over and over in her mind, though each time with a different emphasis. It changed from question, to exclamation, to resignation, to pain. On and on it repeated, different each time.

"Mrs. Fallon? Mrs. Fallon? Are you okay, Mrs. Fallon?" Wilma Hargrove asked when she turned.

"Oregon?" Gabrielle asked.

Puzzled, Mrs. Hargrove answered, "Why yes."

Taking a deep breath, Gabrielle tried to gather her wits about her.

"I know the feeling. On the journey here, I never knew where I was from one day to the next. Once we finally arrived, it was hard to believe we were finally settled. While it was a mighty big relief to be off the trail and settled, it had been so long it took a bit of adjustment time. Course we kept so busy tryin' to get set up before winter, not knowin' what to expect, that there weren't no time to ponder where I was. I expect your husband's busy preppin' a spot to build a home. Is that why he sent you to search for the, uh, whatever it is you're looking for."

Gabrielle stopped and stared at Mrs. Hargrove. "Husband...Kyle...lost..." she stammered, attempting to interrupt the jumbled thoughts swirling through her mind.

"Oh, you poor child! You lost your husband on the trip here. Such a pity. Come all this way and find yourself alone. Not an easy thing for a woman. Are you alone? Do you have any children?"

Gabrielle's bewildered, gyrating mind refused to focus. She managed an anguished, "Children—Francis, Alyson, Nicholas—lost...water...oh, Lord God!"

"Oh, you poor, poor dear. Three little ones and your husband too! All drowned in a river crossing. No wonder you seem confused. We must do whatever we can to help. What about your things? Were they all lost?"

"Things?" a confused Gabrielle felt as though she were grasping at straws.

Wilma put her arms around Gabrielle and held her. "Now, now, we'll find something for you. Don't you worry. I know it seems not to matter in light of your loss, but you'll need…" Leaving a bewildered Gabrielle and heading to the barn, she called to her husband. Gabrielle could hear through her muddled mind as Mrs. Hargrove explained to her husband what she assumed the situation to be, before insisting he take the ill-fated young woman into town. They may know of a place for her.

During the long, jarring wagon ride to town, Mr. Hargrove said little. Gabrielle had the impression he left the talking to his wife. Since Mrs. Hargrove stayed home to care for the stock and continue "puttin' up for the winter," Gabrielle had plenty of time to ponder her circumstances.

Even more disturbing than the odd way of life her hosts had chosen, was the location, Oregon. How did she get here? Could she have been unconscious for long enough for someone to have taken her to Oregon? But why would they? Kyle's occasional allegations of insanity came to mind.

She had learned through their years together that the best way to deal with Kyle's regular outbursts was with calm patience. However, being the strategist he was, he had adapted. His accusations and harassment became more extreme, going on and on, until she responded in anger. Kyle would then become very calm. Utilizing a gentle voice, he would tell her, "You really do need to calm down. You seriously need help. You really should be committed."

Could this be part of a plan to carry through with his overt threats to commit her to an asylum? No. This would take planning. It would be difficult to achieve with the children present. It would require money, which was always in short supply, thanks to Kyle's emergencies.

While Kyle made a good wage, each time Gabrielle would catch up on bills, he had an emergency need. One month it was a sudden need to join the gym, which included not only the initiation fee, but also several appropriate outfits, plus several pairs of shoes, and large, expensive containers of protein powders. Though his enthusiasm for the gym soon waned, the monthly fee did not. A couple of months later, he needed a belt. One reasonably priced belt would not suffice. He brought home a full bag of designer belts, most of which he never wore. Then he found the Tiffany lamp of his dreams at an antique shop. All non-returnable. All of this before paying bills, forcing Gabrielle to juggle them in an attempt to stay afloat. Each time, she prayed for time to catch up before the next emergency. Most of the time, she stayed only a short step ahead of the bill collectors.

Gabrielle took a deep breath, trying to relax and to think. The planning involved in such an illusion would be intense. Plus, he could not have planned her accident with the whirlpool, which would have necessitated a reason for her to be unconscious. Her head reeled just thinking about it. It occurred to her that perhaps in this line of thinking, she was proving his point; she sounded insane. Unlike Kyle, she was a terrible strategist. How long had she been out? Planning this would have taken days or even weeks.

Turning to her quiet companion, Gabrielle asked, "Mr. Hargrove, can you tell me the date?"

"I believe it's the twentieth of September, 1847."

"1847?"

"Why, yes, amazing isn't it?"

For several minutes Gabrielle felt as though her head was spinning. She held the wagon seat to keep from falling. Reminding herself to breathe, she took slow, deep breaths and attempted to relax her shoulders. All the relaxation techniques failed.

"You okay, Mrs. Fallon?"

Gabrielle could no more answer the man than she could explain what had happened. With great effort, she nodded. Her world had somehow turned upside down and inside out, changed color and form, exploded and imploded, all in unison. How could she be okay?

After several minutes of conscious breathing, Gabrielle gathered her thoughts. Could Kyle pull off a hoax this big? The resources and time needed were far beyond his means. Was he right? Was she mentally ill? Despite the current circumstances, she still did not think so. Does one know when they are insane? Considering the circumstances, she didn't bother to deliberate if "insane" was a politically correct term or not. Who cared anyway? Though she did not know the answer, she continued on the premise that her sanity was intact.

Arriving in Calapooia should provide answers. After all, a whole town could not be in on this, whatever it was. If this was the Hargrove's lifestyle choice, surely a whole town full of people would not be participating. If they were, there would undoubtedly be a few modern conveniences to allow them to communicate with the outside world. Even some sects of the Amish allowed phones for business use.

As the wagon bounced over the field, it really could not be called a road, Gabrielle planned. First step, find a phone. Kyle would be frantic by now—or furious. If he wasn't angry now, he would be when she got home. How would she explain this? She didn't understand it herself. Regardless what the answers turned out to be, Kyle would blame her. He would declare she should have stayed at the picnic site; she shouldn't have been reading, if she were a better mother she would have been with her children, and of course, if she were a better wife...

Closing her eyes and taking a deep breath, she again attempted to relax. She relaxed her shoulders, and said a prayer, asking for guidance and protection for her children. Afterward, as she ended every prayer, she prayed for Kyle and asked the Lord to help her love her husband as a wife should.

After several hours of bone-jarring travel, which Gabrielle figured she would feel for a week, Mr. Hargrove pointed, "That there's Kirk's Ferry. We'll be reachin' Brown's general store afore long."

Gabrielle's gaze followed his pointing finger. Amazed at the sight of the genuine, old-fashioned ferry, and knowing it would be a rare experience, the history buff in her yearned to use it, but after realizing there would undoubtedly be a cost involved, she was thankful their trip did not necessitate the ferry's use. These thoughts brought the realization to mind that she had been encountering many new, or rather, antique occurrences. In fact, life in its entirety had been straight out of a history book since she had arrived at the Hargrove's cabin. She must be dreaming.

As they topped a small hill, a minute group of buildings in the distance took shape, and though they had passed a couple of farms, both as small or smaller than the Hargrove's, this had a different appearance. At this distance, Gabrielle could not discern the difference but watched with curiosity as the tiny buildings slowly grew. A sense of foreboding crept up her spine and released a kaleidoscope of butterflies in her stomach. *Town? It can't be!*

With the wagon rolling along the main street of Calapooia, Gabrielle attempted to wrench coherent thoughts from her bewildered brain. Nothing. Blank. Vacant. Forcing herself to draw a large breath, then slowly release it, Gabrielle told herself, *One step at a time*. "So this is Calapooia," she said, making it sound like more of a question than a statement of fact.

"Yep. That there's the church, and that's the livery, over there's a boarding house, feed store's down there, and next to the general store there's a seamstress. Weren't too long ago we didn't have nothin' but a store and a ferry. Good to see the town growin' so big."

So big?

After stopping in front of the general store, Mr. Hargrove reached up to assist Gabrielle down from the wagon. She smiled, despite the strange and trying circumstances. Unaccustomed to assistance in any aspect of her life, this small gesture was like a welcome balm to an aching soul.

Clutching the nightgown Mrs. Hargrove insisted she take, Gabrielle followed Mr. Hargrove into the general store. Looking about, she was unable to keep herself from staring. This small building differed from what she knew as a store. It was different even, from the television and movie general stores, which looked so welcoming. Shelves lined the dark room, which held an assortment of items from lanterns to canned goods. Near the center was a small, cast-iron wood stove, which, by the smoky aroma of the place, didn't draw too well. In front of one bank of shelves was a counter, which included scales and a few small jars filled with hard candies. Scattered throughout the store were barrels and large bags, presumably holding things like pickles and flour.

"Hargrove! Surprised to see you about. Didn't expect you in for at least another month."

Mr. Hargrove walked over and spoke with the short, portly gentleman behind the counter, explaining Gabrielle's circumstances as he understood them. Meanwhile, Gabrielle tried not to look like an awestruck child as she took in her surroundings. "Astonishing!" she murmured. Despite her confusion and distress, the history buff in her couldn't help being fascinated.

Coming to her senses, she hurried to the counter, where the two men were in a hushed exchange. "Sir, I'm sorry to interrupt, but do you have a telephone?"

"A what?" The puzzled man blurted.

Realizing this must be a full community of whatever these people were, she changed her strategy, "Can you tell me where the nearest modern city is?" Anxiety was getting the best of her. Mr. Hargrove's stated year of 1847 unnerved her.

40

Coupled with the strain of worry over Kyle's response to the accident, Gabrielle felt the order and calm she had endeavored to achieve in her life slipping away; panic was taking a grip on her.

"Modern city, ma'am? Far as I know, you'd have to go back east where you just came from to find a modern city. The west just ain't that developed yet. But if you're needin' to order somethin', I can get it here in a few months, or at least by spring. I don't believe I've seen that tele-thing you asked about in the catalogs, but we can sure check."

Gabrielle tried to grasp reality as the world seemed to spin in the midst of a bad dream. "Sir, can you please tell me the year?"

"Why, it's 1847, ma'am." After a pause and a puzzled look at the woman, who had turned pale, he continued. "Can I get you something? Or perhaps you would like to sit down."

Taking a deep breath and grabbing the counter for support, her words came almost as a whisper, "Yes, please."

Sitting on a sack of something, Gabrielle nodded as Mr. Hargrove told her he needed to head back, but Mr. and Mrs. Brown would help her. In her numbed state, she nodded and lifted her hand, though didn't manage a wave. "Thank you again," she said automatically.

"Mr. Brown, is this really 1847, or is this some sort of experiment or project. I desperately need to know the truth," asked Gabrielle, her voice dull, without emotion.

"Of course it's 1847! You've had quite a shock, and it's understandin' you'd be a bit befuddled. Let me get the missus. She'll figure out what to do."

Watching Mr. Brown as he stepped through a door at the back of the store, Gabrielle tried to concentrate. She knew what seemed to be was impossible, but could not imagine a solution to her dilemma. Whatever, wherever, and whoever this community was, they were determined to remain in their world of 1847. Worse yet, they seemed just as determined that she was a part of their world.

Perhaps if she asked about traveling to Portland, or even to San Francisco, it might break the ice. If she was truly in Oregon, surely she could make her way to Portland. If she had to walk, at least then she could go home to her children.

At the thought of her children, Gabrielle's throat and chest constricted. Panic rose as tears slipped down her cheeks. Her hands twisted the only solid reality she could comprehend, the nightgown given to her by Mrs. Hargrove.

Just then, a tall, thin woman, with startling blue eyes, entered the store through the door which Mr. Brown had exited. Several years younger than Mr. Brown, her long brown skirt almost touched the floor. Frizzy, carrot-red hair attempting, and oft times succeeding, in escaping its French twist, she rushed to Gabrielle, grasping her trembling hands in a sign of comfort.

"Mrs. Fallon, my husband told me of your tragic loss. I am so, so sorry. I know there's nothing to eradicate the pain you're suffering, but we'll do our best to assist you." With a look at the door to the street, Mrs. Brown continued. "Come, let us adjourn to our living quarters. I'll fix you some tea. My mother always claimed tea to be helpful in any situation. While I'm not sure of that, it does give the maker and those drinking it something to do, which can be helpful."

With a slight lift of the hand she was still holding, Mrs. Brown indicated Gabrielle should rise, and then led her into a tiny room, no larger than eight-by-ten feet. The beautiful bed in the opposite corner from where they entered seemed out of place. Covered in elaborate quilts and fluffy pillows, the contrast from the Hargrove's cabin was readily apparent. Straight ahead stood a cook stove. It was small, but the similarity to the one she had seen that morning stopped there, as the other was simple and this one ornate. This cute little stove had four burners, rather than two, and a shelf on the bottom. Glancing around the tiny room, Gabrielle noted that though there was not much–it would not hold much–what was there was of fine quality.

"My husband says once the store is more established, he'll build a second story on the store, to use as living quarters. Meanwhile, we live in this small stockroom. The rest of our things are in the larger stockroom, along with supplies for the store. I don't mind though. He went through so much to bring things for my comfort, how could I complain?" As though realizing what she was saying and who she was speaking with, Mrs. Brown looked stricken. "Oh my! What am I going on about? Of course, I can't complain. Please, sit." She gestured toward a small, fine, drop-leaf table with two matching chairs.

Despite her befuddled brain, Gabrielle recognized them as Duncan Phyfe. She fell in love with a similar one while antiquing with Kyle, though the cost had been prohibitive. She had not told Kyle how much she liked it for fear he would purchase it as a gift for her. He loved the magnanimousness of giving expensive gifts, and then forever after used them as weapons against her. After identifying the table as Duncan Phyfe, she was almost positive the bed was also Duncan Phyfe.

Taking advantage of the momentary silence, Gabrielle asked, "How far is it to Portland?"

"Portland? I'm not sure, but my husband would know. Our things and the stock for the store were shipped there, though we came overland, so he's been there and would know. I remember he said he took five days in the wagon to arrive. Do you have family there?" she asked.

"No, but I was hoping with a more modern city to find a telephone."

"Hmmm, what is this telephone? My husband said you wanted a tele-something. If I remember my Greek, the root words would mean distant sound. Am I close?"

A small, brief smile came to Gabrielle. She liked this warm, gracious woman, who seemed utterly out of place in these simple circumstances. "Something tells me you didn't learn Greek here. Yes, you are close. It's a device that allows you to talk to someone else, anywhere in the world, as long as they have a telephone also." Noting the reaction on the woman's face, she thought, *These people really have no idea what a telephone is.*

"But that's impossible! While I admit, it would be an amazing and wonderful convenience; it will never happen. Where did you get the idea for such a thing? And why did you think we might have one?" Without waiting for a response, she continued dreamily. "Oh, wouldn't it be wonderful if such a thing existed. I could speak to my family! Oh, and my school chums! A telephone would make life here less lonely. Hmm, I might even be able to arrange social gatherings with our neighbors. O-o-oh, and what a help it would be for my husband in the store! He could take customer orders over the telephone and have them ready to go when they arrived. Oh, and he could even place orders with supply companies back East and have them here so much sooner for pick-up, with customers making only one trip." She continued excitedly, obviously enjoying the moment of fantasy. She paused, and a slight look of concern marred the excitement on her face. "But then people wouldn't come to the store as often, which would mean we would get to see people even less than we do now, and that would be even lonelier. Hum, I suppose there are two sides to every coin, as they say. But it is rather fun to think of the possibilities, don't you think?"

Gabrielle gave a small laugh, in spite of herself. It had been enjoyable to watch and listen to the excitement on the young woman's face and in her voice as she brainstormed the idea of a telephone. Obviously a very intelligent, educated, and imaginative person, Gabrielle wondered what she was doing here.

"Yes, I suppose it is enjoyable. You seem to miss your loved ones a great deal. How did you end up here, if you don't mind my asking?"

"Coming west was my husband's plan. I met him when he visited our church. At twenty-three, I had never had a gentleman caller, and my family feared I would be a spinster. Between my height and my bright hair, men just smiled and kept going. Clement Brown was different. His eyes sparkled when he looked at me. Being nine inches shorter didn't seem to faze him at all. He would look up at me, smile, and actually talk to me."

As she spoke, Gabrielle saw the smile of remembrance and heard the dreamy tone of her voice.

"When he asked my father if he could come courting, we were all thrilled. At first, I thought father might object, due to Clement's lack of education, but Daddy liked Clement's ambition and respected the years of hard work and saving to build on his dream of opening his own store. When Clement asked me to marry him, I thought my heart would explode. Though we didn't have a long courtship, it had been long enough to discover his name fit–it means gentle.

"Although I knew marrying him meant a move West, since opening a store in the East was unaffordable for him, he was worth it. I do miss my family and friends, but Clement has made a wonderful home here for us."

"You have such lovely things."

"A wedding gift from my parents. They knew Clement needed all his funds to stock the store and they wanted me to live in comfort, so they shipped all of our household needs around the Horn, providing a teamster to assist Clement in freighting them here from Portland along with the store supplies."

"That was very generous. They must miss you a great deal."

"The feeling is mutual. Still, they are thrilled for us. When we arrived late last summer, there was a letter waiting for me when Clement went to Portland to haul the furniture and store goods to Calapooia. Then I received another one late this summer. I've read them so many times, I almost have them memorized."

"Do you help in the store?"

"Occasionally, when one of the wives come in, but I'm kept busy keeping our home. Plus, I make things for Clement to stock in the store. Canned goods, quilts, doilies, clothes, items the newcomers and the men may need but haven't time to do themselves.

"Enough about me! Please tell me some about yourself, Mrs. Fallon. Is there anyone you know here? Or is your plan to return East? By the way, my name is Rose. Rose Brown, a very colorful name, wouldn't you say?"

"I think it's a lovely name. I'm Gabrielle Fallon. And no, I know no one here; nor do I have anyone in the East to return to. I don't know what I am to do."

Upon voicing these words, Gabrielle realized that somehow, as impossible as it seemed, she had accepted that it was now 1847. How she could believe such a far-fetched notion, she did not know, but suddenly, with every fiber of her being, she knew she was in the year 1847!

The realization of the deeper meaning–she could not return to her children–flooded her as violently as the whirlpool had. "Oh, my God…" With this unfinished prayer, tears flowed and uncontrollable sobs wrenched forth from deep within her. She leaned forward in the chair, laid her face in her hands, and wept with abandon, unaware of those who might hear.

Spent with sorrow, the sobs came less as Gabrielle once again noticed her surroundings. The hand stroking her hair was small comfort but comfort nevertheless. Struggling to gasp for breath, she could feel the stroking stop and looked up, seeing a man's red handkerchief. Taking it, she wiped her face and blew her nose, several times.

When done, she took a deep breath and said, "I'm so sorry." No other words could come. Any attempt at further speech would only start the sobbing again, especially when she saw Rose wiping away her tears of sympathy.

"Gabrielle, there is no need to apologize. You need to let it out; you have been through so much and, well, you should know I'm here for you. We'll help you find a place. My Clement has a heart of gold; he'll want to help." Taking the handkerchief, Rose deposited it in a low basket of soiled laundry she pulled from under the bed and then handed Gabrielle a clean one. "Just in case."

"Thank you."

"One more thing," Rose hugged her, "you are not alone here; you have me."

3

Gathered at the small table after supper that evening with Rose and Clement Brown, Gabrielle gave thanks for this loving, tender couple. They had taken on her dilemma—as they perceived it—as their own. While Gabrielle's guilt for not telling them the full truth ate at her, she recognized how insane it sounded.

Could Kyle have been right? Had she gone off the deep end and 1847 was all a bizarre illusion created by a mind out of touch with reality? Though uncertain how or why, she discerned her mind was sound, and that she was, indeed, in 1847.

"...you know we would love to have you stay here with us, don't you? Unfortunately, until Clement builds our second story living quarters, there is barely enough room for the two of us." The unshed tears pooling in Rose's eyes bore witness to the pain it caused her not to house Gabrielle.

With a gentle pat on his wife's hand, Clement Brown said, "Now don't you worry none; we'll find a place for Mrs. Fallon."

"While I'm in no position to be choosy, it would be nice if I could earn my keep, really be needed."

With brows knit in thought, he sighed and shook his head.

"What is it, Clement?" His wife asked.

"There is one family in need. Wife died winter before last. Left him with three children, one barely walkin'."

"Clement, dear, it sounds like the perfect answer to both problems. Why do you look so concerned?"

"Mr. Volstead is not a good-humored sort. Plus, while I've never seen his children, nor his wife before she passed, he's also not the tidy type. Don't take too good care of hisself, if you know what I mean." With a glance toward Gabrielle, he continued, "I apologize if it seems I'm talkin' poorly about my neighbors, but I'm just tryin' to think how I'd feel if my wife were to go there. Can't say I'd like to see it happen."

"Mr. Brown, how well do you know Mr. Volstead?" Gabrielle asked.

"Not well. He comes into the store about once a season. Don't stay and chat, so I haven't been able to get to know him. He told me how his wife up and died on him though, seemed irritated with her. Complained the oldest had to spend too much time caring for the young-un, instead of helping on the farm."

"But it sounds like I'm needed. Do you know where he lives? Is it far?" Though she knew she was in no position to be choosy, Gabrielle hoped she could visit Rose. They just met, but she felt an immediate connection with this open and loving woman. It would be nice to have a friend. Kyle outright discouraged any friendships, proclaiming that she only needed family.

"When he first came in, he said his place was eight miles south. If you're sure this is something you'd like to try, I'll take you out to find it in the morning."

"Yes, please. Will you go too?" Gabrielle looked at Rose.

"I wish I could, but with Clement gone, I need to mind the store. If someone comes all the way into town and finds it closed, we could be perceived as undependable."

"Of course. I'm sorry, I wasn't thinking."

Later that evening, Mr. Brown looked at his wife. "If you can get me one of those spare blankets, I'll just sleep on a couple of those bags of beans out there."

"Oh, no! Please let me sleep on the beans."

Before Gabrielle could say another word, Mr. Brown raised his hand to stop her. "I'm not about to let a woman sleep on a sack of beans. You enjoy that nice bed. Not bein' sure what Mr. Volstead will have for you in the way of sleeping quarters, it may be the last comfortable night's sleep you get."

A gripping fear of the unknown seized Gabrielle, with panic threatening to overcome her. She wished she could stay with these wonderful, relaxed people, at least long enough to adjust to this strange world and the loss of her children. With thoughts of her children, came the welling of tears.

"Oh Clement, now you've scared her!" Rose said, taking Gabrielle's hand.

Gabrielle shook her head. "It's okay, Rose. It wasn't anything he said. I, well," she could barely say the words, "it's, it's my children."

At this burst of words, Gabrielle wept in earnest, turning from her hosts. Unable to stop herself, she dashed through the door which led to the store and stumbled without purpose, collapsing against the first thing that beckoned, the bags of beans. Losing herself in sobs that racked her entire body, she surrendered to the pain which only so deep a loss can produce.

Memories of scenes with the children overwhelmed her. Walks, talks, skating, schooling, skiing, reading to them, it all played like a slide show in her tortured mind. Then the picnic, their delight with the scavenger hunt, Nicholas helping to set the table, Alyson saying Mom was nice, Francis's offers of help. Hugs, lots of hugs and cuddles.

Her thoughts swayed to Kyle: his temper, his manipulations, his explosions, his constant broken promises. What would happen to her children without her there to protect them and keep Kyle on an even keel? "Oh God, please protect my children." Her prayer sounded like a plea. "I don't know if I can do this. Help me…" As if in answer to prayer, she remembered God would never give her more than she could handle. "But God, I don't think I'm strong enough for this." At this, she recalled the verse, "I can do all things through Christ who strengthens me." Breathing slowed, eyes closed, she relaxed her shoulders and remained still for several moments as she focused on calming. "Thank you, Lord."

Pulling the handkerchief Rose had given her earlier from her pocket, she blew her nose and wiped her face. After one more deep breath, she stood and walked around the dark store, lit only by the light of the moon. A look out the front window of the store revealed a small glow of light at the boarding house. "Wow!" was all she said in response to the wonder of her situation, the place, and the time.

Returning to the living space, Gabrielle apologized.

"Now Gabrielle, there's no reason to be sorry." Rose gave her a small squeeze.

"Matter of fact, we been havin' a bit of a discussion." Clement sounded cheerful. "We think it would be best if we wait before goin' to Volstead's. Won't hurt nothin' to be cozy for a few days, and then we'll go Sunday, when the store's closed anyhow. That way the Missus can come too. So, with that decided, I'll take this here blanket and go find me a bag of beans. Night, ladies." The two women watched as he grabbed a quilt off the bed and marched into the store.

Rose explained. "You have been through so much. Anyone would feel overwhelmed. Then we spoke of you moving tomorrow to a stranger's house to care for his children. Your reaction is understandable. I must admit, there is a tad bit of selfishness involved. I'm so enjoying the company of another woman; I know we will be the best of friends. Does this meet with your approval?"

A lump grew in her throat as she considered the kindness of this wonderful couple. Gabrielle nodded. "Yes."

As they prepared for bed, Rose offered Gabrielle the use of her tooth powder. Gabrielle watched as Rose scrubbed her teeth with the tooth powder, using her finger in place of a toothbrush. Following Rose's example, it felt good to clean her teeth, in even this makeshift manner. Then Rose showed Gabrielle the outhouse, twenty feet out the back door. Like at the Hargrove's, there was a pile of clean rags next to the hole, with a bucket of water on the floor. This bucket also held rags, which assured her they were for wiping. Good thing, drip-drying wasn't an option this time.

After changing, Rose said, "I wondered about the bundle you carried. Is it all that remains of your things?"

Gabrielle smiled. "Mrs. Hargrove insisted I accept it. Her extra. Her mother told her you never knew when an extra would come in handy."

Rose giggled and studied Gabrielle as if in thought. "So you only have the clothes you're wearing and that nightgown?" At the nod of Gabrielle's head, she continued, "Tomorrow we will busy ourselves by making over something of mine." She held up a hand. "Before you say anything, I have plenty. My parents insisted on shipping all of my clothes along with the furniture, other than what I carried with me on the trip here, of course. Where I will wear a few of the gowns, I can't imagine."

Gabrielle chuckled. "Thank you, Rose. I can't imagine what I would do without you and your husband."

She settled under the beautiful quilts on Rose's bed and thought nothing could feel as good, except her children snuggled safely in her loving arms.

As the few days with the Browns progressed, Gabrielle helped, observing what Rose did, how she did it, and when she did it. Though an accomplished homemaker in the twenty-first century, not having modern conveniences and a cookbook turned Gabrielle into a novice, needing instructions for practically every chore.

Accompanying Rose to the larger storeroom to search through the trunks containing additional clothing, Gabrielle was astonished at the many beautiful things. In addition to trunks of clothing, a whole houseful of fine furnishings awaited a home.

Rose pulled an exquisite dress with wide, vertical stripes, in white and pale blue, with puff sleeves from a trunk. "You'll need one nice dress; this will do for Calapooia." With a momentary glance at Gabrielle's attire, she continued. "For daily, you need an option, something warmer, how about this?" She pulled out a brown, wool skirt. "And let's see..." She rifled deeper. "this." Out came a brick-red blouse, or as Gabrielle would learn, bodice. Continuing to the second trunk, Rose pulled more items. "This is a serviceable petticoat..."

Gabrielle thought, *slip*.

"... then this simple corset, pantaloons, and of course a chemise."

Pantaloons?

Rose hauled out a heavy woolen shawl and a simple, neutral colored bonnet. Looking at Gabrielle's tiny feet and then at her own, clearly meant to carry a woman over six feet tall, Rose said, "I'm sorry, but I won't be able to help with shoes." They both laughed. "But these stockings will help." She held up a pair of wool socks. "Oh, you'll need an apron." She pulled out a full-length apron.

"Oh, and one more thing." Rose pulled a length of flannel from yet another trunk. Ripping it into a pile of rags, she handed them to Gabrielle. "You'll need these."

Perplexed, Gabrielle reached for them, "What..."

"For your monthly."

Then it came to her, there would be no tampons or even pads available. She recalled reading this was the origin of the phrase, "on the rag."

Holding the dress to its full length necessitated the raising of Gabrielle's arms above her head. "Looks like we have some work ahead of us."

"On the bright side, we'll have spare material."

The two spent the remainder of the day cutting and hemming, when not preparing meals. Gabrielle was thankful for the sewing lesson Mrs. Hargrove had given. Though long, the bodice was not tightly fitted, allowing the extra length to accommodate Gabrielle's fuller bosom. This limited alterations to hemlines.

When they completed their work and folded Gabrielle's new clothes into a neat pile, Rose said, "Hmmm," and then headed for the large storeroom. She returned carrying a small satchel. "You'll need something in which to carry your things."

"But then you won't have one."

"I have another." She gave a guilty shrug at this statement.

"Thank you."

When Rose said they would need to iron the next day, since they had sewn on Tuesday, Gabrielle was reminded of the daily chores she had seen on antique dishtowels and realized it must truly be the way of homemakers in 1847.

After breakfast the next morning, Gabrielle watched as Rose placed two sadirons on the stove. Then she spread a sheet on the table. Taking a basket from under the bed, she removed a shirt and smoothed it onto the sheet, picked up one sadiron, held the bottom of it so it faced her other hand and held her hand about four inches from the sadiron before ironing the shirt. Soon, she replaced the sadiron on the stove, picked up the second one and went through the same process before continuing to iron the shirt. When she had ironed for a while, Rose moved the sadiron she had just placed on the stove to a spot with less direct heat and held the hot one in her hand for a bit before ironing again. She adjusted for temperature, assuring the iron would not be too hot and scorch the shirt.

After observing for a short while, Gabrielle took over, freeing Rose for other chores. As Gabrielle ironed, she continued to watch Rose work, absorbing and committing to memory all she saw.

The next morning, Gabrielle couldn't remember the chores assigned to each day. "So what will we be doing today?"

"In the city, most will go to market today, but I live at the market, so it doesn't make much sense. Instead, I usually do some extra sewing on items we can sell ready-made in the store. Would you like to help?"

The two women spent a relaxing day sewing, cooking meals, and getting acquainted. Gabrielle wished with all her heart she could tell Rose her true origin. But fear of the consequences prevented full disclosure.

On Friday, Rose told Gabrielle it was one of her favorite days. "With a place this small, there isn't much to clean, making this one of the lightest days for work. With two of us, it will be even lighter."

Saturday, Rose told her husband she needed more flour for baking. After breakfast, Gabrielle watched as Rose mixed the bread dough, adding to, using, and replacing the sourdough starter. Gabrielle liked the rhythm and feel of kneading the dough. She ruined many loaves attempting to make homemade bread at home but enjoyed the flow of the kneading process. She had learned to bake a decent loaf of bread, but this provided a rare opportunity to learn from a master.

After placing the bowl of dough on a shelf above the stove, Rose brought out cornmeal for cornbread. She appeared to just toss ingredients in without measuring. This amazed Gabrielle until she realized the limited foods available meant little variety, so learning the recipes by heart came quickly. Rose wasn't merely tossing the ingredients in, but from repetition, used correct amounts according to the bowl and the quantity in her hand.

Rose inserted the cornbread into the oven and suggested they make a pie as a special treat to celebrate their time together. Happy to learn, Gabrielle thanked Rose for the thoughtful gesture. Both women peeled apples, eating a few of the skins as they worked and chatted, solidifying a new and strong friendship.

Removing the cornbread from the oven and replacing it with two apple pies, Rose took the bowl of bread dough from the shelf above the stove. Through the hard work of the yeast, it had risen from half-full to over the top of the bowl. She placed her fist in the center, pushed down, and it seemed as though the air went out of the risen bread. With a gentle rhythm, she kneaded it, formed two round loaves on a board, covered them with a towel, and placed them back on the shelf to rise again.

As the pies baked and the bread rose, Gabrielle breathed in the aromas. Cornbread, apple pie, sourdough, and woodstove combined to create such a homey fragrance she relaxed, feeling at home in this strange time and place. As the ladies chatted, Rose shared stories of her trip west. The first-hand account of life on a wagon train fascinated Gabrielle.

But as Rose removed the pies from the oven, Mr. Brown's voice boomed from the store, "Volstead! Didn't expect you today. Matter of fact, we were planning to visit you tomorrow."

After the initial greeting, the women heard no more, but it was enough. Gabrielle took a slow, deep breath to steady her nerves. Rose gave her an encouraging smile. Then, taking one of the cooling pies, she wrapped a towel around it. After cutting the cornbread in half, she also wrapped it in a towel, which she placed next to the pie.

Later, when Clement Brown entered the room with Mr. Volstead, concern showed on his face. "Well, Volstead here says he sure needs the help but expects you'll want to be marryin' first."

"Marry?" Gabrielle was astonished. "No, I'm sorry, but I don't know you. I couldn't possibly marry you. I would be happy to work for you though."

"Can't afford to pay nobody."

"I don't expect pay, Mr. Volstead. Room and board would be enough."

"Our cabin's small; I guess you could sleep on the floor."

At this statement, the look of annoyance on Clement Brown's face spoke volumes. Mr. Volstead should have offered to sleep on the floor while Gabrielle took his bed, as any gentleman would.

"I appreciate the job, Mr. Volstead, so the floor will be fine."

Rose put her arm protectively around Gabrielle. It was clear she did not want Gabrielle to go with this man, but what choice did she have?

"Long trip back. Already loaded my supplies in the wagon." As Mr. Volstead spoke, he headed for his wagon.

Gabrielle hugged Rose, grabbed the satchel containing both the clothes Rose had given her and Mrs. Hargrove's nightgown and headed out. Mr. Volstead sat in the wagon, so Mr. Brown took the satchel from her, placed it in the back of the wagon, and helped Gabrielle up to the seat.

"Wait!" Rose hurried back inside and returned with a quilt topped with the wrapped pie and cornbread. "Remember, we're here if you need us," she said to Gabrielle, with a squeeze of her hand.

"Thank you so very much," Gabrielle shouted back and waved, as Mr. Volstead had already started the oxen on their way.

4

Mr. Volstead remained silent the entire trip. Too afraid to initiate conversation, Gabrielle tried to console herself that he was nervous as well. Admittedly, she would have crossed the street to avoid him in her time. His filthy hair may have been cut sometime in the last year, with a knife by the looks of it, though he had yet to remove his hat. A revolting, full beard could have something living in it. Ragged clothes matched the hair and beard. The odor emitting from him prompted a desire to plug her nose, if not prevented by manners.

Early that evening, they stopped at a cabin. Unlike the Hargrove's well-built home, light shone between the logs. Gabrielle breathed in, but could not seem to exhale. This was not the Hargrove's tidy farm.

Mr. Volstead did not stop to help her as Mr. Hargrove had done. With the long skirt and the height and awkwardness of the wagon, she understood as she climbed down why it was proper for gentlemen to assist a lady. Gabrielle grasped the satchel and balanced the pie and cornbread on top of the quilt before walking to the tiny cabin and pushing the door open with her foot.

The mess and stench which greeted her did not assuage her fears. Three dirty, unkempt children sat on a rickety bench at a table comprised of a bare board coming out of a chink in the wall with two branches for legs. Mr. Volstead already sat on a stump, dishing beans into his bowl.

"Hello." Gabrielle smiled, placing her burdens on one of two beds. "Perhaps cornbread would be nice with those beans." As she placed the cornbread on the table, Mr. Volstead grabbed it, took half, and continued shoveling food without speaking.

"Who's she?" The oldest asked, her voice thick with contempt. She appeared to be about twelve. Long, dirty, dull, blond hair hung in stringy wads, making Gabrielle think of dreadlocks that hadn't worked. While quite thin, she looked strong for a young girl. Several rips were noticeable in her tight clothing, which was no cleaner than her father's.

Ignoring her, the man continued eating as though he hadn't seen food for a week.

"I'm Gabrielle Fallon. I've come to help."

The girl looked furious. "Help! Pa, we don't need no help. I do just fine takin' care o' things."

"Yea, we're just fine," seconded a boy, about eight. His hair so dirty and matted she hesitated but thought it brown. His stocky build contrasted with his sister's slenderness, but for one so young, he looked muscular. Though better fitted, his clothing was also soiled beyond anything Gabrielle had ever seen.

Mr. Volstead stopped shoveling food. "I need you out with me. With her doin' the woman's work and watchin' that..." He pointed toward the youngest child, a small, disheveled girl about two years of age. "you can work with me."

"Ah, Pa..." A mere glance stopped further speech. Her face spoke of fear and regret at having spoken.

"Cornbread?" Gabrielle gave each child an equal portion, with the same amount for herself. "Now, why don't you tell me your names?" Taking the last dish and spoon from the end of the table, she dished a small amount for herself. She would need to overcome her natural reluctance and forge ahead. While the cornbread was excellent, the beans were hard and too salty.

Glaring at Gabrielle, the oldest girl said, "I'm Wanda, he's Earl, and that there's Daria. Why you here? Why ain't you with your own folks? Don't you have any? Or don't nobody want you?"

Gabrielle swallowed. "I lost my family coming here."

"Lucky them." Wanda's scowl spoke volumes.

It pained Gabrielle to see one so young full of anger and negativity.

"Where she gonna sleep?" asked Earl. "I ain' sharin' the bed with nobody else."

"I'll sleep on the floor." Looking down, Gabrielle winced. This was not the nice, clean, hardpack Mrs. Hargrove kept. She chided herself. *Be grateful.*

The exchange took place while the family hurried through the meal. Manners were non-existent: food dripped from chins, then wiped on filthy sleeves; words spoken through full mouths, which didn't close as they chewed; and each person focused only on themselves, failing to pass food or inquire if anyone needed more before slopping what remained on their plate.

"Chores," Mr. Volstead said before wiping his dripping mouth on his sleeve and standing.

Wanda and Earl followed him outside.

Gabrielle glanced around the cabin and then at Daria. Though not much bigger than a one-year-old, she was obviously older. Gabrielle guessed two, perhaps three. Her long, dark hair had not been washed for an indeterminate amount of time, nor had it been brushed. The dirt on her face made it difficult to ascertain whether her complexion was dark or fair. Her ragged dress looked like she must have worn it for at least a year, by the size and condition of it. Gabrielle ached for this tiny girl and determined to provide a better life for her.

Gathering the dishes to wash, but not seeing any water, Gabrielle took Daria's hand, snatched a bucket and went outside. No well. As Wanda passed, she asked her, "Where do I get water?"

"The creek, where you 'spect?"

"And where would that be?"

"That way."

"How far?"

Wanda walked off.

Grabbing the lantern and holding Daria's grimy little hand, Gabrielle started in the direction of the creek. Just as she despaired of finding it, they came upon a slight slope with water running at the bottom of it.

After filling the bucket, Gabrielle took Daria's hand, led her to the creek, fished the handkerchief from her pocket, rinsed it thoroughly, and then proceeded to wash the child with gentle strokes. Though she didn't resist, the scowl on her face made her contempt with the process clear. Daria remained silent. *Unusual for a child of her age.*

Back at the cabin, no fire burned in the small fireplace. At least this explained the hard beans. There was no stove.

Though hesitant to build a fire this late, Gabrielle did want to clean the dishes and pot. Looking for some form of soap and unable to locate any, she settled for pouring water into the pot, and putting the dishes into it. She let it soak as she neatened the cabin.

A search for a broom to sweep the filthy hardpack left her without satisfaction. Frustrated, she looked outside. There, next to the entrance, on the ground, lay what appeared to be a rough attempt at a broom. By appearances, it had lain there for quite some time. Gabrielle took it inside and endeavored to sweep, as Daria observed from atop one of the beds. The rough attempt at a broom provided an equally rough attempt at the floor. *Not great, but better.*

With a smile at Daria, Gabrielle headed outside again. The child followed. Looking around, about twenty feet to the side of the cabin she saw what appeared to be an outhouse. The smell as she neared it told her she guessed correctly. Opening the door, her stomach retched at the overwhelming stench, thick flies, and hanging from a string, a corncob, which appeared to have dried feces on it. Gabrielle closed the door. "No way!" Taking Daria's hand, she walked behind the cabin and squatted. After watching her for a moment, Daria also squatted.

Upon returning to the house, Mr. Volstead was crawling into bed, although the sun had scarcely gone down. Daria inched onto the bed with the other children and lay down across the foot of it. Much to Gabrielle's distress, Wanda gave her a sharp kick, pushing her further away.

Well, early to bed... Gabrielle wondered as she retrieved Rose's quilt how she could sleep, much less live, in such an environment.

Dawn's arrival took forever. Gabrielle slept little. Powerless to stop the tears, she ached for her children. Kyle was pleasant compared to Mr. Volstead. She was reminded to appreciate her life; it could be worse. She prayed for thankfulness for each day's blessings. Perhaps she was here to change this hovel into a home.

When the barest of light peeped in the sky, Mr. Volstead headed outside, carrying a hunk of bread with him, followed by Wanda and Earl. Gabrielle determined she would scrub that cabin top to bottom. Regardless of how many trips to the creek it required, or how much wood she burned in that fireplace, it would be clean before nightfall.

Stepping out, she called, "Wanda, please come here."

Wanda walked to her and glared.

"I need to know where to find a few items: soap, washtub, scrub brush."

After Wanda directed her to the washtub on the side of the house and the scrub brush on a ledge, she said, "Ain't no soap," and left.

She needed water. Taking Daria, she found a second bucket lying in the yard and headed for the creek. By the time she returned to the cabin with the two buckets of water, her body complained at the unaccustomed work, and the day had just begun. After pouring the water into the big pot by the fireplace, she went to find wood. Next to the woodpile, an outdoor fire pit provided a better alternative. After starting a fire, she returned to the cabin for the large pot of water. She waddled toward the fire, stopping to rest and shake out her arms several times. Legs on the bottom of the heavy cast iron pot allowed her to set it on the fire without extinguishing it.

Staring at the outhouse, she remembered her days at Camp Fire camp. When they were on Suzy duty, the camp name for outhouses, they poured lime into the hole to keep odors at bay. Eyes fixed, she thought for a moment, then used a bucket to scoop ashes from the fireplace. When the bucket was full, she headed for the dreaded building. She ripped the offensive string and cob off the wall and dropped them in the hole. After dumping the bucket of ashes in the hole, she headed back for more and repeated the process several times. Satisfied, she thought, *Good, a twofer, helped the smell and cleaned the fireplace at the same time.*

She dipped hot water from the large pot into the bucket in which she had carried ash and poured it around the inside of the outhouse. Then she scrubbed. But flies swarmed around the hole. Next to the woodpile, a thin chunk of wood reminded her of a large shingle. It should fit. After covering the hole, she scoured every inch of that filthy place. When finished, she rinsed it with the last of the water.

Looking around the yard, a heap of rubbish attracted her attention. She pulled a large tin can from the pile to rinse at the creek when she got more water.

Removing the pot from the fire, she lifted the buckets and smiled at Daria, who sat on the ground watching the entire process. "Come on, let's get more water." With an inquisitive stare, Daria joined Gabrielle.

Returning with two more buckets, plus a half a can of water, which Daria carried, Gabrielle placed more wood on the fire, put the pot over it, and poured the buckets into it.

"Daria, could you please set the can of water in the corner of the privy?"

The small girl looked from Gabrielle to the corner, gingerly placed the can in the corner and looked back at Gabrielle.

"Perfect!" Gabrielle smiled at her, noting just the slightest change in the child's expression.

Taking Daria with her, Gabrielle went back to the cabin. Uncomfortable working in other people's homes, she would not normally make herself at home, but she needed rags for the outhouse. Finally, she found a few baby things in a trunk in the corner. While she hated to tear up and use the lovingly made baby items, they were no longer required for their expected purpose. An incomplete gown with a needle caught in it indicated these things weren't Daria's, they were intended for a new baby. Had Volstead's wife died in childbirth?

The few items didn't produce many rags, but they would have to do for now. Though Gabrielle gave brief consideration to using a few of the cloths Rose gave her for her "monthly," she would need them, not knowing other options, so decided better of it. Perhaps with more time to search, something else would present itself. Until then, she could wash the rags more than once a week. Daria trotted after her as she returned to the outhouse and placed the dry rags next to the hole.

The sun was practically overhead, and the family needed lunch, or as the people here called it, dinner. Since they only grabbed a hunk of bread on the way out the door, they would be quite hungry. What was available? What were they accustomed to eating?

As Gabrielle entered the house, Wanda stood at the stove. "Pa saw ya runnin' around outside and figured if we was to eat I'd best come an prepare it." How could a twelve-year-old make her feel so small? This wouldn't happen again.

"My that smells good; what are you cooking?"

"Rabbit."

Gabrielle peered at the skillet. "Mmm. Anything else?"

"Ain't had time."

"We have the pie Mrs. Brown sent. We can have some of it. Do you have potatoes?"

"Ain't time for tatas."

"Hmmm, oh, I know. It there flour? I can make pancakes."

Wanda pointed.

"Since you're finally here, I'll run out an finish what I was doin'. Think you can keep the rabbit from burnin'?" The young girl's sarcastic tone spoke volumes.

"I'll watch it." Gabrielle took a deep breath for patience. The girl's sullen attitude tried her, although Gabrielle knew she should have come in earlier.

After removing the rabbit from the skillet, she covered it with the large cast iron lid and poured the pancake batter. While it cooked, she washed the forgotten dishes. With the table set and the food complete, Gabrielle found a knife, which she cleaned, since it may have been a while, and cut the pie.

She poured the fresh milk Wanda brought with her into cups when Volstead and the older children entered the cabin.

As the family sat at the table, they dispensed with both hand washing and prayer. Did they plan to eat the fried rabbit with their filthy, dirt-encrusted hands? The answer to her question came soon. She tried to console herself with one thought—it was clean dirt. When had they last washed? Quite a change from the germ-phobic attitude of Kyle and his family.

Instead of choosing a piece, Mr. Volstead used his fork and scraped half of the pie onto his plate. Wanda and Earl each snatched a piece, leaving only one. As Daria followed this process, Gabrielle saw the disappointment on the child's face as she stared at the remaining slice and then at Gabrielle, who cut it in two and allowed the girl to choose hers.

As Gabrielle and Daria ate their bits of pie, the others left the cabin. Not a single word had been said. Gabrielle determined to make this a happier, more considerate household. Perhaps if she kept things clean and tidy, fixed good meals on time, and initiated conversation, it would help. At least it would be a start. She began by chatting with Daria. Though the girl's comfort level did not yet allow her to speak, if indeed she could, she nodded or shook her head if asked a question.

First, plan supper. Then clean while it cooked. With its disastrous condition, coupled with the extra time each chore took due to things like fetching and boiling water, the cabin could not be completed in a single day.

Looking at Daria, Gabrielle asked if they had a garden. The child nodded, grabbed Gabrielle's hand, and took off running. Daria was warming to her. Though still reserved, she seemed happy to disclose the garden's whereabouts. Gabrielle wondered if hers were the first positive words the child ever heard.

The garden revealed another monumental task. It appeared as though it had been sown, then forgotten, with weeds as tall as the vegetable plants. *Fifteen minutes.* Fifteen minutes now and every time she came out here spent pulling weeds and hoeing would do the job and still allow completion of her other duties, assuming there was a hoe.

As she weeded, Daria watched. "Want to help?"

With Daria's nod, Gabrielle pointed out the difference between the plants and the weeds. "Think you can recognize which is which? We only want to pull the weeds."

Fifteen minutes later, by Gabrielle's reckoning, she checked the garden for food for supper. Finding green beans, she picked them into her apron and added both tomatoes and overgrown spinach before pulling a few green onions. After a moment's pause, she asked, "Daria, do you know where the meat is?"

Again, the child nodded.

"Let's take these to the house, and then would you show me?"

Another nod.

In the barn, Gabrielle stared at the barrel filled with brine. Not certain what to do, she stuck her arm in up to her bicep and drew out the first thing she touched, a hunk of raw meat. She retched as she realized this method kept the meat from spoiling. Never good with raw meat, she found this revolting, but since freezers had not yet been invented, they needed some way to preserve it.

Back in the cabin, she studied the gathered foods. Lost without a recipe, she needed to think about it. In the meantime, a trip to the creek for a bucket of cold water to keep the meat in while she cleaned was called for.

The afternoon sped by as Gabrielle cleaned every surface of the small cabin. She ached to strip the beds and wash, but it needed to wait. It was time to start supper. She pulled the meat from the bucket and sliced it into thin strips which she coated with flour and fried. She made more pancakes. Unable to locate a small pot, she put the green beans in the skillet with the meat after remembering how her mother used to add bacon to green beans for flavoring. She tossed a small salad using the spinach, tomato, and onions. Supper should be fine.

As darkness set in, the place was clean, and Gabrielle was proud of herself for pulling together a decent-looking meal under such primitive circumstances.

Upon entering the cabin, Mr. Volstead and the children, still dirty from the field, plopped at the table. The man looked at the fare with disdain. "Mighty big supper, ain't it?"

Gabrielle's face fell. Not knowing what to say, she dished food for Daria.

As Wanda chewed, she said, "Didn't wash the meat enough, too salty."

"What's this?" asked Earl.

"A salad."

"We supposed to eat it?"

"Yes."

"Where's my corncob?" Mr. Volstead's bark startled Gabrielle.

"I've replaced it with rags and a can of water. After using it, just put the soiled rag in the can. I'll clean them for reuse when I do the rest of the laundry."

"Pure waste of time!"

As the week progressed, Gabrielle's comprehension of her duties grew, as did her understanding of the wisdom behind one primary job per day with the other chores tucked in around it. Sleeping on the dirt floor wasn't bad; each evening, she fell asleep before a comfort level could be determined. The constant work and complete exhaustion helped stave off the intense pain and anguish resulting from the loss of her children. The inability to have even the smallest civil conversation with Volstead or the two older children wore on her, but at least Daria seemed responsive to her care, though she still would not speak. Nevertheless, Gabrielle continued to make attempts at small talk during meals, despite the silence and occasional rebukes it provoked.

By the end of the first week, she was proud of what she had accomplished. The cabin was clean, though the bedding still needed to be washed. The garden was almost weed-free. The outhouse was clean, and the smell kept at bay through her daily dumping of ashes into it. And her cooking skills, if not great, had yet to poison anyone, though she received only complaints. Prepping vegetables and whatever berries she could locate for drying by laying them on the roof, covered with cheesecloth, became a daily task. But when she created a compost pile, Wanda informed her with scorn that the pigs ate the inedible parts.

Sunday morning, she took Daria, with the only other dress she appeared to have, which was even smaller and shabbier than the one she wore, along with her own change of clothing to the creek. Despite the cold water, it felt fantastic. But then, she had never washed a week's worth of dirt, soot, grime, smoke, and sweat off herself. Though wash was a stretch without soap. She needed to remedy that.

After cleaning her own body and hair as much as she could, she scrubbed Daria, who seemed perplexed by the process. Had this family ever bathed the child? For her hair, Gabrielle made a game of it. Demonstrating the bobs her children executed in swimming lessons, she encouraged Daria to bob in and out of the water. Though reluctant, Daria soon got into the spirit of the new game. But her bobs were too shallow to wet her hair completely, so Gabrielle tried a new tactic.

"Watch, Daria." Gabrielle floated on her back and asked, "Can you do this?"

Daria shook her head.

"Want to learn?"

Daria nodded.

Lifting her, Gabrielle laid Daria back. At this, she flailed in panic. "Daria," Gabrielle said as she pulled her close, "you need to trust me if you want to learn to float. I will hold you and not let anything happen. Can you trust me?"

Daria studied Gabrielle, glanced at the water, slowly returned her eyes to meet Gabrielle's, and nodded.

"Good girl!"

This time Gabrielle picked up Daria and held her in her arms, like a baby. Then she lowered her into the water. "Now point your chin to the sky."

After a sideways peek at Gabrielle, Daria stuck her chin up.

"Good girl! Now stretch your arms out." Daria did as instructed. "One more thing, relax and arch your back a little."

Daria gave Gabrielle a bewildered look.

Holding Daria with one arm, Gabrielle used the other hand to show Daria what an arch was. Daria immediately formed an arc in her back. Gabrielle eased her arm just below the child in the water.

"See, you're floating all by yourself," Gabrielle whispered, with awe, impressed such a young child could trust her and follow instructions so well.

Daria's giggle made her heart sing.

After drying them both with the one small somewhat clean kitchen towel available, Gabrielle dressed in the clothes provided by Rose. She attempted to put the corset on as Rose had. Rose made it look effortless. It wasn't. Though she didn't relish wearing the uncomfortable thing, she needed support while washing her bra. How she wished for a flat chest. While she struggled, Daria put on the clean dress.

When dressed, Gabrielle finger-combed her long hair. Unable to locate a brush or a comb, fingers must suffice. "Can you do this?" She asked Daria.

Daria ran her fingers through the very ends of her hair.

"Good. I'll help when I'm finished."

When a thick braid hung down her back, Gabrielle helped Daria, whose hair consisted of snarls and mats. When had it last been brushed?

Her heart ached for this child. During the week Gabrielle had been with the Volstead's, she had not heard one kind word spoken to Daria, or anyone. There were no hugs, cuddles, or even smiles. Had they always lived this way? Or did it come about after Mrs. Volstead's death?

Daria's wiggles and shrugs increased. She inched away from Gabrielle.

"When we finish, I'll braid your hair, kind of like mine, if you want. It won't tangle as easily that way, plus it will look adorable."

The child set her face in what Gabrielle assumed was her determined look and showed patience far beyond her age. Finally, snarl-free, Gabrielle divided Daria's hair into two equal sections and plaited tight French braids on each side, making sure they hung in the front, so Daria could see them. With a peek at the braids, Daria smiled at Gabrielle.

For the first time since arriving, Gabrielle felt something akin to comfort. As she and Daria strolled back to the cabin, they held hands. "Do you know how to skip?" With the shake of Daria's head, Gabrielle demonstrated. By the time they reached the cabin, they were skipping.

Saturday Gabrielle had made beans, a giant portion of cornbread, and a berry cobbler, which she set aside for Sunday's dinner. Extra cornbread with a salad for supper meant she could avoid cooking on Sunday. Volstead didn't demand anything but bread for breakfast as they headed out. He treated Sunday like any other day.

But tomorrow was Monday, which meant she needed to follow Rose's example and put the laundry in a tub of hot water to soak. Several trips to the creek allowed her to fill the washtub. Then she added her clothes to it, along with several other items.

The next day, she learned that compared to Monday, the remainder of the week was easy. After starting the fire outside, and several trips to the creek, she filled the large pot with water to heat. Despite her aching arms and back, Gabrielle transferred hot water from the heating pot to the washtub; she then returned to the creek for more water to heat, 'which allowed time for the hot water to cool enough to immerse her hands into it and give the items in the washtub a hot soak.

Finally ready to wash, she lifted the washboard from the outside wall of the cabin, placed it in the washtub, and scrubbed the clothes vigorously. During her modern life, she usually washed what would be deemed clean clothes in this era. These were filthy! Lack of soap made the task tricky. When her skirt was clean, she dunked it in the bucket of cold water as a rinse, wrung as much water out as she could, and hung it from the clothesline, strung from the house to the outhouse.

After washing the few items—the Volsteads wore the same clothes continuously without washing—she tackled the big job. In the cabin, she stripped the bedding from the children's bed. The stench as she pulled it off made her gag.

She needed to remove the straw, wash the ticking, and replace the straw with fresh, but that would wait for another day.

Then the real work began. Wringing the heavy, wet bedding by herself was not just difficult, but painful. She hung it near the house to prevent it from weighing the line down. When Daria handed Gabrielle a long stick, she said, "Thank you," smiling at the little girl. The stick had a fork in one end. *Cool,* she thought. Walking to the center of the line, she stuck the fork under the line and stood the stick up. "You're a good helper," she told Daria, wiggling her braid. Daria's ever-so-slight smile and wide open eyes spoke volumes.

Gabrielle pulled the bedding from Mr. Volstead's bed. Impossible as it seemed, it smelled even worse than the children's. Placing them in the washtub of fresh water, she realized her error.

With a look at Daria, she grabbed her hand, "We must hurry. In my zeal to finish the laundry, I forgot about dinner." By the sun's position in the sky, she might have an hour to pull something together. "That can soak until after dinner."

Throwing several things into a pot of water, Gabrielle made soup. Once again she made pancakes, not knowing how to bake biscuits without an oven. By the time the family arrived, dinner was ready and on the table, much to Gabrielle's relief. From now on she would prepare enough on Sunday to cover Monday's meals.

While they ate, she returned to the laundry and finished washing the second set of bedding. After hanging them on the line near the outhouse, she checked the first quilt's dryness. Panic ensued. It was still soaked! Calming herself, since worry wouldn't encourage them to dry faster, she switched tactics. Being doubled over the line slowed the drying, so she removed it and walked part way to the creek where the grass was long. She laid the quilt on the grass, then went back to do the same with the remainder of the bedding. She could only hope and pray for them to dry.

The can from the outhouse was last. Pouring the water off, she dipped boiling water back into the tin and swished it around before dumping it in the outhouse pit. She repeated the process twice. After this, she scrubbed them in the washtub with the washboard. Though this task sickened her, it beat a family corncob. When she finished, Gabrielle placed the rags in the pot to boil. Letting them boil for about twenty minutes, she fished them out and rinsed them again before wringing and hanging them from the line.

She then dumped the water from the pot and added clean water, swished it, dumped it, and added more water, which she let boil for another twenty minutes before dumping it.

That evening she served leftover soup for supper, along with more pancakes. But her concern was the quilts. Since she munched while cooking, as the family ate, she ran outside to check them.

"Oh, thank you, Lord." she prayed when she found them dry. Folding them, she carried them into the cabin and made the beds as the family finished eating. After evening chores, they crawled under the clean covers with the dirt of that day and many others still on them.

5

The days settled into a routine. Though more exhausted than she imagined possible, Gabrielle nevertheless tried to complete an additional task each day. One day, she determined to make lye soap. During the homeschooling of her children, they had read about the process, and she hoped she remembered the steps. First thing in the morning, before lighting a fire, she scooped ash from the fireplace into the kettle, then added water. After lighting the fire, she let it boil for approximately half an hour. Using the ladle she found on the floor in the corner of the room, she skimmed the lye off the top and placed it in a bucket. She then scooped the solids out and placed them in another bucket, which she carried to the outhouse and dumped down the hole. Then she poured the lye solution back into the pot. Unsure of the remainder of the process, she prayed she had it right. Placing the fat drippings she had saved into the lye, she let them boil together, stirring regularly. Though unsure how long it should boil, she felt somewhat confident as she grabbed a small cast iron pan she found in the barn to hold the hot soap. She said a quick prayer as she set it aside to cool.

Life in 1847 was grueling. She had enjoyed watching movies and television shows about this era, but they made this life attractive, romanticized it. People always had time; things and people were sweet and clean, unless they were the bad guys; fantasy avoided the realistic issues, focusing only on the storyline. This life was demanding and often frightening. One sometimes needed to make the difficult and dangerous choice between watching a small child closely or completing the harsh work often required for day-to-day living, for survival. The dangers for children were many; what if someone was injured?

Though only with the Volsteads a brief time, it seemed like forever. The unending work, the tight quarters, the lack of privacy, and the lack of human compassion left Gabrielle appreciating what she had never valued in her life in the future. While her children had been her life, she had resented Kyle and his constant quest for the best of everything. Why did they need so much stuff? Though dishwashers, indoor plumbing, showers, and her washer/dryer sure sounded good now.

Thinking about it, the things she missed most, other than her children, had to do with water. Unending trips to the creek were exhausting, followed by the work which required using water, boiling water, and disposing of water. In the future, if she wanted to bathe, she turned the tap handle. In 1847, bathing meant many trips to and from the creek, boiling several buckets of water, transferring it to the wash tub, which was a tight fit for an adult, and emptying the washtub when done. Then there was watering the garden; rather than hooking a hose to a sprinkler and turning on the faucet, 1847 meant walking through the garden with a bucket of water and using a cup to water each plant. On the other hand, she had grown much stronger since coming here. She was learning she was far tougher—physically, mentally, and emotionally—than she had ever realized.

Now that she had soap, it was time to address the mattresses. When Monday arrived, her project was to open the ticking, wash it, and put clean straw inside after it dried and before sewing it closed. Despite the hard work involved, she assumed completing the job should clear the cabin of the rancid odor she had not been able to eliminate.

Having no desire to place dirty bedding on the clean ticking, she resolved to wash the bedding. To this end, she requested Wanda's assistance when it came time to wring the quilts. With one of them on each end, they twisted the quilts, wringing out the excess water, before laying them on the grass to dry.

"Why bother, they's just gonna git dirty again?" Wanda asked.

"They smell so much better when clean, don't you think?"

Wanda shrugged.

"If you would like to bathe, the creek is still fairly warm. You would be amazed how good it feels to be clean and slip into a clean bed." Encouraged by the lack of retort, Gabrielle continued, "Maybe Earl would even agree to go swimming and get clean."

Wanda said nothing more as they worked together to complete the quilts, but Gabrielle noticed that evening Wanda flopped into the clean bed the same as every other day, covered with weeks of dirt. Gabrielle consoled herself knowing Wanda had listened to her without her usual contemptuous retort. Plus, the cabin did smell much better.

As Gabrielle worked, she talked to Daria and showed her how to perform simple tasks. Daria finally whispered "A" after Gabrielle traced an A in the dirt and told Daria it was an A. Gabrielle could hardly contain her excitement at discovering the little girl could talk. By speaking, Daria had demonstrated her trust, and Gabrielle determined never to violate that trust. Following this breakthrough, Daria spoke quietly to Gabrielle, but only when they were alone.

A quick learner, Daria was soon singing the ABC song. When snapping beans, they practiced counting. Gabrielle wished for books to read to the little girl. Though she still had the book which had been in her pocket when she fell into the whirlpool, she kept it hidden.

Each day grew cooler. Unsure how to store the vegetables from the garden, Gabrielle again asked for Wanda's assistance. With a string of vile words, Alexander Volstead made Gabrielle's incompetence and burdensomeness clear. Gabrielle cringed at the language he used in front of the children.

To Wanda, he said, "Teach her to make biscuits while you're there, and be quick about it. I need you in the fields."

Wanda glared at Gabrielle. "What grown woman can't make biscuits? I'm twelve and I can."

Attempting friendliness, Gabrielle replied, "You make wonderful biscuits, Wanda. Let's make two batches, okay. First, you do it, and I'll pay close attention. Then I'll make a batch."

Wanda glanced at her father. "You can make a second batch on your own; I got work to do."

After the biscuit making lesson, they harvested the garden. Many vegetables could last for extended periods of time when stored properly. With Gabrielle, Wanda, and even Daria helping, the harvest went quickly. After digging the potatoes, they surrounded them with straw in the barn, verifying each potato was in good condition and clean of dirt, though they didn't wash them. Carrots and other root crops, except onions and garlic, were handled in the same way. Wanda demonstrated how to tie the onions and garlic in bunches and hang them from the rafters. They left the beans to dry on the vines before harvesting them but picked all the green tomatoes, peppers, and summer squash, placing them on shelves in the barn. If there wasn't another spell of heat, they would last at least a month. They added winter squash to the stores in the barn as well.

"I gotta go back an help in the field. Keep pickin' the garden 'til it won't give no more. And keep dryin' stuff as long as ya can."

As Wanda hurried away, Gabrielle wondered at this woman-child. She had no childhood. She worked as hard as any man, as did Earl. How Gabrielle wished she could reach the girl on some level. It would be a victory to get just one pleasant word from her, though she ached to help her. At her age, a girl needed a confidant.

Looking at Daria, she said, "Shall we make a pie for supper?

"Blackberry!" said Daria, who now spoke to Gabrielle, but only when they were alone.

As the weeks wore on, Daria slept snuggled next to Gabrielle. While Gabrielle harbored concerns about the child sleeping on the floor, at least she was no longer subjected to kicks and abuses as when she shared the bed with Wanda and Earl. Cuddling with her provided comfort for both of them.

Lessons were squeezed in whenever possible. Daria would be educated. Gabrielle hoped for the opportunity to educate the others.

When she mentioned taking time for schooling Wanda and Earl now that the crops were in, Mr. Volstead exploded. "Them kids don't need no learnin'. I's teachin' um everthang they'll ever need. Don't you be given um no ideas."

His explosion hadn't surprised Gabrielle. It was obvious he viewed the two children as free labor and nothing more. There was no affection, no kindness, no encouragement, no hugs, nothing to indicate a family, other than residing and working together. The only time she heard him speak was to give orders, issue a reprimand, or complain. Thankfully, most of the complaints were directed toward Gabrielle. She wondered if perhaps she had removed some of the harsh load from the children, though she saw the children had learned the hard way not to spark his ire.

More disturbing than his actions and attitude toward her, which went beyond irritating to menacing at times, was the way he referred to Daria. Though he mostly ignored her, the few times he had spoken to Gabrielle about Daria, he had used the term "that." Not as in "that child," but as in "get that outa my way." It seemed to bother Gabrielle more than Daria, who appeared only to fear her father, avoiding and hiding from him as much as possible.

The rain pounded the roof, producing a symphony of its own. As a result, after chores Volstead and the children remained in the cabin. While Wanda practiced stitches on a tiny scrap of cloth, Earl watched every move his father made, helping whenever told. Was it due to a worshipful attitude or fear he would not know how to do as told? Next to the fire, Volstead sat on his wood stump making bullets throughout the afternoon. Having him there all day unnerved Gabrielle, who maintained her usual routine. He watched her every minute he wasn't forming ammunition. The intense scrutiny made her want to shower. Daria hid in the corner by the trunk. Gabrielle had taught her how to trace on the dirt floor with her fingers, so she practiced writing letters, never making a sound.

Despite the ceaseless struggle, Gabrielle grew stronger and more capable, having learned much, some by trial and others shown grudgingly by Wanda. More confident each day, a new and growing sense of self-respect guided her steps. Proud of what she accomplished, the cabin smelled and looked clean. Meals were on time and tasty. It was worth the painful, red, dry, chapped hands, which she moistened with a dab of the butter she churned.

One morning after completing the harvest, Mr. Volstead declared he would go to town.

"Oh, I wish I'd known sooner, it would have been nice to prepare, maybe clean up a bit. But it will be so nice to see

Rose again." Gabrielle's eyes glowed with anticipation. "How soon do we need to be ready?"

"You ain't goin'! Jus' me. You got work to do." He glared as he snapped at her.

Crushed, she hurried after the man, who headed out to hitch the wagon. "Mr. Volstead."

"I done tol' ya, ya ain't goin'!"

"I understand. I just wanted to suggest, if possible, some chickens would be a nice addition. The eggs and meat would provide variety in our diet."

"Doubt I'll find any." His curt reply implied dismissal.

The children needed time off. It would be advisable if they were working when Volstead returned, so Gabrielle planned a half-day. "Wanda, Earl, finish your chores, we're going for a picnic."

"What's a picnic? And is it hard to get?" asked Earl.

Gabrielle's mouth dropped open as moisture rose around her eyes. These poor children only knew work. "We are going to play in the creek and will take our dinner with us, to eat there."

"Why?" asked Earl.

"Because it's fun."

With chores completed, Gabrielle grabbed a blanket, bundled the simple dinner she prepared in it, then got the pan of soap, which never did harden properly, and off they went.

At the creek, the children hesitated. Though cool for swimming, Gabrielle asked, "Do you know how to swim?"

"Swim?"

Their response, in unison, demanded action. Gabrielle pulled off her skirt, shoes, and socks and waded into the water in her chemise and bodice. "Daria, stay right here at the edge of the water, okay." She received a small smile in answer. Daria still did not speak around the other children. "Wanda, Earl, come."

When deep enough, she demonstrated the breaststroke. Upon reaching them, she turned over on her back and floated before doing a backstroke. Then, flipping to her stomach again, she crawled back to them. Every few seconds she glanced at Daria. Despite being well-behaved, such a young child was not to be trusted near water.

"Wow!" Earl shouted louder than necessary. "Can I do that?"

It warmed her to hear the boy's excitement. "Sure you can, but it will take practice to learn. Come here." She had him lean back as she held him, giving him instructions.

He was a good listener. Volstead expected to tell the children only once before turning a duty over to them. To not listen well meant suffering the consequences, of which she had seen evidence more than once. In her time, those consequences would have garnered a visit from Child Protective Services.

Earl soon floated on his back. A glance revealed Wanda attempting the same thing. "Point your chin to the sky."

"How do I move?" Earl asked.

She showed him how to stroke his arms.

"More, show me more!" Earl demanded.

"First you work on your backstroke, and I will work with Daria."

With time, Daria had progressed to dog paddling. When Earl saw, he demanded to be shown. "Earl, I'm happy to show you, but you need to ask nicely, not order me to show you."

"Why?"

"It shows respect for another person." The children heard only orders from Volstead. Earl learned to speak from his father. "What you should say is, will you please show me how to do that?"

With a scowl and an irritated voice, Earl said, "Will you please show me how to do that?"

The swimming lessons continued with the children making fantastic progress. When they seemed too tired to proceed, Gabrielle retrieved the pan of soap.

"Before we eat, I would like you to wash. You can scrub your clothes while you wash your body and hair."

"Why?" Earl appeared taken with the liberty of asking why.

"So you will be clean and smell good. Try it; it feels marvelous."

Though Earl appeared unconvinced, he followed orders. In his world, children dare not think of disobedience. Gabrielle observed Volstead take a switch to Earl for perceived wrongs more than once, and the man wasn't gentle about it. In fact, he gave the distinct impression he delighted in the process.

After eating, Gabrielle gathered their things, and they walked back to the cabin. By the time they reached it, they were nearly dry due to the unseasonably warm day and pleasant breeze.

That evening Alexander Volstead returned with two chickens. While not the flock she hoped for, Gabrielle was grateful and surprised he brought them. Volstead dumped them from a gunny sack onto the ground and then walked away, taking the gunny sack with him.

"Thank you," Gabrielle called after him.

The chickens would roam free in the yard, but what would keep them from wandering off? Walking into the cabin, Gabrielle grabbed a handful of cornmeal, went back out, called to the chickens, and spread it in a small line. She hoped this would ensure they would stay.

"Woman!" Gabrielle jumped at Volstead's summons.

"Yes," she said with a kindness he did not seem to possess.

"Made me a decision whilst I was gone. I ain't gonna live with a woman who ain't in my bed. We'll go to town on Sunday and marry."

The revulsion this statement produced eliminated any intimidation. "No, we will not marry! I have no intention of marrying you. I work for you in exchange for room and board, but there will be nothing more, now or ever!" Unable to conceal her anger, her balled fists rested on her hips.

"Any woman sleepin' in my house will be sleepin' in my bed."

Drawing a deep breath, Gabrielle struggled for control. "Fine! I shall sleep in the barn."

His eyes blazed. For a moment she feared he would strike her. "Take *that* with you!" He ordered, scarcely containing his fury and pointing at Daria.

"You would make your own daughter sleep in the barn?"

"Ain't no daughter o' mine."

"What do you mean?"

"My woman died, and I married a widder woman on the trail. She came with *that*." He again pointed at Daria. "Only to up and die and stick me with *that*." He pointed one last time at the small girl and stomped back to the cabin.

Heartbroken for Daria, Gabrielle picked up the child and held her close, with tears falling unrestrained. "I love you, Daria."

After supper, she gathered her possessions, took Daria's hand, and headed for the barn. She threw fresh straw on an available spot and laid the beautiful, but now worn and dirty quilt on it. Lying down, she beckoned to the child. Daria's smile glowed in the dark barn as she lay at Gabrielle's side. Gabrielle then pulled half the quilt on top of them.

Despite the concerns of mice, bugs, snakes, and other unwelcome critters, sleeping in the barn provided peace, of sorts. It allowed a welcome privacy after the close quarters of the cabin. To escape Volstead's leering and constant watch provided relaxation unavailable inside the cabin.

With the harvest complete and more time on hand, Gabrielle dug in the trunk again. Daria's threadbare dresses needed replacing. Though Gabrielle wanted to go through it earlier, there had not been enough hours in each day. Deep in the bottom, she found a woman's dress. Made of a pleasant yellow calico, it was small, not much larger than Wanda. This would make a perfect dress for Wanda. With hemming, it should fit her for some time. Perhaps it might lead to an open relationship with the hardened girl.

Digging deeper, with dreams of locating another quilt, which she and Daria could certainly use, Gabrielle continued her search in the trunk. Though no quilt showed itself, a well-worn Bible did.

She opened the cover to see the name, Emma Grace Howard. Following Howard, but clearly written at a different time, Davis. Then after Davis, Volstead. On the next page, a family tree indicated she married Arthur Ambrose Davis on March 9, 1842. Daria Grace Davis was born September 2, 1844, making her barely three years old at the time of Gabrielle's arrival. Arthur died on July 15, 1845. Emma noted he died of cholera and was much loved. Gabrielle's heart broke as she read how on July 16, 1845, Emma married Alexander Volstead, whose wife, she noted, had died in the same epidemic. Alone on the trail to Oregon, Emma hadn't known what else to do. *I wonder if she knew what sort of man she was marrying?* It included no listing of her date of death; Gabrielle was sure the Volstead family did not read or write.

Daria's family. This Bible belonged to Daria. Gabrielle suffered no guilt when she tucked the Bible into the pocket of her skirt to stash with her novel in the barn. Someday Daria would want to learn about her birth family, perhaps search for relatives in the East, and the information in the Bible would help her. For now, Gabrielle could read it to Daria, providing much-needed inspiration.

While the household ran much smoother, no progress had been made in reaching Volstead or the older children, beyond the day of the picnic. Though Gabrielle attempted conversation, it was met with silence or contemptuous comments and insults.

On the morning she completed hemming the yellow dress, Gabrielle insisted Wanda go to the creek and bathe. Volstead was hunting, so they would have time before his return. Gabrielle restrained her joy when Wanda returned clean with washed hair and busied herself with dinner as the girl changed. Turning, Gabrielle gasped. "Wanda, you look lovely." She wished for a mirror so Wanda could see how lovely she looked.

"It'll only take a day in the fields to ruin it, anyway." The hardness of her tone held a hint of sadness.

Gabrielle cringed at the reality of the statement. Wanda's other clothing was so small she could no longer wear it. With no other material available, it was impossible to make her more work clothes. Then an idea struck. In the trunk, lay a set of men's clothing; Gabrielle guessed it had belonged to Daria's father, Ambrose Davis. While she had planned it for Earl, his clothes were still serviceable, so she would make work clothes for Wanda.

Removing the shirt and pants from the trunk, she had Wanda try them on. Gabrielle cuffed the hem and marked where to move the button. Then she marked where to shorten the shirt, thinking this would give her some extra material, maybe enough to put together something for Daria.

"Pants?" Contempt seeped into Wanda's tone.

"You'll find them easier for working. And you'll have clothes for work and clothes for nice."

"And just when will I wear the nice?"

The truth of the barbed question saddened Gabrielle. "You never know when an opportunity will arise. At least you'll have an option when I wash your work clothes." Even as she said it, she realized the absurdity of it, since the family had not changed out of the clothes they wore since her arrival.

Gabrielle had Wanda remove the pants while she moved the button and added a few stitches to hold the cuff, and then Wanda tried them again. She looked cute. Gabrielle gave silent thanks when Wanda allowed her hair to be braided. She was a very attractive girl.

Just then, Volstead and Earl entered the cabin. He threw a rabbit and two grouse on the clean table next to the food. Upon seeing Wanda, Volstead grunted, sat, and shoveled food into his mouth. Gabrielle could see the barest flash of disappointment on Wanda's face before she joined them. As she looked on, Gabrielle said a silent prayer to forgive and remove the contempt she felt for this man.

When they finished their meal, the three headed back to the fields, with Wanda wearing her new pants and shirt. While small, Gabrielle rejoiced at the breakthrough. Other than swimming, it was the first time since arriving at the Volstead's that Wanda had shown the tiniest bit of interest or spoken to her with anything but contempt. Perhaps with time.

Looking at the three dead animals still on the table, Gabrielle knew she was expected to clean them. Kyle considered himself quite the outdoorsman, though he had never hunted. But together they watched multitudes of documentaries telling what to do with wild game. Under the current circumstances, she gave thanks for the memorable lesson on dressing a grouse.

Thoughts of Kyle made her understand how comparatively good life had been with him. Despite the need to beware of anything that may set him off, during his sane times he treated her well. He conducted himself as a gentleman. He bought her little gifts. He even complimented her. He led the family in devotions. *I miss family devotions.*

Focusing on the dead animals, she laid the grouse on its back on the floor, spread the wings, and stepped on them with her feet right next to the body. She gripped the legs close to the body, took a deep breath, and with a slow, steady pull, the legs, feathers, and head came off the bird. After stopping a moment to take a steadying breath, she cut the legs off the rest and set them on the table. Picking the body and wings off the floor, she scooped the entrails out, pulled the hunk of hanging feathers off the bird, and cut the wings off the body. She then sliced down the back, filleting the breast meat from one side and then the other.

Though she hadn't completed the job as smoothly nor as neatly as the man in the movie, she was satisfied. After repeating the process with the other bird, she set aside the entrails for the pigs. Then she looked at the rabbit. No rabbit dressing movies. Baffled, she decided to tackle the task like a fish.

Hoping to preserve the hide, she made a long slit up the stomach. It peeled off the rabbit, much like a banana. She had expected to need to cut it from the flesh. After cutting the hide from the head and legs, she ran the knife along the belly, being careful not to cut too deeply; she knew she needed to avoid cutting into the intestines. Her stomach wrenched as she gently scooped the intestines out of the animal, adding them to the entrails for the pigs. Seeing the liver, kidneys, and heart, she removed them, saving them aside for food. She retched as she cut off the head and the feet, leaving the legs attached, and the contents of her stomach outside the cabin.

Surprised at her work, she had done an acceptable job. She certainly never expected to need such knowledge. But then, she had done a lot of things since coming here she never expected to do.

She would ask Volstead about tanning the rabbit hide. Perhaps he would teach them all. She assumed he would know how. If she saved several, she could sew them together and make a coat for Daria, or with many, a blanket.

After washing all the meat, she left the rabbit in a cold bucket of water with salt, for tomorrow's dinner. The grouse she chopped and combined with vegetables and potatoes in a stir-fry for supper.

During supper, she asked about tanning the rabbit hide, Volstead looked at Earl and told him to take care of it, since the helpless woman couldn't. Gabrielle didn't know why she was surprised that an eight-year-old would know how to tan a rabbit hide, he did everything else the grown man did. She would watch as he worked on it, so she could learn.

As the weather grew colder, the drafts in the cabin became increasingly intolerable. Unlike the Hargrove's cozy little place, the logs were not fit tightly together. It looked as though someone had begun to chink it, but stopped. Without chinking to fill the considerable gaps, light and air easily entered the cabin. Surprised, though she didn't know why, that they had tolerated two winters without completing the job, Gabrielle determined to finish the chinking. With time in short supply, she decided the method she used in the garden would work well. Each day she mixed one bucket of mud, broke bits of straw into it, and chinked the walls of the cabin. Before long, the completed job resulted in a cabin far less drafty, warmer, and requiring less wood to heat.

On Monday, as Gabrielle readied the laundry, she eyed the dress Wanda had outgrown. When washed, perhaps she could make Daria a dress or a shirt for Earl. Due to the extreme filth of the article, she rinsed it in the creek when fetching water. To begin its washing in the washtub would necessitate the immediate changing of water.

Gabrielle saved the dress for last. As she added soap and scrubbed it on the washboard, the old, soiled dress disintegrated. Wool may have survived the constant wearing and filth, but her efforts revealed it was probably made from old flour sacks, which could not withstand the abuse. What little of the material remained intact, she sadly cut and added to the outhouse rag pile.

I miss toilet paper. Who knew a roll of thin paper could make such a difference in life? How long before Sears and Roebuck put out their catalogs? While that scratchy paper didn't sound pleasant, it held more appeal than washing rags every week. But then, she assumed the early catalogs were black and white on thin paper, rather than the high gloss, colored paper of later years. Gabrielle remembered her mother saying that her great-grandparents didn't get plumbing until the late 1960s and they kept a Sears and Roebuck catalog in the outhouse. It had sounded odd. Now she understood.

Gabrielle's disappointment was keen. While she understood people of this era made do with little, the lack of certain essentials was unacceptable. With the hard work this family put forth, the farm produced well. No doubt Clement Brown would gladly trade yard goods for its products. Perhaps she could speak to Volstead about it.

If necessary, she would use the material from the beautiful dress Rose had given her. Since she had specified its use, Gabrielle hated to cut it apart, but Rose would understand. First, she would try Volstead.

At supper that night, Gabrielle dared to approach the subject. "You may have noticed I was able to come up with new clothes for Wanda."

Rather than respond, Volstead merely looked at Gabrielle as he continued shoveling food into his mouth.

"Earl and Daria also need clothes. They are outgrowing theirs, which are quite threadbare. I'm sure you would also enjoy a fresh change of clothing. Additional bedding would be helpful with the weather getting colder."

Still no response, though he had stopped shoveling food and sat looking at her, suspicion in his eyes.

Gabrielle decided flattery may help, so she continued. "With all your hard work this farm seems to produce far more than we need, I thought perhaps you could trade a bit for some yard goods."

Volstead said nothing and resumed eating. At least he didn't refuse, so she chose to see it in a positive light.

When the garden had given all it could, and Gabrielle had picked all the dried beans, she pulled the remnants. She grabbed a shovel and loaded a roughly fashioned wheelbarrow with manure from behind the barn. At the garden, she spread the manure over the soil, then repeated the process three more times.

During dinner, she asked Volstead, "Would it be possible for you to till it into the soil?"

"Why the fool did ya do that?" He growled while glaring at her.

"To fertilize the garden, helping to produce better next year."

"Foolishness."

After clearing the dinner mess, Gabrielle grabbed a hoe and shovel, turning the manure into the garden, thankful she had hoed it on a regular basis since her arrival. She continued until time to prepare supper, hoping it was mixed well enough. The next day, she laid a layer of straw on top, to help deter weed growth and provide added compost material to work with the manure, before adding leaves from nearby trees. Hopefully, the extra effort would make an easier, more productive plot in the spring.

With the prepping of the garden, the thought of remaining with the Volsteads season after season, maybe years, jarred Gabrielle. *Oh Kyle, I'm so sorry for not appreciating the good in you.* She had yet to find any form of good in Volstead, except perhaps that he took her on, but taking her on was for his benefit only, not hers.

Late, too late in the year to still be traveling, a wagon with a young couple arrived. After speaking with Volstead, the man spoke briefly with his wife, helped her down, unhitched his team, and went to help Volstead.

After so long without seeing another soul, Gabrielle stared, unmoving. She soon recovered her composure and ventured out to greet the young woman.

She was quite beautiful. Her strawberry blonde hair glowed like a halo from beneath her bonnet. Despite being on the trail, she was clean and well dressed, with a lovely shade of pale blue calico peaking from under a cloak. *Sweet,* thought Gabrielle. *This young woman looks sweet.* What gave that impression, Gabrielle didn't know, but it stuck with her. As she approached the woman, Gabrielle understood. It wasn't the clothes, her hair, her cleanliness, or even the way she stood. It was the serene expression on her face. Peaceful. In Gabrielle's harsh, new world, this woman was a pure ray of sunshine.

"Welcome! I'm Gabrielle Fallon. It's so good to meet you. You're the first people I've seen since coming to work here. You are, as they say, a sight for sore eyes."

With a slight curtsy, the woman introduced herself. "Good afternoon. So pleased to meet you, Mrs. Fallon, I'm Mrs. Elsie Wicks. My husband is Mr. Daniel Wicks. It appears we will be here for a while as he does some work for your husband."

Gabrielle hastened to correct her misconception. "Oh no, he's not my husband, I'm employed here. His name is Volstead, Alexander Volstead. He lost his wife some time ago, and I needed a place to stay, so he hired me to run the household."

"Oh! Excuse me; I assumed you were married."

"Understandable mistake. Please, don't worry about it. Actually, I sleep in the barn and would as soon be buried in it before marrying *him*." Gabrielle cringed. "I'm sorry, that was unkind. Where are my manners? Please, come in out of the cold."

As they walked inside, Gabrielle became mindful of her appearance. Though she attempted to keep up her hygiene, with all the hard and dirty work, it was difficult.

"Could I offer you some coffee?"

"No, thank you. What you can do is tell me how I can help. We are apparently going to be here a few days in exchange for supplies, and I do hope to be of assistance to you."

"Oh, it will be wonderful to have another woman around. I was just about to begin supper. Unfortunately, I'm not the best cook. How are your cooking skills?"

"Mr. Wicks teases that he wed me for my cooking, so I better be proficient. My baskets were always one of the first to sell at the socials."

Gabrielle perceived the speed at which her baskets sold may have had as much to do with the cook as the food. "Fabulous! Perhaps while you're here, you can teach me a few things."

"I would love to! I'll be right back." With this, she walked to her wagon, retrieved an adorable apron, returned, and took charge.

Gabrielle marveled at her self-confidence. Even in a stranger's home, with unfamiliar people, and cooking over a fireplace, she appeared right at home. *Amazing*, thought Gabrielle. *If only I had a smidgen of her self-assurance.*

Conversation was light and enjoyable as the two women worked together. Elsie Wicks was a patient and thorough instructor. Gabrielle, an eager learner. She wished Wanda could be in on this, both for the cooking lesson and the social instruction, but she was doing chores for Volstead.

At supper, it became apparent the Wicks were not only well suited for one another but saw only the best in everyone. They didn't seem to notice the lack of positive social banter from Volstead, or if they did, they chose to pretend otherwise. They told of their travels and seemed to think the harshness of the trip west to be a great adventure.

"Surely the train came long afore now. Why you 'rive so late?" Volstead inquired.

"It's an unfortunate story," Mr. Wicks began. "We made what we thought were wonderful friends on the trail. After arriving, we found adjoining parcels, which would allow us to help one another, and provide a built-in social life for us and our families, when the time comes. We found a beautiful spot and built the other family's cabin first, since they had two children and another on the way. Built them a nice, snug cabin, spacious enough for their expanding family. Then, as long as we were in the area, the man suggested we go ahead and erect their barn before starting on our cabin. 'Won't take long,' he said. Though I wanted to provide a cabin for the Mrs., he assured me it wouldn't be long before we'd start on our cabin. Well, we built that family a nice barn to go with that fine cabin. The women finished chinking the cabin while we built the barn."

"Might neighborly o' ya," Volstead said. The expression on his face clearly stated he considered the man an idiot, but then, as though an idea seized him, his countenance brightened as he nodded.

"Once we completed that barn and it was time to start on our place, the man's tune changed. He insisted he didn't know what I was talking about. Said he didn't have time to build someone else's cabin; he had work to do to get his family set for winter. I tell you, I was flabbergasted! Until then, they seemed to be such a wonderful family. Looked like we had found lifetime friends. Well, Mrs. Wicks and I discussed it and determined we didn't want to live near such neighbors. After all, when we have children, what kind of influence would their children be? I was angry. Here we were, so late in the season and no roof over my wife's head. I didn't want to see him ever again. So the Mrs. and I loaded up and took off. We figured there is a lot of land left and we would find a fitting place elsewhere. I must admit; I am concerned about getting shelter up.

"Now darling, there's no need to worry. I have already told you, if we need to spend the winter in the wagon, we will be fine."

"Not going to happen. We'll soon find a place, and I will build us a nice little cabin."

Gabrielle appreciated seeing the obvious love the couple shared. She enjoyed hearing conversation at the table. It had been so long since she had heard anything but slurping, chewing, grunts, burps, and complaints; it was refreshing.

After the meal, Volstead offered to help Mr. Wicks set up for the night, surprising Gabrielle. He always crawled into bed after supper.

Mrs. Wicks helped clear the table and wash the dishes before excusing herself for the evening.

Taking Daria's hand, Gabrielle headed for the barn. She was amazed to see Volstead helping Mr. Wicks and chatting on like they were old buddies.

Odd, she thought.

The next day was productive. Elsie Wicks taught Gabrielle a few more cooking techniques, and they took turns standing guard while the other bathed in the washtub in front of the fire. The hot bath was a delight. Since it became too cold to bathe in the creek, Gabrielle limited herself to hurried sponge baths in the mornings after breakfast. She hadn't felt truly clean for weeks.

Conversation flowed as the two women worked. Elsie Wicks was easy to talk to. While the relationship felt different than her relationship with Rose Brown, it was relaxed. Better yet, it was positive. It was so lovely to have such optimistic people around again.

Oddly, Volstead was nicer. Far more peculiar, he bathed! Gabrielle hoped it was because the Wicks brought out the good in him, but suspected there was more to it than that. Meals were bastions of conversation. Gabrielle was shocked how sociable Volstead could be when he chose to be. Instead of working the fields with him, Volstead had Wanda and Earl cleaning the yard and creating order outside.

The following morning Elsie Wicks surprised Gabrielle, "We may be neighbors if the parcel next to this is still available."

"What?" Gabrielle's jaw dropped as she asked for clarification.

"Mr. Volstead has kindly offered to help us if we should choose to build nearby. He said he must finish harvesting the winter wheat crop, but if Mr. Wicks helps, they will finish in no time and then build us a cabin."

Understanding dawned on Gabrielle. Now she knew why Volstead had unexpectedly and shockingly grown so sociable. Why he was so chatty and kind. Why he was so complimentary. Why the children had been cleaning the yard. She could not allow this wonderful, trusting, naïve couple to be swindled again. "Mrs. Wicks," Gabrielle clasped her new friend's hand. "I would dearly love to have you and Mr. Wicks as neighbors. You are wonderful, kind, and loving people. You are also very trusting. Some might say," she hesitated, "gullible."

Elsie Wicks eyes enlarged, and her head went back as though she had been slapped.

"Please, I beg of you, do not take offense. I mean what I say in the nicest way. I must tell you what I have seen, heard, and experienced since coming here so you can make an informed decision regarding your future."

Gabrielle told of the conditions she had found upon arrival: cabin, outhouse, garden, yard, barn, and children. She described his treatment of the children, animals, and herself. Finally, she revealed the change which came over Volstead from the moment he heard Mr. Wicks' telling of the cabin built for their previous neighbors.

"Mrs. Wicks, though I have no desire to speak ill of anyone, I have lived this horrible existence for months. Alexander Volstead is not a nice man. I would not suggest to my worst enemy to align themselves with him. I am here because I have nowhere else to go. If I did, I would not be here. Please, discuss this with your husband before taking Volstead up on his proposal. I fear you will once again be left homeless."

The next morning, after making their excuses to Volstead, the Wicks collected a small amount of food for all the work they had contributed, packed their wagon, said their goodbyes, and left.

Gabrielle ached as she watched them drive away. She enjoyed the companionship of Elsie Wicks. The conversation during meals was a delight. The improvements Volstead made in just two days were considerable. But her relief that they would not once again be taken advantage of by an unscrupulous and selfish man overshadowed any regrets. She prayed for them as they drove away, asking the Lord to keep and protect them.

As the weeks progressed, each night, Gabrielle piled all of her clothing on top of the quilt, in an attempt to keep them both warm. She grew concerned as winter neared. As the temperature dropped, she laid straw on top of the quilt and clothes. Though the roof kept the barn dry, the floor sprouted an ooze. She added more straw beneath them.

When the cold spell arrived, leaving frost covering the ground and a thin layer of ice on the puddles, Gabrielle awoke chilled to the bone. She wrapped her shawl around Daria as they trudged stiffly to the cabin and resolved to move them back inside–under her terms.

Though not warm by twenty-first century standards, the warmth of the fire felt incredible. The chinking helped considerably. After warming, Gabrielle said, "Mr. Volstead, it is below freezing out there and impossible to stay warm in the barn with only one blanket. We must be permitted to resume sleeping on the cabin floor."

With a malicious glint in his eyes, he said, "You know my terms."

"I will cook and clean, but nothing more. That will not change."

Grabbing her arm, he pulled her close. "You'll do as I say!"

Gabrielle jerked away. "You will not touch me, Mr. Volstead!"

At this statement, he pulled her to him and mashed his vile mouth against her soft lips in what she assumed he thought was a kiss. It reminded Gabrielle of his repulsive approach to eating. When he released her, she backed away. "You keep your filthy hands off of me!" Though with every fiber of her being, she wanted to slap him as they did in the movies, her awareness of the children's observation precluded such dramatics.

His fury showed as he rammed her against the wall, and slammed his work-hardened right fist into her delicate face, followed by a massive left fist into her stomach.

Gabrielle collapsed as her breath left her. Blood poured from her nose and the corner of her mouth. She gasped for breath as she felt a rib-cracking kick in her side. Dizzy with the intense pain, nausea overwhelmed her. Closing her eyes, she took several slow deep breaths, attempting to gain control of both her emotions and the pain. When she opened her eyes, only Daria remained in the cabin.

Tears streaked Daria's little face as she stood with her hand on Gabrielle's shoulder. Taking the towel Daria proffered, Gabrielle first dried Daria's tears, and then worked to staunch the flow of blood coming from her nose. Gabrielle winced with each touch.

The blood finally ceased its flow. Gabrielle managed to stand, and with a steadying hand stumbled to the shelf and pulled off a clean towel, then staggered to the bucket of fresh water. With the wet towel and delicate touches, she washed her face free of blood. Once again soaking the towel in the refreshing, cold water, she held it to her face, cautious of her nose. The already substantial swelling told her it was broken.

Daria's tears still flowed, but no a sound came forth. She had learned the lesson well, to avoid being seen, never be heard. Gabrielle held her arms out to her. Daria rushed in. Embracing her, Gabrielle felt her sobs but heard no sound.

When the crying ceased, Gabrielle made eye contact. "Sweetheart, I know that was scary, and it did hurt a lot, but we have a long day ahead of us. We will walk to town. Do you think you can do that?"

Daria nodded.

"Good girl."

Gabrielle rinsed the towel, wrung it out, and handed it to Daria before grabbing a loaf of bread, which she wrapped in a clean towel, and peeked out the cabin door to see Volstead and the other children chopping and stacking firewood. Taking Daria's hand, she scurried to the barn. Gabrielle took four apples and added them, along with the loaf of bread, to the satchel of her clothes. She tied the wet towel to the handle.

After putting Daria's extra dress over the one she was wearing to provide added warmth, Gabrielle studied Daria. Momentary reluctance seized her. The little girl wore two threadbare dresses and had no shoes. How could she possibly walk to town in the freezing weather? With conviction, Gabrielle dug her blue skirt out of the satchel. Removing the brown wool skirt given to her by Rose, she put on the blue one. After buttoning her flannel shirt on Daria, Gabrielle gave thanks for the button attached to the middle of the arm to allow rolling of the sleeve, which made the sleeve only slightly too long for Daria. She then placed the wool skirt over Daria's head, and buttoned it at her neck, creating a cape. It was too long for the small child, so Gabrielle found a piece of twine in the barn and belted it around Daria's waist, leaving the top blousy to take up the length of the skirt/cape and allow her room to move her arms. Removing the beautiful wool socks Rose gave her and replacing them with her ankle socks, she slipped her feet back into her shoes. She put the wool socks on Daria and folded them back over her feet, creating a double layer. A piece of twine at each ankle secured the socks on her feet. Another at the toe tip of the sock kept it from rolling.

Gabrielle told Daria to remain in the barn until she returned. At the fear in Daria's eyes, she hugged her. "It's okay; I'll be right back."

With a fortifying breath, Gabrielle opened the door with purpose and marched toward the woodpile. A prudent ten feet from Volstead, she stopped. "I'm leaving."

"Suits me fine. Take that brat with you."

At this hoped-for statement, Gabrielle retreated to the barn but hesitated a moment before entering to study Wanda and Earl, who remained focused on stacking the firewood. Though guilt plagued her for abandoning them to Volstead, she had no option. For Daria's safety and her own, she had to flee. They were his children; she could not take them. In the barn, she tied the shawl on Daria's head, draped the quilt around her own head and shoulders, picked up the satchel, pulled Daria's hand through the slit of the skirt beneath the button to hold, and walked out the door, headed for town.

The small child and battered woman struggled through the long, arduous walk. Gabrielle occasionally carried Daria. Though lightweight, the satchel, quilt, and possibly broken ribs made holding her difficult. They rested on a regular basis.

Gabrielle glanced back frequently, out of fear Volstead would change his mind and force them to return.

When crossing a small creek, they quenched their growing thirst. Gabrielle seized the opportunity to bathe her bloodied and swollen face in the cold water. After several splashes of water to her face, she took the towel from the satchel handle, soaked it in the water, and held it on her face, enjoying the soothing feel. She hoped it would reduce, or at least limit, the swelling. Breathing was becoming difficult and the interference with her vision problematic.

"Daria, would you like a piece of bread?"

Daria nodded. She was back to nodding, shaking, pointing, and the other non-verbal signals used when Gabrielle first arrived at the Volstead's. Witnessing Volstead's violent actions that morning, coupled with the amount of resulting blood, had traumatized her.

"Daria, do you know where we are going?"

Daria shook her head.

"To town! Have you ever been to town?"

Another shake.

"I have wonderful friends there who will help us. Their home is cozy and safe. My friends, Mr. and Mrs. Brown, are kind, gentle people, who smile and laugh a lot. Does that sound nice?"

Daria slowly nodded her head in reply.

Perhaps the child didn't comprehend the permanence of the departure from the Volstead's, so Gabrielle attempted to explain. "You know, we won't be returning to that farm ever again. We are safe now. I will always take care of you and won't let anyone hurt you. You won't ever have to see them again. Does that make you feel better?"

The child nodded and hugged Gabrielle.

Gabrielle held her tightly. "Ah, Daria, I love you. Everything will be just fine."

As Gabrielle said the words, she hoped they were correct. With her relief at escaping Volstead and being able to take Daria with her, she had somehow forgotten she was once again homeless in a strange time and place. Now it wasn't just her, but the two of them, in winter. Saying a silent prayer, she found peace knowing they weren't alone.

After again washing her face and soothing it with the wet towel, Gabrielle tied it around the handle of the satchel. With a painful attempt at a smile for Daria, they continued on their journey.

Remembering the games she played in the car with her children on long trips, Gabrielle and Daria had a scavenger hunt, played the ABC game, sang songs, and told stories. Or at least Gabrielle sang and talked. Daria only pointed and watched. When they paused to rest, they snacked on apple or bread. On one break, Daria napped. Gabrielle contemplated the regret of leaving the other children to such a life, especially after seeing glimpses of light in them, but she had to save Daria and herself. After a good cry, Gabrielle joined Daria in a brief nap.

Around noon, a misty rain started.

Thankful she paid close attention to landmarks on the way to the Volstead farm, Gabrielle was reasonably sure they were near their destination as the sun reached the horizon. Finally, with the last trace of light, she saw it in the distance.

Squatting, she pointed. "Daria, look, not much further," She tried to smile around the pain and swelling.

A little hand reached up and gingerly touched her sore and swollen face. She then kissed the better side. As tears filled Gabrielle's eyes, she struggled to maintain her composure. With a kiss on the little hand, she held it and said, "Let's hurry."

6

Prompted by the dark store, they walked to the back door, which opened to the living quarters. As she knocked, Gabrielle attempted a smile at Daria, who clung to her hand.

At the sight of Rose, Gabrielle finally felt secure.

Replaced by shock, anger, and sorrow in succession, the joy and surprise left Rose's face. "Oh my!" Tears pooled at the sight of her friend. Pulling her inside, she called her husband. "Clement…"

Upon seeing Gabrielle, Clement's expression set into a hard look, but his kind voice held regret. "Oh, Mrs. Fallon, I'm so sorry. I didn't know."

"You have no reason to apologize. Please don't feel guilty."

As Rose assisted Gabrielle onto a chair to allow a better look at the damage to her face, she noticed Daria, "What? Who?"

"This is Daria. Daria, this is Mr. and Mrs. Brown."

The little girl did her best to hide behind Gabrielle, fear revealed on her pale face.

"It's okay, Daria. These are the nice people I told you about. We're safe here."

Realizing they had walked all day, Rose helped remove their sodden, makeshift wraps. "You two must be hungry. We were about to sit down to supper. Let me add a few things, and we'll eat in no time."

As they finished eating, Daria's eyes drooped, and her head fell against the chair back. Gabrielle said, "I can't thank you enough for taking us in. It's been a long, rough day, and we're worn out. Could we find a place to sleep?"

"The two of you just bed down in here with Rose; I'll sleep on the beans in the store."

"I appreciate the offer, but perhaps we could set up a place in the storeroom. It might be easier for Daria."

"But it's cold in there, and the floor is hard," Rose grasped Gabrielle's arm as she objected.

"Believe me; it will be luxury. We've slept in the barn for some time now." Looking at the quilt, laid aside when they arrived, she continued, "Though I deeply regret the condition of the lovely quilt you gave me, I must express my heartfelt appreciation. It was all we had for sleeping."

With her tears returning, Rose said, "Don't you worry about the quilt; there's more where it came from, and it's washable. I'm so sorry I didn't send more with you, or that you were there at all." She reached toward Gabrielle's battered face, withdrawing her hand before touching it.

Mr. Brown moved a few bushels of beans to create a bed for them in the storeroom, while Rose dug several quilts out of a trunk. Then Gabrielle laid Daria on the makeshift bed.

"Thank you." Gabrielle's voice caught, preventing her from saying more. It was nice to be around gracious, compassionate people again. Even in the irrational life with Kyle, there were moments and occasional days of fun and laughter. He could be loving and kind when he chose. With the Volsteads, any form of kindness, compassion, or graciousness was nonexistent.

As Gabrielle finished changing into her nightgown, Rose tapped on the storeroom door before entering. "I thought you might like this." She handed Gabrielle a wet cloth and a glass of water. "I had Clement get cold water from the well."

"Ah, Rose, what would I do without you? Thank you so much."

"Does it hurt terribly?"

"Yes, but I know it could have been worse, so I'm thankful. Though I think my nose is broken. Does it look as bad as it feels?"

"Both of your eyes are black and puffy, your nose is swollen to twice its normal size, and you have scrapes and bruises on your left cheek."

"That's where he punched me. His massive fist got the nose as well." Gabrielle shuddered at the memory of his fists hitting her. "I'm just thankful he stopped after two punches and a kick."

"He hit you twice? And kicked you?"

"The second blow was in the stomach."

The anger and revulsion evident on Rose's face came out in her voice. "We need to do something about this. He can't get away with it!"

"Rose, unless there is some form of law here, I don't think anything can be done." Considering the era, she continued, "Even then, I'm not sure they would do anything. I worry though, about the two remaining children. Even at eight and twelve, they've already developed many of his characteristics. During the months I was there, I could not get through to them on anything but the basest level."

Rose hugged Gabrielle. "I'll let you sleep now. In the morning you can tell me how Daria came to be with you."

"Thank you again, Rose."

In the middle of the night, Gabrielle woke while trying to scream, but no sound came forth. She gasped as though unable to breathe. The nightmare left her shaking and frightened. Although she just awoke, she could not remember most of it. But she did remember both Kyle and Volstead were there. For some reason, she was being forced to return to them both. Shivers crawled up her spine at the thought.

The realization that she feared returning to Kyle, even if she could get back to her own time, was a shock. He had seemed so perfect until a few months into her pregnancy with Nicholas. Then he changed. Or perhaps he began showing his true self. It was like living with Dr. Jekyll and Mr. Hyde. Only this Jekyll was too sweet, sickeningly so. She despised him as much as Hyde. At least with Hyde, she wasn't waiting for the ball to drop. She knew he was crazy and would say or do anything. With Jekyll, it was all lies, one big act.

The notion of her beautiful children living alone with that man induced a cascade of tears. What would happen to them? Would they be safe without her to keep him calm? Who would love them? Kyle possessed no concept of the word. The months of unshed tears flowed uncontrollably. Weeping as she had not since the initial realization that she could not return to them, Gabrielle grieved the loss of her children.

When at last the tears ceased, Gabrielle realized a small hand stroked her back. Such an amazing blessing, this child, this gift from God. While trading three children for one would not have been her choice, she could not imagine her life without Daria.

Lifting the cloth Rose provided, she wiped her face and nose, realizing she had chosen the worst of moments to vent her grief. Her throbbing, swollen nose didn't take kindly to the attempt to wipe it. Instinct and common sense told her it would not be a good time to blow it. After a tender wipe, she cuddled Daria and fell back to sleep.

Waking early, with Daria still asleep, Gabrielle heard the Browns busy in the other room. Wrapped in her shawl, she made her way through the store and tapped on the door of the living quarters.

"Oh good, you're awake." Rose greeted her as she opened the door. "I thought you might enjoy a bath, so we've been hauling and heating water. The washtub is almost ready. Clement will work in the store until you're finished."

"That sounds wonderful! Thank you. But what if Daria awakens?"

"Clement will keep the storeroom door open and if she wakes will send her in here."

After Mr. Brown left, Gabrielle removed her clothing and squeezed cross-legged into the washtub. While it wasn't the roomy, relaxing soak of her century, it felt heavenly.

Since the weather had gotten too cold for bathing in the creek, she and Daria had been taking sponge baths in the cabin after the others left for work. Using the washtub had been out of the question, since Volstead could, and would enter at any time. Unaware of any time the others had bathed during her months there, other than the day of the picnic, when she gave the dress to Wanda, and during the Wicks visit, she was determined to teach Daria basic hygiene.

Rose handed Gabrielle a bar of soap, which had a delicate scent of lilacs. "I thought you might appreciate something feminine right now. Use it on your hair also, and then I'll pour the rinse water."

After her bath, Gabrielle realized her things were still in the storeroom. Rose reassured her. "I noticed last night blood covered the bodice, so we'll give yours a good washing before you wear them again. I dug out some of my clean things for you and put a few basting stitches in the skirt. Oh, and feel free to use the tooth powder if you want; I would venture to guess the Volstead didn't stock any. If you think of anything else you need, just ask."

As Gabrielle finger-combed her hair, Rose moved her hand and combed it for her, using a beautiful, tortoiseshell comb.

"Tell me about Daria." Rose prompted.

"It's amazing, considering I'm homeless and unable to care for myself, but I consider that child a gift from God."

"When I first arrived at Volstead's, the little attention they paid her shocked me. The way they treated her appalled me, never a kind word or a smidgen of love shown; it was heartbreaking. They provided the absolute bare minimum for her. During the rare occasion Mr. Volstead referred to her, he said 'that.' Not that child, not Daria, not her, but just 'that.' It wasn't until after the crops were in and he came to town that Daria and I slept in the barn. He planned for us to go to town the next Sunday and wed. I refused, saying I would work for him, but marriage was out of the question. He said any woman who lived in his cabin would share his bed. So I countered by telling him I would sleep in the barn. He ordered me to take Daria. I was shocked that he would have his daughter sleep in the barn, until he told me she wasn't his. His wife died, so he married Daria's mother, a widow, who died soon after, leaving him with Daria. When the freeze came, I insisted we return to the cabin. He said only on his terms and grabbed me. When I tried to shake him off, he became violent. The children saw the whole thing, Daria included. Afterward, when he and the other children went out to work, I got the bleeding stopped, grabbed a loaf of bread, took Daria to the barn, packed our things, added apples, and told Daria to stay put. I then told Volstead I was leaving. He said to take that brat with me, just as I hoped. I could not have left her there." The story burst forth in a non-stop flood. It felt so good to share the nightmare with her friend. Rose remained quiet for some time before speaking. "We must make clothes for her. Poor thing, she's wearing rags."

"I wanted to make something for her but lacked material. As you saw, I wore my lightweight skirt yesterday so she could wear the wool one as a cloak. She didn't have a coat or shoes, so I fashioned some for her from the socks you gave me. I'm afraid they are ruined."

"Good. We'll find another pair for you, and…" Rose's eyes filled with tears.

"I'd better check Daria." In the storeroom, Gabrielle found what she feared. Daria was awake and still, afraid to make a noise. "Good morning, Daria. It's okay; I was in the next room taking a bath. Let's go get you cleaned up; there's more water heating."

Daria's sad eyes looked at Gabrielle's face.

"I'm okay, sweetie. It doesn't hurt as much now, and I feel so much better now that I'm clean. You will too." Taking her hand, she led her to the other room.

The wash tub fit Daria much better. Though she had no memory of ever bathing in a wash tub before meeting Gabrielle, it didn't take long for her to enjoy the experience. While she bathed, Rose found a camisole for her to wear. "This will do if we tie the straps while we make a proper dress."

After breakfast, Rose took out the lengths of material cut from Gabrielle's clothes. "Do you think we could incorporate these into something for Daria? She might enjoy having dresses like you."

"Rose, that's a splendid idea!"

As they busied themselves making Daria a dress, they encouraged her to relax and smile. However, the timid smile refused to show itself until they completed two dresses. One included the brown wool used in Gabrielle's skirt; the other included the white cotton of Gabrielle's petticoat.

At supper that evening, they discussed Gabrielle's situation. As hopeless as she felt, the Brown's positive attitudes lifted her spirits.

"We'll find something," Clement Brown said. "This time though, I'll investigate to confirm it's a safe and wholesome environment."

"For now, you rest and heal. We are fine with you here." Rose smiled at the little girl. "This gives us an opportunity to get to know Daria,"

As the days wore on, Daria grew more comfortable with the Browns, though she still resisted speaking. After a week, Gabrielle determined it was time. Upon waking, Gabrielle asked Daria which dress she would like to wear. Daria's answer was to point at the desired dress. "No, Daria, you know how to talk. You need to use your words. Tell me the color." Daria again pointed. "Daria, sweetheart, I understand you were very scared by what happened at the Volsteads' cabin. But look at my face; it looks much better, doesn't it?" Daria nodded. "The Brown's are kind and welcoming, aren't they?" Daria nodded. "We are both safe now. There is no reason to be afraid. You will always stay with me. I won't let anyone hurt you or take you from me. I love you."

Daria studied Gabrielle before a tear slid down her cheek. The child put her arms around Gabrielle and whispered, "I love you."

Gabrielle's heart squeezed. The joy of this child was immeasurable, just as losing her own was unbearable. She looked at Daria with a slight smile, "Do you trust me?"

Daria nodded, and then with a look from Gabrielle said, "Yes."

"Good. Can you try to trust the Browns enough to speak to them?"

"Okay," she said with a slow and quiet voice.

"That's my good and very brave girl."

Shocked to discover both Thanksgiving and Christmas had come and gone while she was at the Volstead's without the tiniest sign or mention, Gabrielle thought, *How sad to know the celebration of the Lord's birth meant nothing to the man.* At this thought, Gabrielle's heart wrenched, thinking of his two young children who knew nothing of love, or faith, or even happiness, only work. How she wished she could have gotten through to them, and to him. To live such a life was so very sad. What meaning was there to it?

As her thoughts wandered, as she had so many times before, she wondered what God's purpose in bringing her to this time could have been. To save Daria? But what of Francis, Nicholas, and Alyson? Didn't they need her also? Or was there a lesson there for Kyle? She prayed he might learn whatever lessons the Lord had for him. Admittedly, she had no feelings for him. Whatever feelings there once were, he had stomped out with his abusiveness. She had prayed relentlessly to love her husband. Did she still need to pray that prayer although she could no longer be with him?

7

After Gabrielle's face healed sufficiently, the Browns introduced her to the townspeople. They first visited the modest boarding house. Gabrielle loved its gingham curtains and delightful baking aromas; its charm surpassed only by Mrs. Butler, the woman who ran it. How she would enjoy working there, but Clement Brown had spoken with Mrs. Butler just after Gabrielle arrived in Calapooia. With the town still becoming established, the boarding house barely scraped by and could not afford help, even at the cost of only room and board. Now with Daria, it was clear they would only stop to say hello.

Gabrielle had a distinct feeling Harriett Butler would fit well in the twenty-first century. Despite the hardships of life in this era, she bore a cultivated look. While possessed of all the refinement and manners any lady of the period hoped to achieve, her determined and driven ambitions for the small boarding house and the town of Calapooia were significant. Though a gracious hostess, she held her own in any situation. As Mrs. Butler told her story of how this cultured woman fell for a trapper and resolved to fuse their two lifestyles, Gabrielle listened with fascination. Mrs. Butler's need for interaction with others appeared to be at variance with his passion for the solitude provided by a trapper's lifestyle, so she resolved to find a solution which satisfied both their needs. After building a boarding house in the middle of the wilderness, her husband taught her the skills needed for surviving alone, possibly for months at a time. Now she could shoot, chop wood, and fix a roof as well as any man.

Despite missing Mr. Butler during the weeks and months he was gone, her enthusiasm for life in Calapooia never waned. Gabrielle got the impression Mrs. Butler loved the challenges as much as the people and would have been a corporate CEO in the twenty-first century. She ran the cozy boarding house in an efficient and firm manner, allowing for time to chat with guests and to remain active in the growing community. Gabrielle had learned enough about keeping house in this era to understand doing both was a monumental feat. Mrs. Butler impressed Gabrielle.

On another day, Rose took Gabrielle to meet the seamstress. "Don't let Mrs. Harolds get to you. Despite her gruff manner, her skills with a needle are incomparable. The only time she seems happy is when she is sewing. She and Mr. Harolds came on the wagon train with us. The tragedy of losing all of their children on the way here was almost more than she could bear. Mistook water hemlock for wild parsnips, you know. She was good-natured and devoted to her children before the tragedy. Since then, well, she's different. She blames herself. She was the one who picked the water hemlock. It's amazing the entire family didn't die, but she fed the children early that night."

"I suppose she would be different after such an experience," Gabrielle said, her words infused with sadness.

"Oh Gabrielle, I'm sorry. Of course you understand."

Despite its cutting like a knife, Gabrielle smiled weakly at Rose. "You have no reason to be sorry. I'm blessed with Daria. She helps make it easier. Perhaps if Mrs. Harolds still had a child around, it might be easier for her. Come, let's call on her. Maybe spending time with Daria will help."

Bitterness kept Mrs. Harolds in its grip. It showed in her posture, the way she held her face, the tension in her shoulders. Gabrielle recognized it for what it was. Consumed with anger instead of sadness, those around the poor woman couldn't understand she was suffering from what they knew as melancholy, but in the future, would be referred to as clinical depression.

"Can't believe you'd bring that child in here!" Mrs. Harolds shrieked, causing Daria to hide behind Gabrielle's skirt.

"Mrs. Harolds, this is Mrs. Fallon. She's the woman I told you about who lost her whole family, her husband and three children, on a river crossing on the way here. The child is Daria, she was orphaned shortly after arriving, and Mrs. Fallon has taken responsibility for her."

"How can you?" she asked, with a bewildered expression, as she looked at Gabrielle.

"The idea of caring for children was almost unbearable. When I saw Daria and the other children where she was living, I felt as though I couldn't breathe. How could I give myself over to other children when I struggle each minute to accept the loss of my own? But Daria has been a miraculous gift. She gives me focus, and I know I need to think of her, not spend time feeling sorry for myself." With a sigh and eyes filled with tears, she continued. "My children will always be in my heart, but if I let their loss consume me, I would be saying the time we had together couldn't be sufficient to sustain me." Tears flowed unchecked. "Francis, Nicholas, and Alyson will always be my children. They will always be a part of me, regardless of this indescribable loss. I hope to honor them by my conduct and by giving Daria what I can no longer give them."

"I suppose it's easy when you have a child to replace them." Mrs. Harolds' expression matched her bitter tone.

"Easy? Not at all. Even Daria could never replace my children. Items are replaceable, but children are special unto themselves. I could have twenty children with me, or even give birth to more children, and still miss my three. To replace a child is impossible. To open my heart to chance loving another child is terrifying. But to close myself off from loving and caring for others would turn me into someone my children wouldn't know, and when I see them again in the great hereafter, I want them to know me."

At this, Mrs. Harolds face changed. Tears welled and flowed, softening the hardness. Rocking back and forth in her chair, with her sewing clenched in her hands, she wailed and wept with all the desperate anguish she had known and repressed since losing her children.

When Rose saw Daria hide deeper in Gabrielle's skirt, she picked her up, hugged her close, and stepped out of the shop, turning the open sign around as she left.

Gabrielle put her arms around the grief-stricken woman and stroked her back, her own tears coursing down her cheeks. Soon, a man Gabrielle assumed was Mr. Harolds rushed into the shop. He kneeled and wrapped his arms around his grieving wife. Gabrielle slipped out the door, reaching for the handkerchief Rose gave her, always handy in her pocket.

The following Sunday, Gabrielle and Daria joined the Browns at church. The simple building, though modest, was warm and dry, thanks to a little stove in the corner. Wooden benches formed neat rows. On a shorter bench, several children occupied the first row. Facing the room was a small desk, on top of which a disproportionately large bell sat. Gabrielle assumed the church also served as a school.

The pastor welcomed them as they entered, greeting the newcomers with warmth and enthusiasm. Another family arrived behind them, so they moved on after only a brief introduction.

Despite a lack of hymnals, Gabrielle joined in the singing of the opening hymn, *Rock of Ages*, glad she knew it reasonably well. Though in modern time she preferred praise music, her church still included a couple of the old hymns in most services. There was something solid and sustaining about them.

During the service, a few children went to the front and quoted memorized Bible verses. Each child knew their verse. However, the presenters varied in self-confidence, as evidenced in the manner of speaking: from the stilted delivery, to the barely audible, to the shake-the-rafters volume.

Gabrielle once again gave thanks during the sermon. Pastor Harris's sermon style combined Bible teaching, application, and conviction. He was teaching from James, one of her favorite books of the Bible. James's direct manner of speech and lack of hesitancy to say what needed to be said appealed to her. He reminded her to consider it joy when facing trials and to persevere no matter the situation. Pastor Harris added that regardless of what the trial or hardship is, she must not panic or fear, she must trust God. As happened so many times in her Christian walk, the Lord provided that particular message for her at the perfect time. She gave thanks for the blessing of the provision of his message.

Following the service, Gabrielle thanked Pastor Harris for his inspiring sermon, telling him how much she enjoyed the service. "And the children recited their verses beautifully."

"Yes, my wife does a magnificent job with the children. She was a schoolteacher when we met, though she stopped teaching when we married. After receiving God's call to come to Oregon, we knew convention need not apply, and she should once again teach, at least until another teacher becomes available. We trust God will soon provide, since come summer he will bless us with a child of our own."

"How wonderful! Congratulations. I will keep both in prayer."

"I understand you are looking for a position. I don't suppose you possess a teaching certificate?"

"Though I taught my children, no I don't. I'm sorry I'm unable to help you." Despite her experience teaching her own children, Gabrielle was aware a teacher of this time must know by heart a great deal of information which she would need textbooks to teach.

"No problem, we trust in God's provision. But, like any good pioneer, we have a contingency plan. I shall substitute until a suitable teacher comes along. While my duties as pastor and husband keep me busy, with Calapooia's small size, I shall endeavor to fill both positions, if the need arises."

Pastor Harris looked at Gabrielle. "While I understand you may still be recovering and perhaps hesitant, I do know of a family separated due to the need of someone to help. Are you interested?"

The Browns had listened politely to the conversation, but at this Mr. Brown spoke. "Pastor, while I trust your judgment, I feel to blame for what happened to Mrs. Fallon and intend to make sure it don't happen again. I plan to check the conditions of any position she might consider thoroughly."

"Understandable, but I can assure you, this is a God-fearing, loving, and reliable family."

"Are they here today?"

"No, due to the circumstances, they are unable to attend church on Sundays. Once they have help, I have no doubt they will be here every Sunday."

Though Gabrielle had listened respectfully to the conversation, due to the help and concern Mr. Brown had shown and Pastor Harris's position, it was time to speak. "What exactly is the family's situation?"

After a brief glance at Mr. Brown and a nod in reply, Pastor Harris looked at Gabrielle. "The Mitchells journeyed on the same wagon train as we did. Hard-working, wonderful couple. Three well-behaved children and expecting another shortly after we arrived. Mr. Mitchell went right to work building a fine cabin so the Mrs. would have a nice home for the birth. He figured they could make do without a barn if need be, but his family needed a warm, dry place. Baby was born about four months ago. Healthy, strong boy. At first, Mrs. Mitchell seemed okay, but then she got weaker and weaker. She died when the baby was about a week old, leaving Mr. Mitchell with four young children. For a hard-working man, caring for children would be difficult, but with a two-year-old and a newborn, well, that's a lot for even a first-rate man like Mr. Mitchell. Another woman on our wagon train gave birth about a month before we arrived. She and her family settled about five miles past Mr. Mitchell. She's acting as wet nurse to the baby and also took in the two-year-old. Mr. Mitchell misses those two children terribly, so twice a week, on Sunday and again on Thursday, he loads the other two children in the wagon, and they visit those two babies. So you understand, Mr. Brown, if they were to come to church, they would only see those two babies on Thursday. We all felt the more Christian thing to do would be to gather his family together."

"Sounds like the man has his priorities right," Mr. Brown nodded.

"Pastor, would it be possible to meet Mr. Mitchell? Oh my, do you think he would consider Daria too much of a burden?"

"Mrs. Fallon, I have a hunch he would take in several children if it meant he could have his babies at home again. Mr. Brown, I know you will want to be there; can you get away from the store tomorrow? It will be an all-day excursion, since they live about six miles out."

"I know the Mrs. will insist on going along also, so I'll close the store for the day and we'll all go."

"But Mr. Brown, what if someone comes to town needing supplies?" Gabrielle remembered they liked to keep regular hours.

"This once, they'll just have to wait for our return. After what happened with Volstead, we aren't about to let you go anywhere without thoroughly and personally checking Mr. Mitchell and the conditions."

Gabrielle smiled at Mr. Brown's protective attitude, choosing to ignore the "let" statement. It was a term Kyle used, which she felt was meant to demean her and keep her in her place. In this instance, she appreciated Mr. Brown's concern and knew he felt a great deal of responsibility for what happened with Volstead.

8

Early the next morning, Gabrielle gathered their things. In her previous life, with the use of cars, the distance was nothing, and she could have returned at an appointed time if the situation looked good. However, 1848 was different. They needed to stay if circumstances warranted.

Rose disagreed. Upon entering the room and seeing Gabrielle packing, she voiced shock. "Surely, you aren't planning to stay today! Please, Gabrielle, let's visit the Mitchells, return home, and discuss it. If appropriate, we can take you back next Sunday, or even the Sunday after."

Gabrielle hugged her friend. "Rose, I appreciate your concern, but if the conditions are safe, we both know I'm called to stay. Mr. Mitchell needs his children home. Can you imagine hardship requiring you to send your children to someone else to raise, even for a short time? It must be excruciating. Besides, it will be better for Daria if we settle sooner, rather than later. And don't forget, I can pack to come back just as easily.

"But…" Rose's attempt to refute her friend's logic left her without an argument. "Okay, if you do stay, we'll visit on Sunday." She paused. "And bring you home if circumstances dictate."

"Excellent compromise." Gabrielle handed Daria a small bag for her things.

"Only this time, you're taking two more quilts." Memories of Gabrielle's story and the worry they prompted made Rose adamant.

"Rose, we can't take all of your spare quilts."

Rose laughed. "Believe me, there's more where those came from. My parents must have thought we would freeze in Oregon; they sent an entire trunk packed tightly with quilts. There were so many, we've even included a couple of them on the shelves in the store."

Once again seated in a wagon on her way to the unknown, Gabrielle thought how different this ride was from the two previous rides. Giving thanks and praise for these devoted friends, a firm and worthy Pastor, and this child who had become her own in every way, Gabrielle wondered if it was wrong to miss and want her own three children so very much. She dismissed the thought as ridiculous. Of course it wasn't wrong! Her pain and loss were excruciating. They were her babies, a part of her; she would always miss them. Closing her eyes, she inhaled deeply, slowly exhaled, and forced herself to relax. She snuggled the delightful child, a gift from God, who was cozied between her legs in the bed of the wagon and once again gave thanks.

It was difficult to think of starting over at another stranger's cabin. The weeks with the Browns had been comforting. More than that, they had been educational. Gabrielle had not hesitated to ask questions. When Rose showed surprise at things she did not know, Gabrielle explained that she had led a somewhat sheltered and privileged life.

If she stayed at the Mitchell's, her cooking would be much improved over what she served at the Volstead's. While her repertoire may be small, she had the necessities down pat. Her bread was turning out beautifully. Her cornbread was as tasty as Rose's. Even better, Rose had instructed her how to make them without an oven, just in case.

Knowing she was far better prepared than before gave Gabrielle some comfort. They had sewn, made soap together, done laundry, ironed, cleaned, and cooked. Even little Daria was learning a few simple jobs. While Gabrielle understood some things may require adaptation due to what supplies and equipment the Mitchells had, she had asked Rose how to do with less, so she still felt equipped to handle life in 1848.

With a shock, Gabrielle realized she accepted her life in the 1800s. At first, she had considered the possibility of trying to locate the river and whirlpool in Montana. But if she miraculously found the spot, jumping into the whirlpool might not work. She might not live through the experience. Or, worse yet, what if she regressed in time even more? She was here, and here she would stay.

"You're quiet." Rose's comment brought Gabrielle out of her contemplation.

"I suppose I am. I was thinking of all the changes in my life over the last several months. What would I have done without you? I don't just mean the help and protection you've given me; rather, in you, I have found a true and trusted friend." A twinge of guilt nudged Gabrielle. Though she trusted Rose, she hadn't trusted her enough to confide the whole truth regarding her origin.

"It is I who am thankful. You, my dear friend, brought more than you know to this relationship. It can be difficult for a woman here. The loneliness can be powerful, overwhelming even. Though Clement is close by in the store, I have ached for another woman to talk to and share with. You gave me that and so much more. Teaching you has helped me feel needed. Although I stay busy most of the time, I don't do enough."

Rose reached for Gabrielle's hand. "I have a secret."

"Share?"

"We will be blessed with a babe come summer."

"Oh Rose, I'm thrilled for you!" Gabrielle smiled. "Something tells me you'll feel needed then."

As the wagon stopped at the Mitchell's cabin, Gabrielle's heart raced. Harboring reservations after her experience with Volstead, she took a calming breath and hugged Daria. *It'll be okay*, she told herself. Still, her taunt nerves produced a deep, jagged breath.

A girl around seven-years-old stepped out of the cabin as they halted. She was neat and clean, with her long, blond hair brushed and braided, though cornmeal dusted her small apron. "Pastor Harris!" Her face brightened. "Papa's out in the stable. He's adding a fourth wall to keep the animals warmer and dryer. The chickens stopped laying, and Lilly isn't giving much milk."

"Hi, Beth. This is Mr. and Mrs. Brown, and that's Mrs. Fallon and Daria. If you could show the women inside and make them comfortable, Mr. Brown and I will go see if we can help your papa."

Beth looked at the ladies. "Nice to meet you. Come in, and I'll put on a pot of coffee." When Daria peeked from behind Gabrielle's skirt, Beth said, "I have a little sister about your age. She's with a neighbor right now, but we visit twice every week. It's okay." She held her hand out to Daria. "I think I can find a cookie if you would like one."

Daria's experience with other children had not been good. She stayed back, clinging to Gabrielle's hand. Gabrielle squatted and looked at Daria. "Daria, Beth is being nice. The proper thing is to say thank you. You need not be afraid. Mrs. Brown and I are right here." Daria managed a peek at Beth and a nod but still clasped Gabrielle's hand.

The tidy cabin amazed Gabrielle. Under the circumstances, she expected a place where a man struggled unsuccessfully to manage by himself, with two young children underfoot. Instead, he seemed to be doing quite well. Capable and mature beyond her years, Beth showed herself to be a fine helper.

There was no cook stove. Something cooked over the fire in the fireplace, which was made of smooth river rock and had a raised hearth. A wooden mantle set into the rock held a few items. Two beds pushed end-to-end against one wall with a trunk at the foot of one of them left just enough space to allow a person to open it. On the opposite wall stood a large table with two benches. Near the fireplace, which covered part of the wall opposite the door, shelves held all manner of kitchen items.

"Here you are, Daria." Beth offered a small cookie to Daria.

As Daria extended her hand, Gabrielle stopped her.

"Daria, if you want the cookie, you will need to say thank you. Otherwise, I'm sorry, but you can't have it."

Gabrielle ached as Daria's eyes took on a frightened look. However, keeping a tight grip on Gabrielle's hand, she turned to Beth and whispered, "Thank you."

"You're welcome." Beth motioned toward another girl. "This is my little sister, Catherine. Catherine, this is Daria."

"Hello, Daria. Would you like to see my doll? My mama made it." She held a rag doll with an intricately embroidered face. "You can hold her. Her name is Ruth."

Daria's questioning look received a nod from Gabrielle. Reaching out, she shyly took the doll, looked at its face, and then hugged it, closing her eyes and rocking. A little tear slid down the child's cheek.

"Daria, what is it?" Gabrielle asked.

Daria handed Ruth back to Catherine. "My baby burned." Her whisper held a tearful choke.

"You had a baby doll?"

Daria nodded. "Sally. He burned her when mama dead." More tears followed.

Gabrielle couldn't stop the welling of tears as she held the child. It seemed there was no end to Volstead's cruelty.

Gabrielle heard movement, followed by Beth speaking. "Daria, I'm too old for dolls now. My poor Barbara just lays there waiting for me to care for her. She needs someone with more time. Would you like to be Barbara's new mama?"

Daria and Gabrielle both turned to see Beth holding her own beautifully made rag doll out to Daria. A choking sob escaped Gabrielle at the kindness this little girl was showing a stranger child. To practice such generosity and compassion at this young age, Beth must have learned by example. Gabrielle knew at that moment, if Mr. Mitchell agreed, she had found a home. A glance at Rose told her Rose also knew.

The two women amused themselves playing with the children and helping Beth with her duties. Though Daria relaxed enough to play with the girls, when Catherine offered for her to help search for eggs, Daria's eyes filled with fear and she shook her head no.

Beth said, "Catherine, I think Daria would rather stay inside and play with the marbles Papa made for us." Gabrielle sensed Beth was wise beyond her years.

As the girls played with the marbles, Gabrielle wondered about the father who, despite a hard and busy life, would take the time and effort to make marbles for his children. His children showed kindness and generosity. She looked forward to meeting him.

Soon, dinner was ready, and Beth sent Catherine to "fetch Papa." Gabrielle stilled the nerves which sprang from nowhere. She said a quick prayer of thanks for these wonderful children and His guidance through the day's decisions.

Pastor Harris entered the cabin. "Well, I see you ladies are getting along just fine. Something sure smells good."

Daria looked up and smiled at Pastor, then spied the man entering behind him. Upon seeing him, she jumped up from her play and ran to Gabrielle, hiding behind her skirt.

"We have a shy one." The man tilted his head as he commented.

"Unfortunately, she's frightened." Pastor Harris's sadness showed in his quiet voice.

The look of pain crossed the man's face when he realized the situation. Wisely, he left it alone.

"Mr. Mitchell, I don't believe you've met Mrs. Brown."

The man turned to Rose. "So glad to make your acquaintance, ma'am." He removed his hat and nodded.

"And this is Mrs. Fallon and Daria."

"Mrs. Fallon, Daria, nice to meet you both," he said with another nod.

"Mr. Mitchell." At a loss for words, Gabrielle bent and looked at Daria. "Do you remember what we talked about when meeting people?"

Daria nodded.

"Well…"

"Nice to meet you." The barely audible and shaky greeting came out as Daria stared wide-eyed at Mr. Mitchell.

This tiny voice received a smile and a wink in return.

Daria's expression of fear changed to a look of question and concern.

While the cabin was somewhat larger than the other living quarters she had seen until now, with seven people it was cozy. At first, Gabrielle was surprised the table could hold all of them, until she realized they would have been a family of six, had his wife survived. While it was apparently made from local materials after their arrival, care had been taken, and it was a fine table. Matching benches on each side completed the set.

When Rose put out the peach pies she brought, Mr. Mitchell exclaimed over them. "My favorite! I love peach pie, and it's been ages since I've seen one. Can't tell you how much I appreciate your thoughtfulness."

Mr. Mitchell opened the door and grabbed a stump of wood, one of two just outside the door, and brought it to the end of the table. A chunk cut out of the top formed a seat, leaving a portion sticking up, creating a back. Pastor Harris moved the second one to the other end of the table. Gabrielle realized they had anticipated the need for additional seating and carried them to the door as they came to the house. These were not new. Mr. Mitchell must have made them months ago. However, they lacked the finished look of the table and benches. The significance of this saddened her; he must have been making them when his wife died, so never returned to complete them.

Careful to avoid the appearance of staring, Gabrielle looked at Mr. Mitchell. Though not tall, probably 5'10", he possessed the muscular build of a man used to hard labor, with broad shoulders and a barrel chest, making him appear taller. His massive, work-hardened hands demonstrated tenderness as they stroked Catherine's head. Gabrielle had the distinct feeling he had been attempting to cut his own hair since losing his wife, but at least it was clean and reasonable. It was time for a new attempt. His eyes, a rather indistinct color, looked worn and tired. He sported a grow-out beard, as though a week had passed since he last shaved.

The men washed using the soap and water at the wash basin. After sitting, Mr. Mitchell and his two girls held hands and reached for the hands of those sitting next to them before he said grace. Gabrielle noted the difference between this household and that of the Volsteads, clean hands at the table and prayers, plus conversation. She wondered if perhaps it was due to Pastor Harris being there, but realized the children had grasped hands automatically. This was, indeed, their family way.

Though Mr. Mitchell didn't talk a great deal, what he said was cheerful, friendly, and positive. He appeared to be of quick wit, creating laughter around the table without trying to be funny. *Thank goodness*, Gabrielle thought; though she loved a good sense of humor, she couldn't abide people who *thought* they were funny but weren't. She noted he spoke positively to the girls and even managed to include Daria in a discreet manner, to avoid frightening her.

When they finished eating, the men returned to the barn to finish the fourth wall. While it may result in arriving home in the dark, they felt they should stay and assist in the completion of the project.

"If need be, we'll just bed down here and leave at dawn, if you don't mind," Mr. Brown insisted when Mr. Mitchell voiced concern about traveling in the dark.

"Tell me about your other sister and your new brother," Gabrielle said to Beth and Catherine as they cleaned up after dinner.

"Our sister's name is Annabelle, but we call her Anna," said Beth. "She's two and a half. I miss her so much. She likes to hear stories and cuddle. But she doesn't like getting her hair brushed."

"And our baby brother's name is Journey, on account of he was born after the end of our journey here." Catherine piped up, eager to contribute something knowledgeable to the conversation.

"I said I could take care of Journey, but Papa thought it's too much for me. I sure wish he could live here with us. But Papa said when he's able to eat and drink from a cup, maybe he can come home. I'm afraid he'll be half grown by then and won't know we're his family, even though we go see him twice every week." Beth seemed to be venting, frustrated at not having all of her family at home. "He looks a lot like Papa, you know. Us girls got Mama's blue eyes and blond hair, but not Journey; he has Papa's brown hair and hazel eyes."

Through the remainder of the afternoon, the women planned to help the little girls with their duties around the cabin, and then play with them for a while, but this changed when Beth realized they were almost out of soap. She was disappointed because her Papa would have to do it, since she wasn't allowed to make it by herself.

"Papa works so hard all the time. I wish I could do more to help."

"Why don't we spend our afternoon making soap?" Gabrielle's suggestion provoked an expression on Beth's face which conveyed her relief.

Before beginning, they took a walk to the creek and brought back water. They would need water for the soap. Gabrielle was relieved they had more than two buckets. While capable of carrying only two, additional buckets would come in handy.

As they walked, Gabrielle appreciated the beautiful spot the Mitchells had chosen for their homestead. It was a combination of fields and trees. The fields needed almost no clearing for Mr. Mitchell to ready them for planting. Rather than being flat, like the Volstead's land, there was a gentle roll to them. The tree-covered hills began at the edge of the fields. She liked the hills. The trees, mostly oak and fir, added beauty to the place, and she was sure they made it easier to get wood for fuel.

When they returned, Beth showed the women where they stored the animal fat. She said they burned mostly oak in their fireplace, so the ash from it would work well. She also brought out a box her father had made to pour the soap into for forming bars.

Gabrielle was astounded how much this young child knew about running a household and commented on it.

"I always liked to help Mama with chores. Papa's shown me some things since she died." Her tone was matter-of-fact. "I could make the soap, but Papa wants me to wait until I'm stronger. He said it's too dangerous, with the lye and all."

While the women and Beth, who insisted on helping, worked, Catherine and Daria played with their dolls. Knowing the numbers one through ten, Daria taught them to Catherine and the dollies, before teaching them the nursery rhyme Gabrielle had taught her. "One, two, buckle my shoe…" After the nursery rhyme, Daria moved on to colors. Catherine was able to help and even taught Daria some colors. It was delightful to hear the little girls playing. Astounded how rapidly Daria warmed to Catherine, Gabrielle supposed it was due to their being so near in age, as well as the gentle, amiable manner with which Catherine conducted herself.

With a box of soap hardening and a pail of soft soap on the shelf, the women set about supper. "Now Beth, you are a wonderful help, but why don't you play with the little girls for a while and let Mrs. Fallon and me prepare supper. You should have some play time also." Rose encouraged the child.

"But it wouldn't be polite to let company do all the work."

"It will make us very happy to see you relax and play for a while. Besides, the stew is quick and easy, and the biscuits won't take much time at all. There isn't enough work left for three people. Maybe you can get the little girls to help you set the table."

Beth smiled at Rose and did as she asked. This extraordinary child, mature beyond her years, enjoyed mothering the younger children. With much of mothering for pioneers of the 1800s consisting of passing on knowledge of how to function and to survive to children who had little time for play, Beth gained a great deal of pleasure from this small chore, which seemed more like play than work to all three girls.

After setting the table, the girls brought out a string with its ends tied together and taught Daria to play cat's cradle. Daria watched, concentrating on the different moves, delighting in the various forms the string could take. When Beth and Catherine finally made a mess of the string, Beth asked Catherine to prepare the cat's cradle so she could help Daria, showing her the two X's and how to use her thumb and index finger to grab them, go under, and back up, with Catherine releasing. Daria beamed with joy when, after three tries, she achieved a single X, without dropping the string.

Gabrielle delighted in watching the children play. She had taught the game to her own children, as far as she could remember it. Seeing Beth and Catherine take it much further than she remembered, she looked forward to playing with them. But greater than her delight with the simple game, was her pleasure with Daria's quick acceptance of the girls.

As it grew dark, Beth lit the lamp with a twig from the fireplace. "Sometimes Papa doesn't come in until well after dark. He has a lantern in the barn for work. He told us to go ahead and eat when he works late, but I'm not sure, with company and all, if we should. I'll go ask." With this, she ran to the barn.

After returning with the news the men would be at least another hour, perhaps two, the women and girls helped themselves to supper. Beth also brought news. With the late hour, the guests would spend the night. The womenfolk would sleep in the two beds in the house, and the men would sleep in the barn.

Remembering the cold and damp at the Volstead's barn, Gabrielle voiced concern, but Beth told her not to worry, they were making a nice little room in the barn.

When the men returned from their long day, they ate and then each grabbed a wool blanket off the beds and headed for the barn. Mr. Brown had brought Gabrielle's things in from the wagon, including the three quilts. After spreading them out to replace the now missing blankets, they prepared for bed.

146

"Oh, pretty! They really brighten the cabin." Beth's excitement was infectious.

Gabrielle took great joy in brushing the girls' hair. She had loved brushing her own daughters' hair. *Odd,* she thought, *how something can bring so much pleasure and such intense pain at the same time.*

Crawling under the covers, Gabrielle commented how good the bed felt.

"Papa made the rope beds as soon as he finished the cabin. We brought the mattresses with us from Ohio." Beth was obviously proud of her Papa and everything he did. To have accomplished so much in so little time spoke of the long, hard hours the man worked.

Rising early the next morning, the women hurried to dress and fix breakfast, in preparation for the return to town. Nothing had been said regarding her staying with the Mitchells. Though time with Mr. Mitchell had been limited, Gabrielle already felt a fondness for his daughters and hoped to stay.

When the men came in, Mr. Brown said, "Rose, we need to hurry home. Though I hadn't expected to stay the night, I'm sure glad we did. Mitchell now has a fully enclosed barn which includes a small room for him to sleep. While stopping to chink took more time, we figured the room would stay warmer and dryer that way, making one less thing to worry about."

"Papa, why are you going to sleep in the barn?"

"Well, kiddo, I guess we got carried away and forgot to check and make sure this would happen." He then turned to

Gabrielle, "Mrs. Fallon, I'd be thankful for you to stay and help, if you would like. I understand you had a bad experience, but you may rest assured, you are safe here. While I'm sure there are those who would suggest we marry, I understand why this is not an option. I am, however, concerned to protect your reputation, so I will sleep in the new room in the barn, while you may have the bed. If tongues wag, I'll put a quick stop to it."

Relief flooded Gabrielle, and she appreciated his regard for her reputation. "Thank you, Mr. Mitchell. I would love to stay and help. You must be aware; there's a lot I still need to learn."

"You just ask, and we'll figure stuff out as we come to it."

Beth's eyes got big. "Mrs. Fallon will live here? Daria, too?"

Mr. Mitchell laughed and gave a light tug on Beth's braid. "Yes, Daria too."

Beth turned around and hugged Daria, who had hidden behind Gabrielle when the men entered the cabin. "You're going to live with us; we'll be like sisters!"

9

Gabrielle took a refreshing, deep breath as she watched the wagon with Pastor Harris, Mr. Brown, and Rose pull away from the cabin as the sky began to lighten. Letting the air out, she relaxed her shoulders and told herself it would be okay. The Browns, though seemingly confident with the situation, were still not comfortable, and planned to visit on Sunday, so if things weren't working, Gabrielle and Daria could return with them. She wavered, questioning her determination to stay. Daria clung to her skirt. *Perhaps I should have given her more time. Time to relax at the Brown's. Time to heal. Time to grow at ease with others.* But in her heart, Gabrielle knew she and Daria had found a home.

"Daria, would you like to help me wash the breakfast dishes?"

Daria nodded, an indication of her nerves. Her silence spoke volumes. Bending, Gabrielle took the small child in her arms and held her, then looked up upon hearing Mr. Mitchell approach.

"Mrs. Fallon, will you need anything before I head to the fields?"

Gabrielle, with thoughts of modern conveniences, wanted to laugh at the absurdity of the question. "I think I'll be fine. Beth seems capable; she's amazing."

Mr. Mitchell shuffled his feet and smiled toward the cabin where his daughter had retreated. "She's a good girl." Despite the smile, there was sadness in his eyes.

"Thank you for staying." He headed to the field.

Beth ran back out. "Papa?"

"Yes?"

"Does this mean Anna and Journey will come home?"

"Anna should be able to come home. We may need to wait to bring Journey home. He still needs to stay with Mrs. Ralston until he can drink from a cup."

The disappointment on Beth and Catherine's faces at the news of Journey staying with the Ralstons was heartbreaking.

"Mr. Mitchell, isn't there a way we can feed Journey here? Couldn't we bottle feed him?" Gabrielle asked.

"Bottle feed?" He looked at her with questioning eyes.

"Yes. If you have a bottle, we could fashion a nipple out of leather or perhaps even cloth and feed Journey cow's milk."

"Hmmm, I do have an empty glass bottle which held medicinal alcohol."

"May I see it?"

"Of course." He headed to the barn to retrieve it. Gabrielle had learned barns were used primarily for storage rather than to house animals.

Upon his return, he looked dubious as he handed the bottle to Gabrielle. "There's leather and cloth in the steamer trunk."

After putting water in the bottle, Gabrielle wound a string around the top with a small piece of soft, thin leather attached, forming a nipple. "Who wants to try it?"

Both Beth and Catherine volunteered. Since Catherine was quicker, she got to test it.

"I'm not getting anything," she said, disappointed.

"Wait. Let the water saturate the leather," Papa told her.

Soon, her eyes brightened. "I'm getting some!"

"See how much you get and how long it takes," Gabrielle said, noting how much water was in the bottle to start.

After a few minutes, they looked at the level of water in the bottle again and were pleased.

"Mr. Mitchell, I do need to tell you that cow's milk will not be as good for Journey as mother's milk. Cow's milk is richer, and it's possible he may not accept the bottle."

"He's had four months of mother's milk; if he will take the bottle, he needs his family as much as we need him here. That is, if you think you can handle everything with the extra work a baby brings."

"I have wonderful helpers; I'm sure we'll manage."

"Good. Then we'll prepare to bring Anna and Journey home on Thursday."

"Yay!" Beth and Catherine danced around the room.

A look of concern crossed Beth's face. "But Papa, Lilly hasn't been giving as much milk. What if she dries up?"

"I've put her in the barn; the warmth will help her milk production. If required, I'll trade for milk from the neighbors. We need our family together. Though I'm thankful for their help, I'm sure the Ralstons will appreciate two less mouths to feed."

Gabrielle watched as he headed for the field, his stride showing more confidence than his speech. She closed her eyes, took a deep breath, and slowly released it. Opening them, she took Daria's hand and dug deep for courage as she led the child into the cabin, their new home.

The three days sped by as the family prepared to bring the two youngest home. The entire family invested long hours preparing ahead in anticipation of the extra work the baby would require. From the barn, Mr. Mitchell retrieved a cradle, which Beth said came all the way from Ohio. Beth would share the bed with Gabrielle, while Daria would sleep with the two younger girls, assuming she wasn't too timid. Extra wood was cut, extra water brought from the creek, extra bread and cornbread made, and extra beans cooked for leftovers. The laundry was done again on Wednesday to assure as little work as possible during the busy first week home.

Anna loved cookies, so Beth insisted on making a batch to welcome her home. Catherine showed Daria how to churn the butter, since Lilly had already begun giving more milk. Mr. Mitchell took one of the unfinished stump chairs out to the barn to finish as time allowed, leaving the other in place for now.

They worked together with ease. Daria grew comfortable with the girls, though she still shied away from Mr. Mitchell. It was as though this family was meant to be.

Thursday morning, the family gathered in the wagon. Mr. Mitchell led them in prayer before departing. A bottle of milk packed away allowed for a test with Journey before taking him home. Extra blankets and a wooden crate in which Journey could sleep during the trip had been included. Just before leaving, Mr. Mitchell placed a carved set of wall sconces on the blankets in the crate.

"After the Ralstons first took Anna and Journey in, I carved these whenever I found a few moments of time. I figured I'd give them as a thank-you for helping us."

"They're beautiful! I'm sure they will appreciate them. I baked an extra pie for them," Gabrielle said.

The family's cheer and excitement intensified with each mile. Gabrielle looked forward to meeting the two remaining Mitchell children. The bumping wagon seemed like a carnival ride as the children laughed and played in the back. Like Mr. Hargrove, Mr. Mitchell was a quiet sort, though he did point out landmarks along the way and was quick to laugh and joke with the children.

Pulling in front of the Ralston cabin, the door opened, and a small girl came running out. "Papa! I missed you, Papa."

"Annabelle!" Mr. Mitchell jumped out of the wagon and picked up his daughter, twirling and hugging her. "You need not miss me anymore. We've come to take you home."

"Home, yippee! Home, I'm going home." The happy child flung her arms around her papa's neck.

While at the Ralston's, they tested the bottle of milk to assure Journey would take it. Though he looked confused, at the first taste of milk, he made an odd face, then seemingly resigned, appeared determined to finish the contents as fast as possible. This boy liked to eat! Soon, however, he fell asleep, with plenty left for his next feeding on the way home.

With this accomplished, they needed to head back. Though the Ralston's sought to convince the family to stay for dinner, Mr. Mitchell declined. They needed to get home before dark and do chores. They also wanted to take advantage of Journey sleeping. If they waited, he might need to eat again before leaving.

Mr. Mitchell thanked the Ralstons for their generosity in keeping the children, and let them know if they ever needed anything, he would be there. After presenting the sconces, he looked embarrassed as the Ralstons exclaimed over them. Gabrielle gave them the blackberry pie made from dried blackberries, and Beth gave them a batch of cookies. Mrs. Ralston, with tears in her eyes, hugged Anna and kissed Journey on the forehead, so as not to wake him. After placing Journey in the box bed, they loaded the children, all their things, and headed for home.

That evening, after changing and feeding Journey, Mr. Mitchell played with his son, his joy at having him home evident. Then he laid the baby in the cradle next to Gabrielle's bed. Surprised, Gabrielle thought men of this century viewed caring for children as woman's work.

Looking at Gabrielle, he said, "Thank you for this."

"It is I who needs to thank you. You have given Daria and me a home." She glanced at Journey sleeping in the cradle. "I'm looking forward to having a baby around again; it's been a while."

"How old were your children?"

"Francis is," she caught herself, "was, nine. Nicholas was eight, and Alyson was six." Gabrielle closed her eyes and willed the tears to stay away. But they insisted on making an appearance.

"I'm sorry. I didn't mean to cause you pain."

"Please don't apologize. I like to talk about them, though I wish I could do so without crying."

"Time is supposed to help."

"So I understand, but I'm still waiting. I suppose it has become easier in ways. I now accept they are lost to me, that I'll never see them again. At first, a lot of hard work helped me not to cry myself to sleep each night, since I was so tired I couldn't remember my head hitting the pillow. I'm thankful for Daria, and now your children; they do make it easier. I can't help but fall in love with them. At least I'm not left alone." Gabrielle had babbled when she should have just agreed. She mentally kicked herself.

"Yes, work helps, the children do too," he said, then kissed each of his girls goodnight. Daria shied away whenever he came near, so he smiled and told her goodnight. But then he did something surprising. He said, "Daria, may I give Barbara a goodnight hug?"

Daria's astonished expression matched Gabrielle's. She nodded and handed the doll to Mr. Mitchell, who held the rag doll like a real baby, gave it a hug and kiss, and whispered, "Goodnight, Barbara," before tenderly returning the doll to Daria.

As he headed out the door, Gabrielle let out her breath. What a stunning thing for a rugged farmer to do for a child. But it would take a while before Daria could trust him, or any man.

While she no longer hid from Mr. Brown, she still could not relax with him. It saddened Gabrielle to see how Volstead had traumatized the girl. Hopefully, Mr. Mitchell's tenderness would eventually break through the shameful memories which had so scarred the small child.

Will the gentleness last? Kyle was sweet and gentle at first. Considerate and nice. He impressed everyone he met as almost too-good-to-be-true. During Gabrielle's pregnancy with Nicholas, the true Kyle emerged, though he still put on a good act for others. But time revealed the truth. There was no "almost" in the too-good-to-be-true.

Once again, the thought of her precious children alone with that monster incited fear. Helplessness overwhelmed her. Oh, at first he would play the poor bereaved widower to the hilt. He loved to be the victim. He could act, and he would perform his tragic role. He even believed it, for a while. It was when the "while" ended that concerned her.

His world was whatever he felt at the moment. Reality held no bearing. If something "was" at that moment, then it was always that way in his mind; he could not be convinced otherwise. If he felt different an hour later, then his reality changed. She remembered cleaning and shining all day to make the house perfect, but when she hadn't had time to put away the folded clothing laying on the laundry counter, he ranted that the "house was always a pigsty." This was a common occurrence.

She took measures to protect the children from his uncontrollable anger but was too slow on occasion. When at four years of age, Francis left her toy camera on the floor, an enraged Kyle threw it past her at the wall, breaking it into several pieces. Stepping in to protect Francis, Gabrielle took the verbal brunt of his anger.

Overwhelmed by the memories and knowing she could no longer protect her children, Gabrielle stepped outside. Tears weren't enough. Racking sobs shook her body as she crumpled to the ground. "God, please protect them." Her soft cries sounded loud in the quiet night. Then a warmth seemed to hold her, as though in a hug, despite the chill of the cold night air. With the sensation came peace.

The tears stopped as quickly as they had begun. She inhaled and wiped her tears with her handkerchief. Looking at the clear night sky, with the beauty of its multitude of stars, she whispered, "Thank you."

As she stood outside the cabin door, attempting to relax from her loss of control, she looked around the farm and gave thanks for the provision of a good home. Through the darkness, she saw the shadow of Mr. Mitchell outside the barn. He appeared to be watching her. It would take her time to trust also.

10

Aware of the baby sleeping in the cradle next to her, Gabrielle awoke as he fussed. She slipped out of bed and whispered to him as she prepared to change his diaper. Perhaps with the close living quarters and demanding life, people of this era were accustomed to sleeping through noise, but with four other children sleeping in the room, she hoped to avoid their waking each time the baby woke.

Though it was rather dark in the cabin, with no light other than the remaining small fire burning in the fireplace, the experienced diaper changer had no trouble. Despite the modern approach to diapers in the twenty-first century, Gabrielle used cloth diapers with all three of her children. While expense may have been a contributing factor, the feel of cloth against skin sounded much more appealing to her. Nor could she justify the throwaway nature of disposable diapers when she supported the "reduce, reuse, and recycle" philosophy. Odd to find herself in a time and place where this was a way of life, but without the catchy name.

As she slid the stubborn diaper pin through her hair, using the natural oils to lubricate it, making it easier to pin the diaper, Gabrielle whispered to Journey. He responded with small smiles and a careful observation of her.

Lifting him, she reveled in the feel of a baby in her arms. She had always wanted a large family, but Kyle objected, declaring they would stop as soon as he got his son. There was a part of her that had hoped to have a whole string of girls before having a boy to satisfy her desire, but his reaction to the news that Francis was a girl dashed that hope. One would have thought she had gone behind his back and ordered a girl. It was the first real glimpse she had of his true nature, though at the time she passed it off as a one-time reaction of disappointment. She fervently prayed for a boy when pregnant with Nicholas. After the ultrasound showed he had his son, he declared they were done. They had the perfect family, a boy and a girl, just like his parents. There was no discussion, no consideration of her feelings, he simply made his decree. When, despite taking precautions, they discovered she was pregnant with Alyson, he accused her of planning the pregnancy behind his back and even went so far as to claim the baby wasn't his. The accusations and insults continued full force until his parents were told there would be another grandchild. With their excitement, it was suddenly Kyle who had found it necessary to convince Gabrielle to have another child, "she's not much into mothering, you know."

As Gabrielle cradled Journey in her arms and watched him devour the contents of the makeshift bottle, she wondered if she would ever be able to let the nightmarish memories go. She determined to push the bad times from her mind and focus on the good. There were good times, she reminded herself, and she was going to make a concerted effort to remember them.

A small smile appeared as she realized, thanks to Kyle, she could name nearly every bird she saw. And, due to his introducing her to his interest in antiques, she knew who made Rose's furniture. She also knew how to clean and sanitize better than anyone she knew. *Okay*, she thought, *not a good start on the positive, but it was a start.*

Wondering about the time, Gabrielle burped Journey and then laid him back in his cradle. *I wish I knew what time it is*, she thought, *I don't know whether to stay up or go back to bed.* She crawled back into the bed and snuggled under the quilts, watching the baby reach for his feet and listening to his babbles.

The remainder of the week was busy, with the entire family adjusting to the extra work and time a baby in the household required. Gabrielle found, despite the large stack of diapers available, she needed to do an extra wash day. Perhaps it was a result of her obsessive attitude regarding dry diapers on a baby, but wet was wet, and she certainly couldn't leave him wet. Though she restricted the extra washing to diapers, it still consumed a great deal of time. Plus, on rainy days, of which there were many, the diapers hanging across the cabin could be in the way at times. However, on sunny days, Beth enjoyed hanging the diapers on the low line her papa had installed outside and then collecting them when they were dry. Gabrielle also showed her how to fold them, amazed by how well she did.

Catherine finally convinced Daria to help her look for eggs, and was excited when they returned with two. Though two eggs wouldn't go far with seven people, it was a relief to know the hens were laying again.

Anna and Daria played well together. From the moment they met, it was as though they had always been together. At first, Gabrielle was astonished at Daria's acceptance of Anna. There seemed to be no hesitation at all. After a bit of thought and observance, it made sense; Anna was even younger than Daria. This meant she was no threat. Anna was someone for Daria to mother. Gabrielle was thankful that, being the loving child she was, Daria was not inclined to treat Anna the way the Volsteads had treated her. In fact, she seemed to take her role as the elder very seriously. As she had done with the rag dolls, she began teaching Anna to count. When Anna neared the fireplace, Daria gently took her hand and pulled her away, saying "Stay back, Anna, hot!"

Evenings were pleasant. Since it grew dark quite early, they often played with the children and relaxed or worked on projects. While Gabrielle sewed or mended, she taught the girls to sew, beginning with samplers. Due to the early teachings of her mother, Beth had progressed to simple sewing projects, such as an apron with embroidered flowers on the bib.

Gabrielle enjoyed listening as Mr. Mitchell played his harmonica. Watching his patience as he taught Beth to play a song increased her opinion of him. They all smiled as Catherine and Anna both tried the harmonica. Daria was still unable to bring herself to trust the man sufficiently to get close enough to try, but had progressed so she no longer hid behind Gabrielle when he came into the cabin.

Each night, when giving hugs and kisses goodnight, Mr. Mitchell continued to give Barbara a kiss and hug in Daria's stead.

On Saturday morning, before heading back to the barn for chores, Mr. Mitchell said, "We no longer need to visit the children on Sundays, so let's load up bright and early in the morning and head for church. You should pack a dinner."

Surprised, Gabrielle said, "But, Mr. and Mrs. Brown planned to visit us tomorrow. We'll miss them."

"Mr. Brown mentioned the plan, but I let him know if we didn't yet have both children home, we would be at the Ralston's, and if we had both children, we would see them at church."

"Oh, good." Gabrielle looked forward to seeing her friend.

The next morning, they loaded the wagon in the dark. Though the sky was clear, it was cold. Remembering having read about potatoes making good hand warmers, Gabrielle had risen early and baked some in the fire, so they would each have a potato to take in their pocket. This also provided additional food for dinner. As each child headed out the door, Gabrielle stuffed one in their pockets and then handed one to Mr. Mitchell.

The wagon rolled out of the yard as the sky lightened. "We made better time leaving than I thought we would, we may be early." Mr. Mitchell seemed pleased.

Gabrielle beamed. She knew how to assure the family was ready to leave at the appointed time. At least that hadn't changed with the century.

Arriving at church, only a few families waited. Despite the early hour, Gabrielle spied Rose and her husband waiting. Rose rushed to Gabrielle.

"You got the baby!"

"Yes, on Thursday. He's such a sweetheart."

"But, how are you feeding him?"

"We fashioned a bottle from an empty whiskey bottle and a nipple from a piece of thin leather."

"What an ingenious idea! Was it yours?"

"I suppose you could say that." Gabrielle's slight smile restrained the giggle within.

As Mr. Mitchell and the children continued inside, in a quiet voice, Rose asked, "How is it? Is he treating you well? You don't have to stay; you can come back with us. Clement and I talked it over, and we can arrange a small part of the storeroom for you and Daria to live in until we build the second story. He said we could order a stove to keep it warm."

"Oh Rose, you are such a wonderful friend, but you need not worry. Mr. Mitchell is every inch a gentleman. In fact, I was amazed that he helps with Journey's care. Changes diapers and everything. He truly is a gentle man."

"What a relief! But know you have a home with us if needed."

"You are both incredible to think of it; I appreciate it. But I like living there. The children are amazing, Daria loves it there, and I like being needed and appreciated. Every evening he thanks me. I keep telling him he need not thank me; after all, it's beneficial to both of us, but I think he's so overjoyed to have his family together again that he feels the need to do more."

Taking Gabrielle's free hand, Rose smiled. "I'm so pleased. We must take our seats, but first, you will join us for dinner after service, won't you?"

"We did pack dinner, but I will extend your invitation to Mr. Mitchell and we will if he is agreeable."

Gabrielle then took a seat next to Daria, who, as expected, sat as far from Mr. Mitchell as she could. But she had continued inside with him and the other children rather than clinging to Gabrielle's skirt. Especially surprising was her willingness to leave Gabrielle's side in a room filled with strangers. However, Gabrielle did notice Daria's tight grip on Catherine's hand.

Gabrielle enjoyed the service as much as she had the previous Sunday. Pastor Harris possessed a genuine heart for the Lord and a gift for teaching. At the close of service, she thanked him for introducing her to the Mitchells.

"No need, Mr. Mitchell already thanked me. I've tried to keep in touch with him since he lost his wife, and this is the most content I've seen him. I take it the arrangement is working well."

"Yes, very. Thank you again."

With Mr. Mitchell agreeable to joining the Brown's for dinner, they headed for the Brown's store. Upon entering, Gabrielle wondered how they would fit in the tiny residence. She soon had her answer. With some rearranging in the large storeroom and adding goods to the store itself, they had fashioned a living area with Rose's furniture and a large table from crates and shelving boards. Over this lay one of Rose's lovely tablecloths. Several rounds of wood and more shelving boards provided benches.

"This is amazing, but hasn't it left you short on storage room?" Gabrielle wondered aloud.

"Perhaps, but it will be nice to have a place for Rose to receive guests, and I just rearranged a bit. I stocked more in the store and piled higher in here." Clement Brown grinned.

Rose continued excitedly, "After we saw the effect, Clement decided to move the storage items into the small storage room and move our living quarters in here. I'm so excited to have more space, and comfortable seating will be nice too. The most difficult part will be moving the stove, but Clement said not to worry, he would manage."

"Makes perfect sense. There's no way the cradle would have fit in the other room. There's barely enough space to walk as it is."

"Cradle?" Mr. Mitchell asked.

"Yep, baby should arrive this summer." Clement Brown beamed with pride and excitement. From his expression, one would think they were the only couple to have ever accomplished such a feat.

"Congratulations!" With a look at Gabrielle, Mr. Mitchell continued, "You must have known; you don't seem surprised."

"Yes, Rose told me on the way to your cabin. I would have told you, but it wasn't my news to tell."

With a slight smile and a nod at Gabrielle, he turned to Mr. Brown again. "You will love being a papa. It's truly a miracle how this tiny creature can wrap you around their finger and instantly become the center of your world."

"I just couldn't be more excited. And I know Rose here will be the best mama ever."

"You have a cradle already?" Gabrielle asked.

Rose giggled. "Yes, one of the many 'necessities' my parents insisted on shipping. I slept in it as an infant. Gabrielle, would you like to help me bring the food in from the other room?"

Mr. Mitchell rose. "We have a meal in the wagon; we'll add it to the table."

"My missus fixed enough to feed three families, so leave the vittles in your wagon and you'll have supper ready when you arrive home." Mr. Brown's insistence stopped Mr. Mitchell.

Rose had indeed fixed more than enough food, including both an apple and a dried blackberry pie, plus a cobbler made from canned peaches. It felt like a holiday with the abundance of food.

"Mr. Brown..." But Mr. Brown cut Gabrielle off.

"Now, now, we're friends here. It's time we sounded like it. I'd be pleased if you'd both call me Clement."

Gabrielle smiled. "Clement it is."

"As long as we're on the subject," Mr. Mitchell added, "Please call me Wade." It was the first time Gabrielle had heard his first name.

The chatter continued throughout the meal, with all agreeing the food was delicious.

While eating the cobbler, Wade turned to Gabrielle. "Can you make this?"

"Not yet, but I will know how before we leave."

"It so easy," Rose insisted. "It's just a cup of this and a cup of that. My cousin Paula taught me to make it."

"I'll need to know what those cups are before we leave." Gabrielle laughed at her friend's idea of a recipe.

As Rose cleared the table, Gabrielle helped. "While we take care of these, you can tell me more about those cups."

Beth, used to the womanly duties, also helped.

"Beth, you're welcome to play with the other children." Rose's gentle voice sounded more like a question than a statement.

"I like doing this, if you don't mind."

"Of course I don't mind, we appreciate the help."

"While you ladies clean up, we'd best go hitch the team. I hate to eat and run, but with these short days, if we don't get going, it'll be past dark before we make it home." Wade and Clement grabbed their coats and headed through the store.

While Gabrielle changed Journey's diaper, she thanked Beth for helping, "This way I can feed Journey before we go and not leave all the work to Mrs. Brown."

"I know you work faster than I do and Papa wants to leave soon, so would you like to help and I'll feed Journey? I'd like to try."

In answer, Gabrielle rose from the rocker and gestured for Beth to sit. Placing Journey in her arms, she handed Beth the bottle. "Watch how much he takes. He likes to drink fast and needs burped frequently. You're a wonderful helper, Beth. Thank you."

The ladies chatted as they cleaned, making frequent trips back to the table from the living quarters, allowing them the opportunity to check on Beth, Journey, and the other children, without seeming to doubt Beth's ability.

The other children each carried an item to the living quarters, and then Catherine asked for a cloth to clean the table.

Not wanting to be left out, Daria offered to sweep. At Anna's look of confusion, Rose handed her a towel for drying the makeshift table.

When finished, they put on their coats to leave, and Rose handed Gabrielle a package. "It's a dress for Daria, made from the length we cut off the dress you are wearing. By the way, you look lovely. Is it the first time you've worn it?"

"Oh, thank you, Rose. She will love it. And yes, it is the first time. I'm not sure why I didn't wear it last Sunday. Maybe I wanted to wait until my face had healed. Thank you so much."

"You look much better. Does it still hurt?"

"My nose is still tender, as are my ribs, but I suppose that is to be expected. They are so much better though, I often forget."

Taking a contented Journey from Beth and checking his diaper one last time, Gabrielle said, "Okay children, time to go; your Papa must have the wagon hitched by now." To Rose, she said, "Thank you again. I'm assuming we will see you next Sunday."

"Absolutely."

Wade helped Gabrielle and the children into the wagon before climbing in himself. With a wave, they headed home. For Gabrielle, it was the most content she had felt since arriving in this time and place.

11

With the start of the new week, Gabrielle established a routine. Though much of the work was exhausting, she enjoyed it. There was something real about becoming a part of the process rather than just loading a machine. Hot water up to her biceps or the squish of dough between her fingers made her feel alive. Dodging drying diapers served as good exercise, but everything of this era seemed to fit that category.

Smelling the wood fire burning gave her a sense of home she had missed for years. Maybe it wasn't so much the smell, as the feeling of coziness, family, and peace. Despite the physical pain of her healing nose and ribs, despite the emotional pain of being separated from her children, she found comfort here. No need to always be on guard. Although the cabin was small for seven people, it was so full of life and love, the size went unnoticed.

Even with five children, sometimes the quiet seemed overwhelming. In modern times, when not teaching, Gabrielle always had a radio, CD, television, or audiobook playing. The silence disturbed her, frightened her. Silence with Kyle foreshadowed disaster. In contrast, while at the Volstead's, silence meant safety. It meant time enjoyed with Daria. It meant not being berated. It meant he was not near. But silence at the Mitchell's had many meanings. Sleeping children, mischief-making, a game of hide-and-seek, rest and sleep in a cozy bed. Mostly though, Gabrielle found silence meant peace. She enjoyed the quiet of a walk, the crackling of the fire as she rocked a child, a quiet evening with Wade nearby as she mended or just rocked after the children fell asleep. She appreciated silence as she caught the small sounds: the peaceful tranquility of Journey breathing as he slept, the wind outside the cabin, the crackle of the fire, the dripping of the rain, the sizzle as the rain coming down the chimney hit the fire.

The initial perception of safeness with Wade frightened her. For the first time since her father died, Gabrielle was not on guard around a man. While she still reminded herself to relax, this was more from habit than her current situation. She cautioned herself that time often reveals a different person. But she sensed this was not the case with Wade Mitchell.

The children slept as Gabrielle and Wade sat in front of the fire. With work on their laps, neither attended to it. The flickering light of the fire absorbed both people.

"May I ask something personal?" Gabrielle's quiet voice broke the silence.

"You may ask anything you like. If I'm uncomfortable answering, I will tell you."

"Would you mind telling me about your wife? I don't even know her name. I thought it might make it easier to help the children remember her if I knew something about her." She had debated if she should inquire, his wife had not been gone long, but something prompted her to ask.

"Sarah. Her name was Sarah Louise Olson Mitchell. She was lovely." Wade stared into the fire as if he could see his wife. Moments later, he asked, "What would you like to know?"

"I'm not sure. Anything you feel comfortable telling me."

"We grew up in the same community in Pennsylvania. Went to the same church. She was several years, five, younger than me, so I didn't pay much attention to her until she suddenly seemed to be there one day after she turned sixteen. I couldn't take my eyes off her. Sarah later told me I noticed her because she started wearing her hair up, like a grown woman. She was shorter than me, though taller than you, and had blond hair. The girls have her hair. We courted for two years. While we courted, my brothers helped me build a little house on our parents' property. When we completed the house, I asked for her hand. We married a week later. I couldn't believe she was mine! She loved sewing and making pretty things for the house. When the babies started coming, she joked if people would quit making things for them, she could make more. She liked to joke. It often seemed contradictory, since she was so soft-spoken, but she had a mischievous bent. All in good fun though. Just before my brother Cale asked Sueann Bunting to marry him, we heard about the free land in Oregon. Knowing Pop didn't have enough land to sustain the families of four boys, we joined the train to Oregon so Cale and Sueann could have the house we built. I thought it would be difficult for Sarah to leave behind all the pretty things she had made, but she said it would give her reason to make more." He paused and took a deep breath. "She never got the chance."

Wade remained silent. Gabrielle wondered if she had been wrong to inquire about Sarah. Perhaps she should have waited for him to bring up the topic of his wife.

Then Wade looked at Gabrielle. "Thank you. That felt good. I haven't been able to say a word about her to anyone since her death. People seem reluctant to mention Sarah. If something is said about her, the subject gets abruptly changed. It's as though they fear I might crack if I talk about her. The problem is, by not talking about her, it's as though she never existed. That hurts even more than losing her."

"I understand. If I allude to my children, people squirm until they can change the topic. My children were my world; I want, no, I need to talk about them."

"Tell me about them."

Gabrielle smiled the smile of memory. She then told Wade about Francis, Nicholas, and Alyson. It felt good. It hurt too. Tears kept slipping out, but at times they combined with laughter as she told an amusing story involving one or more of the children.

Finally, she said, "I can't thank you enough for sharing your precious children with me. They make it easier somehow. While my children are irreplaceable, having children to care for not only fills a need in me but makes me feel needed. They are so full of love and acceptance. They are easy to love."

"It is I who must thank you. One of the hardest parts of losing Sarah was sending Anna and Journey away. I knew Sarah would understand, but she would also hate it."

The two remained quiet for some time before Wade spoke. "Gabrielle, I don't mean to pry, but you don't speak of your husband."

She wondered how to respond. She must remain loyal to her husband, but she could not be dishonest. How to explain without speaking ill of Kyle? She drew a deep breath. "Kyle is, was complex. He could be wonderful when he chose. Generous to a fault. Complimentary. Hard-working." She paused. "But life was not always straightforward. We can all be moody at times, some of us more than others." Stopping, she realized she could not speak further without being harsh. Perhaps she revealed too much already.

They remained quiet for the rest of the evening. Gabrielle assumed Wade understood her dilemma concerning speaking of Kyle. It must be apparent to anyone; while she mourned her children mightily, she said nothing of Kyle. *Forgive me, Lord, if I am not honoring my husband.*

The next day, while laying the ragdoll, Barbara, on the bed, Gabrielle studied her. The stitches were fine and beautifully done. Sarah had, indeed, been quite talented with a needle. *I do well to sew a straight line*, she thought, before realizing she had tried to compare herself to Sarah. *Shame on you! This is not a contest. You are blessed to be in Sarah's home. Thank you, Sarah, for the opportunity to care for and love your children.* Gabrielle shook her head at having compared herself to Sarah even for a moment.

She imagined how Sarah suffered before she perished. She must have known she was dying and wouldn't be there to raise her children. Even if the infection Gabrielle assumed she died from hadn't taken her, her heartbreak over not watching her children grow up surely must have. Gabrielle knew on a daily, nay, minute by minute basis what it was like not to be with her children. It ripped one's heart to shreds. But she would be there for Sarah's children and perhaps, if God willed, a loving woman would be there for Francis, Nicholas, and Alyson.

As she worked, Gabrielle saw Wade's description of Sarah in her daughters. Beth was gentle-spoken. Even at her young age, Anna had a mischievous side to her. Catherine already displayed talent with a needle. Such ability should be nurtured. But Gabrielle didn't possess the skill or knowledge to teach her. Perhaps Rose could provide lessons.

Despite the constant pain of loss she bore like a weight, Gabrielle loved this place, the cabin, the family, the peacefulness, and even the work. Despite its harshness, she felt alive. It kept her busy, which, while she could not forget, made the relentless anguish of missing her children somehow easier to bear.

12

A couple of weeks later, Gabrielle had just finished changing Journey's diaper when she said, "Oh no! Beth, I need your help. Can you go get your Papa?"

Beth ran to the barn where Wade had been mending harness. Gabrielle could hear her shouting, "Papa, Mrs. Fallon needs you."

Wade hurried into the cabin. "What's wrong? Is Journey okay?"

"The children are fine. It's me. I'm getting a visual migraine. If I can lie down in a dark place, it should go away, and I'll be okay, or at least have nothing more than a headache. But if I can't, I'll end up with a horrific migraine and unable to see to do my work."

"By all means, lay down. What's a migraine?"

"It's like an intense headache, only much worse. It can affect vision and cause vomiting. Think of an axe sitting in your head. When I get them, especially with no medication available, I'm out for the remainder of the day. I have too much to do to spend the rest of the day down. While it may not seem light in the cabin, it's still not dark. May I lie down in your room until it's gone? It's dark there, isn't it?"

"Of course. What else can I do to help?"

"Watch the children," she replied quietly. "But first, I'm going to close and cover my eyes from the light, and I need you to lead me to your room."

Wade asked Beth to watch the children for a bit, then tucked Gabrielle's hand in his elbow and led her to the barn as she covered her eyes with her other hand, warning her about any uneven ground on the way there. Arriving in his room, he helped her onto his bed and asked if she needed anything else.

"No, thank you. Oh, this doesn't always work. Occasionally, I will get a migraine anyway."

"You just relax and don't worry about anything, we'll check on you later."

"I'm so sorry."

"Nothing at all to be sorry about. You just rest."

Gabrielle lay on the rope bed with her eyes closed trying not to focus on the swirling colors and lights she couldn't stop seeing. She concentrated on her breathing, hoping it would help her to relax and take her mind off the lights of the migraine. "Oh please, take this from me. I have so much to do," she prayed.

Twenty minutes later the lights ceased, but Gabrielle remained motionless hoping to thwart a threatening headache. At the sound of someone coming, she attempted to rise.

"Lie still, I brought a cold cloth for your head. I thought it might help." Wade placed the cloth on her forehead and another on the back of her neck.

"Thank you. I'll be up soon and get back to work." Years of Kyle's anger at her laziness when this occurred left Gabrielle self-conscious and concerned.

"Don't worry about it. You relax and take care of yourself. When you feel up to it, come back to the cabin and rest. Beth and I have dinner almost ready, and Catherine is conducting school for Daria and Anna. I'll stay around the cabin for the rest of the day and make sure the children are quiet."

Unaccustomed to understanding and kindness from a man, and amazed by the care Wade showed for everyone around him, a tear slipped out the corner of Gabrielle's eye. Wade took the cloth from her forehead, wiped the tear, and replaced the cloth before leaving.

Exhausted from dealing with the lights, Gabrielle dozed. Upon awakening, she expressed relief at only a minor headache, with no migraine. She made her way through the darkened interior room and the barn, before opening the barn door, only to find herself assaulted by the light. Shading her eyes, which would remain sensitive for the remainder of the day, she made her way to the cabin.

Entering the cabin, she halted, stunned. There sat Wade telling a story with the children gathered around him, and Daria on his lap! Though Gabrielle had known Daria was beginning to relax with him, the quick acceptance still astonished her.

"We ate, but I saved you a plate," Wade said when he finished the story.

"Thank you," Gabrielle said in a manner that conveyed she was thanking him for far more than the meal.

"How are you feeling?"

"Better. A bit of a headache, but I'm okay."

"I thought I'd take the children outside to play while Journey is asleep. Let me know when he wakes, and I'll come back in." Wade said as he and the children put on their wraps.

Conscious the children needed more teaching time than the bit of free time she could squeeze in each day, Gabrielle determined to make schooling a priority rather than an extra. With the school so far away and the children so young, it was up to her, regardless of how difficult it might be to find time.

Shortly after she moved in, Wade told Gabrielle to go through everything and use whatever she needed. While doing so, she found a set of the first four McGuffey Readers and four slates. Wade and his wife had obviously made the children a priority when packing for the overland trip to Oregon.

Though Gabrielle had homeschooled her children and was familiar with McGuffey Readers, she had not used them. In the twenty-first century, she had at her disposal many outstanding teaching sources, but here, she would make do with McGuffey and whatever she could design and remember.

She knew teaching would be the easy part, especially with such well-behaved, enthusiastic learners. Scheduling would create the challenge. With days already full, how could she find the time? She would need to be creative, extremely organized, and rely on more help from the children with both teaching and chores. Beth would love to pass her knowledge on to the younger ones.

Perhaps she could create games for the children to play which would teach them certain fundamentals. She had used store bought educational games frequently with her children. The tricky part would be figuring out how to create them without paper or cardboard. Gabrielle enlisted Wade's help. His time was not now as full as it soon would be, with spring planting, so perhaps he could make a game. After describing the game she had in mind, Wade said he would be happy to help; the game should be ready within a week. Though he could make a rougher version sooner, Gabrielle told him a week would be fine. He also added that he would love to help with teaching whenever possible.

While waiting for the game, Gabrielle worked with each child, determining how much they already knew. Though they all knew how to say the alphabet, thanks to the ABC song, their knowledge of the written letters varied. Beth could identify all the letters, and sounds, though she had not yet put the sounds together to read. She told Gabrielle that her mama had intended to get the reader out and teach her after Journey was born. With her knowledge, she could help the younger children with the game, which would be adjustable for all ages. Their familiarity with numbers was similar to letters. They could all count, though some farther than others, just as their ability to identify numbers varied by child. Only Beth and Catherine had any math concepts, and theirs were very basic.

Gabrielle rose earlier in the morning, which allowed her to complete some basic chores before the children woke. Catherine fed Journey his bottle in the morning, much to her delight. This freed Gabrielle to work with Beth in the reader. Beth then played with Journey while Gabrielle taught the younger girls.

After starting dinner, Gabrielle used a tray of rice as a blackboard to demonstrate how to write numbers. She traced the number in the rice, and then the girls practiced by filling their slates with the number. When she was satisfied all of them could write the number, she traced another number. But there was a flaw in her plan. Beth caught on much faster than the other girls; she continually waited for them to finish. So

Gabrielle switched to teaching Beth, who then taught the younger girls. Beth had a slate, which allowed Gabrielle to put away the rice and provided time for other work.

After a week, Wade brought the completed lotto game with him when he arrived for dinner. The quality of craftsmanship impressed Gabrielle. Thirty-six small wooden rounds, each approximately the size of a silver dollar, on which he had burned the lowercase letters of the alphabet with ten of the letters twice, were smooth to the touch. The four larger wooden rounds, each about eight inches in diameter, had nine different uppercase letters burned onto them, were also smooth to touch. Burning the letter gave the wood a three-dimensional effect, adding a pleasing tactile element.

"I'm eager to see how this will work." He placed the game on the table, with the children gathering around to look and touch.

"Children, would you like to try your new game after dinner?" Her question received a chorus of approval.

"What's it called?" asked Beth.

Gabrielle thought, looking at the four log rounds on the table and the smaller rounds that looked just like knots from the logs. "Knots on a Log."

After dinner, Wade helped Gabrielle with the dishes; Beth and Catherine dried and put them away. Then, holding Journey, he sat at the table to watch the game.

Gabrielle gave each girl a larger round and placed the smaller rounds on the table face down. "Catherine, you may start. Pick one of the little rounds and tell us what letter you have drawn."

Catherine drew. After thinking a moment, she showed the letter and said, "K, I drew a K."

"Very good! Now can you find the capital K on your board?"

Studying her board, Catherine pointed. "There it is."

"Wonderful, now place your small K on top of the capital K."

She placed the letter, beaming with pride.

"Daria, it's your turn to draw a letter."

Daria smiled at Gabrielle and chose a small round. Looking intently at it, with a smile she said "I, I drew an I," and immediately placed it on the upper case I on her board.

"Wow, good job!" Wade said, with an amazed look on his face. Gabrielle continued to be amazed at the three-year-old's enthusiasm and ability to learn.

"Beth, it's your turn."

Beth drew her letter and displayed it. "I drew an H," she said, "but there's no H on my board.

"That's right. Since the boards have only nine letters, you won't always get one of yours. When that happens, you place it back, face down, and it's the next person's turn. But first, since you can already identify all the letters, can you tell us what sound your H makes?"

Beth thought for a moment and then made the correct sound.

"Perfect! One of the wonderful things about this game is it will grow with you. After you learn all the sounds, then you'll say the letter, the sound, and a word beginning with that sound. Then later, I'll ask for a noun, a verb, an adjective, or an adverb beginning with that letter."

"Well, I'll be." Wade's tone held notes of wonder.

Since Anna only knew how to identify the letters in her name, she needed assistance, but Gabrielle had made sure A and N were on her board so she could feel excited about knowing some of her letters.

When Daria's letters were all covered, she looked to Gabrielle, "I'm out of letters," she said, with a sad expression.

Gabrielle chuckled. "That means you won!"

"I won? Is that good?"

"Yes, you did. And yes, it's good. Good job, girls. How did you like the game?"

The children all answered with cheers, and Wade said, "I'm impressed. How did you ever think of such a thing?"

"It's a simple lotto game I used to play with my children. As they grew older, I just kept adding to the requirements to make the learning last longer. You did a beautiful job making it. Thank you so much."

"I'm the one who should thank you." Wade suddenly turned away. After a moment, he said, "Okay children, get ready for bed, and we'll have a story."

Wade's stories were delightful. Simple and short, but interesting. Sometimes he told of things that happened while he worked or things he saw. Other times he described how to do things, such as when they would dig a well. But the most interesting of all were his fantasy stories. He would make up stories of knights and dragons with damsels in distress, great mountains with goats and their keepers, or perhaps tiny little people living in the forests. His stories were always fun, designed never to frighten the children. More often than not, they had a moral to teach as well as entertain.

When Wade suggested Gabrielle tell a story, she was stumped. Never one for creativity, she had no talent for making up stories. So, she borrowed from the future. Her stories were fantasy. She told of cars, trains, planes, and far off places. She told a story of men landing on the moon! As a result, the children and Wade believed her to have the world's greatest imagination.

13

Gabrielle welcomed the arrival of spring. Though this also meant more rain, the days between showers were generally warm and beautiful. The extended daylight was also a treat.

At first, she felt sorry for Wade, with the extra-long hours this meant for him, but soon realized he relished the long, hard days. As the wheat and corn sprouted, he gathered the children and Gabrielle to show them. His excitement and satisfaction in seeing his crop growing were contagious. His patience while explaining to the children seemed never-ending.

As the children asked questions, Gabrielle had an idea. "Would you like to see how a seed sprouts?"

Her question received an enthusiastic response.

"How?" Wade whispered to Gabrielle.

"Beans in a damp cloth. We will pull one apart periodically so they can see what's happening, then when they are fully sprouted, we'll plant them so they can watch them grow."

The look of admiration she received from Wade shot a sense of warmth through her. As the months passed, she had come to think it conceivable the kindness in Wade was real. This was a breakthrough for Gabrielle; the years with Kyle taught her men were not to be trusted. For her to acknowledge that perhaps this was the real Wade, as open and honest as she, was a huge step.

Just as Daria needed time to trust and heal, Gabrielle also needed time. While she had recovered physically, the emotional scars were deep. Could she ever overcome them? The developing trust she felt for Wade frightened her with an intensity that made her want to run but also offered hope.

Opening the cabin to the warmth and fresh air revealed a massive chore. Spring cleaning. With the tight living quarters, the ash and smoke from the fireplace, and the inevitable dust from the dirt floor, a thorough cleaning was in order.

On Monday, rather than only doing the regular laundry, she pulled all the bedding for washing. After placing it in the water to soak, she moved the benches and the table outside, then rolled the mattresses, and with the help of the girls, carried them outside to air, placing them across the benches. Later she would beat them with a stick. Having learned her lesson about drying time for quilts, after washing and wringing them, with help from the girls, she spread them on top of the long grass to dry.

She continued moving things out until the house was empty. While she wasn't confident with her method, it was getting done. With a shovel from the barn, she scooped the ash out of the fireplace into a bucket, which she emptied outside. Later, she would use the ash from the pile to make soap. With a bucket of water and a scrub brush, the rock surround of the fireplace was soon clean.

The overhead sun prompted her to ask Catherine, "Will you please set the table outside. We'll have the stew I put on this morning, with some cornbread, and the fried pies I made last night." Catherine enlisted the help of Daria and Anna.

Gabrielle gave thanks for the support the girls offered. Beth was taking care of Journey; she had become accomplished at caring for him and demonstrated a gift with babies.

With the food out of the house, Gabrielle swept the hardpack dirt floor. Satisfied it was as clean as dirt can get, she grabbed a rag for dusting. Realizing her error, she traded the cloth for the broom and swept the rough log walls, then re-swept the floor, being careful not to create dust. Looking around, she was satisfied with the clean cabin.

Outside, Gabrielle found Wade cleaning bed frames. "Wade, don't you have enough to do? I'll take care of that."

"No problem. After I clean these, I can help you take it all inside before going back to the field. Besides," he grinned, "this way we can move the beds back in the house and put the mattresses on them. Then we'll have places to sit for dinner."

"Oh no! I'm sorry. I thought I had it all figured out." Her panicky voice betrayed the nerves her error had provoked.

"Gabrielle." He placed his hand on her shoulder, "It's okay. I thought it was cute. That's quite a job you've taken on. I'm still not sure how you got the beds out here."

Gabrielle tried to ignore the affection and glow she felt from his touch. Together they soon had the beds back in the house, when she stopped. "Oh no!"

"What?"

"I haven't beaten the mattresses yet."

Wade lifted an eyebrow and smirked. "Done."

"Thank you," Gabrielle said, and then rolled the mattresses with Wade's assistance.

After what felt like a picnic, with Journey asleep in the shade of the oak tree which stood in front of the cabin, Beth offered to do the dishes so Gabrielle and Wade could take the furniture back inside.

Wade looked around the cabin. "Looks good. By the way, this morning I prepared the garden space for planting. The seeds are in the trunk; you can start planting tomorrow if you'd like."

Gabrielle's face filled with panic.

"What's wrong?"

"I have a very black thumb; I can't seem to grow the simplest things. What if I use the seeds and nothing comes up? It's not like we can run to the market for food."

"We'll plant the garden together, and I'll teach you how to care for it." Seeing her look of doubt, with a stroke of his thumb against her cheek, he soothed her. "Gabrielle, it's okay, it'll be fine. I have a knack for growing things, and I'll be here."

Gabrielle wondered, but not about the garden.

Early the next morning, Gabrielle and Wade left Beth to care for Journey, with Catherine to assist. With the two little girls tagging along, they took the precious seed packets to the garden plot.

Gabrielle's eyes grew wide. "It's a big garden!"

"There are seven of us." Wade's response was gentle, not judgmental.

"Good point."

As the morning passed, Wade demonstrated how to plant each seed, at what depth, and how far apart. As they planted the rows, cautious with each valuable seed, he described how to care for them until they sprouted and how long it should take for each to sprout. He showed Daria and Anna how to fill a cup with water from the pail and pour it over the seeds they had just sown. This, he explained, would be their chore each morning, unless it rained.

Looking at the freshly turned soil, so dark and rich in appearance, Gabrielle inhaled the sweet aroma. It was so beautiful here. She envied those who could coax life from the soil; perhaps with Wade's tutelage, she too would acquire the knack.

They talked and worked easily together. They had developed a comfortable friendship. It occurred to Gabrielle that she admired Wade. He was a hard worker, an honest man, always willing to lend a hand, and a loving, devoted father. Now that Daria no longer feared him, Gabrielle noted he treated Daria no different than his own children. She had even taken to calling him Papa, as the other children did. If he objected, he gave no indication.

By dinner, the huge garden was planted and watered. Wade congratulated Daria and Anna on a job well done. Turning to Gabrielle, he asked, "Are you feeling more confident about the garden now?"

Gabrielle raised her brows as she giggled. "As long as you're here to supervise, yes. Just don't leave me alone with it, unless you want a year of nothing but corn, wheat, and meat." She enjoyed the sound of Wade's laughter as they headed for the cabin.

Awakened to the patter of rain that night, Gabrielle snuggled into her covers, glad the seeds would have a good and thorough soaking.

In the morning, Daria and Anna expressed disappointment over the drizzly conditions. The excitement of their new responsibility left them eager to prove dependability. They begged to water despite the rain. Gabrielle guessed the chore would grow old long before summer was over, so she discouraged the idea.

After chores, Gabrielle watched the children on the floor of the cabin playing with their marbles. In an era when toys, games, and even playtime were in short supply, she developed a new appreciation for the game. When the girls put the marbles away and turned to their dolls, Gabrielle picked up a missed marble. Shocked at the weight, she asked Beth, "Did you say your papa made these?"

"Yes, they are bullets for his rifle, but he thought they were a good size for marbles. He had extra lead, so he made those. Later he added a few wooden ones."

"Oh, my." Gabrielle put the "marble" back in the pouch and went to look for Wade, taking the pouch with her.

"Wade?" She hesitated, unsure how to phrase what she needed to tell him.

He smiled a welcome and continued sharpening a plow blade.

"I was watching the girls play with the marbles you made them."

"Ran me a bit short on lead, but they sure do enjoy them."

Wade eyed her with concern. "What's wrong?"

"It's the lead itself. It's poisonous and can harm the children."

"I've never heard of such a thing."

"It's not yet well known. We need to take the marbles away or at least the lead ones. Do you think you could create more from a different material?"

"Are you sure about this?"

Gabrielle nodded.

Rising and taking the bag of marbles from Gabrielle, Wade went into the house. As he picked the lead marbles out of the pouch, he said, "I'm so sorry girls, but I'm running short of bullets. I need to take the lead marbles back, but I'll make more wooden ones or find something else. Please forgive your Papa."

"It's okay Papa; we know you wouldn't take them if you didn't need them."

With kisses on the tops of all heads, Wade went back to the barn, taking the lead marbles with him.

Mondays were not her favorite day. Gabrielle reached in the washtub, the hot water scalding her work-roughened hands. Grabbing the first item, she scrubbed it on the washboard. She enjoyed the warmth of the spring weather while completing the laborious chore of laundry.

Wade worked in the distance. He held the plow steady as he readied yet another field for planting. He had told her he divided his land into plots and would continue plowing and planting through the end of July in hopes of continued and late harvests. By that time, with good weather, it should be time to harvest the first of the crops.

When asked why they needed so much, Wade told her he hoped to sell or trade to get items otherwise unavailable to him. She looked in wonder at the man, so industrious, so caring, and so devoted to the children.

In addition to continuing with the fields, he dedicated one day a week to adding to his pile of logs. This began during the winter, and Gabrielle originally thought it would serve as firewood, but the firewood stack seemed separate. When asked, he just smiled, as if she should know. They were not large logs, but they were consistent in size. With a glance toward the cabin to see the little girls at play, Gabrielle noticed the logs were all the same size as the ones used in building the cabin.

That evening at supper, Gabrielle asked, "Are you planning to add to the cabin? Is that what the logs are for?"

Wade chuckled. "I knew you would figure it out. We could certainly use more space. Thought I'd build on that end," he pointed toward the beds, "and make it into two bedrooms. What do you think?"

"Wow! But what would we do with all the extra space?" Gabrielle couldn't believe what she had just said.

"Maybe a living space, with comfortable seating, who knows? But with seven of us, I figured we could use a bit more room, especially as the little ones grow. Don't count on it happening too soon though. Once harvest season starts, the addition will stop until harvest is complete. I'm hoping to have some building done by then, since I'm thinking only two more days of logging will do it, assuming I don't run into problems."

Gabrielle's astonishment at this turn of events was not about the extra space, but that this man, who had so much to do just to feed his family and work the farm, would add to it for the mere comfort of his family, and all while sleeping in the barn! With each passing day, her respect for Wade grew. This growing respect also increased her sense of wariness. It was difficult to lose the memory of "too good to be true."

With the cycle of the spring rains and warm sunshine, the world around them soon turned into a blanket of varying shades of lush green. Fresh new leaves on the deciduous trees blazed bright green against the established dark green of their evergreen relatives. The sprouting fields and garden, surrounded by contrasting rich brown soil, flashed a multitude of greens, edged by the bright green of new grass.

In contrast to the abundant greens of the world around them, their store of supplies seemed dull and lifeless. Little was left and much of it barely usable. Gabrielle wondered if the food would last until they could begin harvesting again.

However, it would seem that even in this, God made amazing provision. Along with all the fresh sprouts, deer, rabbit, and other creatures came out in abundance. Wade's expertise with his rifle soon had them preparing meat and hides. Some meat was placed in the brine barrel, while the remainder was made into jerky. Wade busied himself in the evenings tanning hides. Nothing must be wasted.

Once again Gabrielle considered the abundance of things and the exorbitant waste she and those around her had been conditioned to expect and accept in the twenty-first century. Almost nothing was expected in this hard life in which she had found herself. Yet, despite the hardships and constant work, there existed a satisfaction which seemed to be missing in the environment of high expectations and crowds of shoppers she had left behind. It occurred to her; perhaps accumulation of goods filled the void created by the lack of gratification achieved from the physical exhaustion of providing for yourself. While she knew people of her time worked hard, it was a different type of work and the consequences of not working for even a short period of time were quite different. The rewards were also different.

One evening, Gabrielle watched as Wade told the children a story, heard their prayers, and tucked them into bed. In no time, they slept. When they weren't helping with the work, they were playing, and with the good weather, their play usually consisted of active outdoor games. After Gabrielle scratched a hopscotch in the dirt and taught them how to play, the game seemed to rule their play time.

As he waited for them to fall asleep, Wade sat in the stump chair whittling a piece of wood. Looking closer, Gabrielle realized he was carving a marble.

Wade stopped his whittling and looked at Gabrielle. "Gabrielle, it's a beautiful evening. Would you like to walk?" Wade's offer wasn't unusual since the weather had improved, though with all the meat to prepare, it had been a while since they had found an opportunity to take a walk. They always remained near the cabin so they could hear if one of the children awoke.

Gabrielle nodded. She enjoyed their walks. She appreciated Wade and enjoyed spending time with him, but refused to admit she felt anything other than friendship. Ignoring the warm feelings that flooded her when he came in from the fields and the electric charge she felt whenever they happened to touch was becoming difficult. But she had no choice.

The night air was warm for April. With the clear sky, the stars, more than she had ever seen in her own time, were breathtaking. The moon lit the world around her, providing a subdued and tranquil light source. She breathed in deeply, relishing this life and the unpretentious beauty of it. As they walked near the field full of tiny corn stalks, Gabrielle could smell the tilled earth. Odd how she noticed little things here that her senses seemed to miss in the twenty-first century, where the joys and attractions of the simple and miraculous were sadly overlooked due to the many electronic and motorized distractions.

Pointing, Wade said, "Look, an owl."

Gabrielle saw but did not hear as an owl swooped down and picked something from the field.

"They help keep the mice down."

"I know something about owls. Their wing feathers are serrated, allowing the wind to be distributed, which is why their flight is silent." Gabrielle paused. "We studied them when I homeschooled my children."

"You are so good with the children." Wade looked at her. "I've been thinking. We've come to know each other since you've been here. We're no longer strangers. I care a great deal for you." He took a breath. "I think we should be married."

Gabrielle stopped, stunned. "Married?"

While she had pushed all thoughts of a relationship with Wade from her mind, she knew the quickening of her heart revealed feelings far deeper than they should be. For one joyous moment, she almost said yes.

"Wade," she hesitated as she thought how to say what must be said. "I also admire you, and I'm quite happy and content in this home you've built, but I'm sorry, I cannot marry." At this, she turned and walked back to the cabin, leaving him alone next to the field. As she walked, tears trickled down her cheeks.

The moment Wade suggested they wed, Gabrielle became conscious of feelings she had suppressed, but could no longer ignore. Previously, she viewed him as an employer of sorts. While she admired, respected, and was grateful for him, thoughts of romance could not be permitted; they simply hadn't gone in that direction. How could they? She was already married.

It had been six months since Wade's wife died. Though not long by modern standards, for these pioneers, she now recognized the difficulty of being alone with a family. The amount of work to live a so-called simple life and the time it took demanded a partner. There was no time for lengthy mourning periods. This life was not simple at all; it was hard, very hard. She was unsure if Wade felt ready to move on or if he was more interested in propriety. Knowing there had been some talk circulating regarding their living together and not being married, despite Wade's room in the barn, Gabrielle wondered if that was what prompted the proposal. Not that it mattered.

Wade and everyone else assumed it had been seven months since Kyle's death. But Kyle didn't die. He was still alive. Looking at the wedding ring she still wore, she realized her dilemma had no solution. Even if Kyle did die, she had no way of knowing. She chastised herself as she realized the idea of Kyle dying prompted no feelings. None.

Overwhelmed by the realization of the strong feelings she held for Wade, regardless of there being no physical demonstration of those feelings, meant she was being unfaithful to her husband, sending Gabrielle to her knees. She prayed fervently to love her husband and only her husband. She beseeched God for guidance and wisdom. With tears streaming, she prayed for Wade, that he should know peace and He may provide for him a helpmate worthy of such a kind and gentle spirit.

The wise thing to do would be to leave, to follow Joseph's example and run from temptation, but it would not be right to leave Wade without help. She cringed at the irony of it all. She was caught in not one, but two catch-twenty-twos. As a married woman, she could not possibly be with her husband, who despite her many prayers, she nearly despised. Nor could she marry the man she had grown to love and who wanted to marry her, because she already had a husband in another century. To top that off, she could not continue to live here considering her adulterous feelings, but to leave would cause great hardship for Wade and the children, which she couldn't possibly do.

"Oh Lord, what would you have me do?"

14

As the weeks passed, the awkwardness Gabrielle felt around Wade subsided. Though she occasionally noticed him gazing her way with a perplexed look, nothing seemed to change. He still treated her with the same kindness and respect he had from the beginning.

The garden, like the fields, sprouted and was growing, much to the children's delight and Gabrielle's surprise. Daria and Anna were faithful in their watering duties, not yet growing weary of the chore. Beth and Catherine had been given the daily chore of weeding, while Gabrielle made sure to spare fifteen minutes each day to hoe and weed.

Journey was beginning to crawl. Gabrielle was glad that Wade had built a raised hearth for the fireplace, knowing it had taken extra time and work. When she commented on it, he told her they had a friend in Ohio whose baby had been burned due to the ease of accessibility. He wasn't taking any chances.

Gabrielle wished there were more books available. Beth was reading quite well now, but it was a big leap from reading McGuffey to the family's King James Bible. It would be nice to have some children's books at her disposal. *If we only had a small portion of the library I had accumulated for my children by going to garage sales and friends-of-the-library sales.*

One Sunday at church, Gabrielle noticed how much Rose had grown. Realizing the baby would arrive within a couple of months, and seeing how happy Rose looked, she was eager to spend time together and learn how Rose was doing. Her once tucked-in bodice now hung over her skirt, and Gabrielle realized why skirts were made so adjustable in the waist and the bodice so loose fitting.

After service, they greeted each other warmly, always looking forward to their time together on Sundays.

"My parents received the news about the baby. They are excited. They must have forgotten about sending baby clothes and other needs with the furniture and shipped a package containing a whole layette. This baby won't lack for things to wear. As you can imagine, I haven't been able to stop myself from making a few items."

Raised voices near Wade and Clement distracted Gabrielle. "Be careful what you say, Foster. I'll not have you slandering Mrs. Fallon that way. Mr. Brown and Pastor Harris helped me build a room in my barn, and that is where I sleep. Mrs. Fallon has been a godsend to my children and is every inch a Christian lady. You will apologize."

Unable to hear the rest of the conversation, Gabrielle guessed what must have happened. Their living arrangements were not only the subject of gossip, but apparently Mr. Foster had alluded to them.

Rose took Gabrielle's arm and guided her toward the store. "He's a crass man. Think nothing of what just occurred; he likes to stir up trouble. He's lonely and needs companionship."

"Wade is conscious of the talk."

Rose looked at Gabrielle. "Did he say something?

"He suggested we marry."

"Gabrielle, that's marvelous! He's such a good man. When will the wedding be?"

"Rose, I can't marry Wade." The sadness in Gabrielle's voice could not be missed.

"Why? Is there something you haven't told us? He's not different at home, is he?"

"Wade is wonderful, but I simply can't marry. I'm sorry Rose, but I can't tell you more."

Gabrielle was uncomfortable for the remainder of the visit. She wanted to tell Rose she was already married, but then instead of thinking of her as a woman of questionable repute, people would have no doubt she was insane.

The ride home was warm. It seemed summer had arrived early. After supper, Wade's suggestion that they all go to the creek was met with enthusiasm. Everyone changed from their Sunday clothes and Wade grabbed a blanket before heading for the creek.

Gabrielle gave thanks Wade and their friends didn't subscribe to the old-fashioned idea that nothing but worship must happen on Sundays. Not only was this the Lord's Day for worship, but a day he created as a day of rest. Sitting quietly on hard chairs acting pious all day didn't sound the least bit restful to Gabrielle.

After playing in the creek with the girls, Wade picked up Journey from the blanket where Gabrielle had been playing with him. He then reached a hand to assist Gabrielle. "Come in the creek with us." His smile held a look of contentment.

As she accepted his assistance in rising, the combination of his hand holding hers and his beautiful smile caused Gabrielle's breath to catch. She must get a grip on herself! With a deep breath, she rose, kicked off the tennis shoes she still wore, and with a lift of her skirt waded into the creek.

Wade stayed at the edge, dipping Journey's feet into the water, while Gabrielle hiked her skirt higher and joined the girls in the splashing. Daria, who was scrubbing her hair in the water, remembered floating and asked for help. Soon Gabrielle was giving floating lessons to all four girls. They caught on quickly, even little Anna.

Gabrielle joined the girls. The water was brisk but refreshing. She closed her eyes as the water caressed her face and cradled her in its embrace. Rising, Wade stood next to her, with Journey lying on his back in the water.

"The creek's rather cold for him, don't you think?"

"He loves it. Just a bit more and then we'll wrap him in the blanket to warm him. It's nice that you taught the girls to float."

"I'll teach them to swim this summer. Though not many women do, it's important."

"You swim. Is that what saved you?"

For a moment Gabrielle didn't understand, but then realized he was referring to the supposed river crossing accident. "My skirt kept me from swimming; I guess you could say it was a miracle." At the memory of the whirlpool, Gabrielle's eyes glistened with thoughts of her children.

"I shouldn't have mentioned it."

"It's okay. We should feel free to speak of our past lives."

"You've never spoken of the accident."

Gabrielle stopped. How to speak of an accident that didn't happen? Guilt ate at her for allowing her friends to continue their mistaken assumption of how she came to be alone here. Closing her eyes, she inhaled. When she opened them again, Wade had Journey out of the water heading for shore.

As she neared him, Wade said, "I'm sorry; I didn't intend to cause you pain."

"It's okay. Perhaps someday I'll tell you how I found myself here, but not yet."

As they talked, they gathered the children and headed to the cabin. While walking, Gabrielle's awareness of her wet skirt clinging to her body brought color to her face and neck. She attempted to loosen it, with little success. Wade chuckled. In return, she gave him her best "look." At this, both laughed.

Back at the cabin, the tired children prepared for bed, and then Gabrielle told them a story. As happened many nights, she borrowed from the future. Sometimes speaking of actual events, other times copying stories from favorite books not yet written. Tonight she shared one of her favorite children's stories, *The Red Ripe Strawberry and the Big Hungry Bear*. Having read it to her children many times, she told the story verbatim.

After kisses and hugs all around, she faced Wade, who had diapered and dressed Journey and was laying him in his cradle. "That was fun. Thank you for suggesting it." Gabrielle kept her voice low, to avoid disturbing the children.

"We'll need to remember it through the summer. It's easy to get busy and collapse into bed after supper."

Wade studied Gabrielle. "Why can't you marry?"

Shocked by his unexpected question, Gabrielle stopped and thought of how to respond. Nothing came to mind. With a sigh, she whispered, "Goodnight, Wade."

For a moment he appeared ready to say something but instead closed his eyes as he exhaled, then walked out of the cabin.

A quiet man, Wade only talked when he had something to say, but as the week progressed, he barely spoke. It was obvious he was upset. Uncertain whether the upset was anger or hurt, Gabrielle felt terrible. She had no desire to distress Wade. But she could think of no way around her dilemma.

She watched as Wade fed mashed beans to Journey. He focused on Journey, with occasional looks or responses to the girls, but he avoided even looking in her direction.

After feeding Journey beans, with bits of cornbread and milk, Wade rose, placed the dishes to be washed, and walked out of the cabin. It was unlike him to leave the children after supper. Gabrielle asked Beth to supervise the dishes and followed him out the door. Though she had no idea what to say or do, the situation interfered with the whole household.

In the barn, Wade chiseled a piece of wood. "Wade, are you angry with me?"

With a quick glance at her, he turned back to his work. "I'm not angry."

"Then why are you avoiding me?" She bent and picked up a few of the wood chips which landed on the floor.

"I'm trying hard to understand. I haven't asked you to marry me for convenience, or even to stop gossip, but because I have feelings for you. I thought you had feelings for me."

"I do, but this is an impossible situation for me."

"Then explain it to me." While speaking, his focus remained on his work.

"I wish I could. But Wade, the children are feeling the tension. If we cannot retain a happy home for their sakes, without you staying away as much as possible, I must find a different place to live. This cannot come between you and your children. By allowing it, well, I'm here to make life better, not worse."

His lack of response spoke volumes. Either explain why she could not marry him, or she needed to leave. She stood watching him for what seemed like an eternity before walking from the barn. Though she struggled to remain stoic, tears slipped out, followed by choking sobs erupting from deep inside her.

She had only just begun to accept the loss of her children. The waves of devastation engulfed her less frequently and were less intense than before, though the pain remained with her. But now came a new loss. Why? She tried to live a good and proper life. Was she being punished for something? It seemed as though she was meant to lose everyone she loved.

At that thought, she stopped as a jarring reality overwhelmed her. Daria. She had adjusted to life here. She had become part of the family, one of the sisters. How could she take Daria from here? Would Wade even want to keep her?

She couldn't lose another child. She couldn't lose these children. She promised Daria she would never leave her. What was she to do?

As she walked, she noticed the wood chips still in her hand. Uniform, square, thin pieces of wood with a slight curl on one edge. She snapped off the curl. These little squares reminded her of something, but her befuddled mind could not grasp what it was.

Back in the cabin, she laid them on the table and helped the children prepare for bed. She loved brushing their hair. With a practiced gentleness, even Anna had grown to accept having her hair brushed. Gabrielle suspected she secretly enjoyed it, but her young, stubborn streak prevented her from admitting it.

While preparing breakfast the next morning, Gabrielle caught sight of the wood squares in her peripheral vision. She stared at them. Seeing them peripherally had caused her to see them as *Scrabble* tiles. Looking at the uniform size, she knew they would work. If Wade could create a board, the letters and board could be burned to create a rustic version of the game.

During breakfast, she asked if he could make more of the chips.

With an odd look, he nodded.

"Can you also make a board about this big?" she asked, holding out her hands.

A hint of a smile accompanied his answer. "Yes. Do you have another game in mind?"

"Yes, I do. Not only can the children play this one, but adults enjoy it as well."

She grabbed a school slate and drew a *Scrabble* board. Since phrases like "double word score" would be difficult to burn into the wood, Gabrielle suggested horizontal, diagonal, vertical, and blacked out squares to indicate these. She guessed the number of squares on the board and chose fifteen by fifteen. She knew the placement of several special spaces but needed to guess on the others. She had played numerous *Scrabble* games with her family. Not only was it a great learning tool, but it provided hours of fun. On a second slate, she wrote the alphabet followed by the number of tiles needed for each letter and the point value. She guessed on several. While the amounts might not have been precise, they were close. J, Q, Z, and X were the easy ones.

"Can you do it?"

"Yes, it should be fairly simple, but it may take time."

"Oh, one more thing. We need four trays that will each hold seven of the chip-tiles."

Despite himself, Wade smiled and shook his head. "You are something, Gabrielle Fallon. Give me a week, maybe two."

"Thank you!" In her excitement, without thinking, she hugged him. Awkwardly, she withdrew and busied herself with chores.

"Keep doing that, and I may become a full-time game-maker," Wade said in a husky voice, which sent forbidden shivers all the way to Gabrielle's toes. She sighed as she watched him retreat out the door.

Gabrielle still had not found a solution to her dilemma a week later when, just after the children had gone to bed and fallen asleep, Wade came into the cabin carrying the game.

"All done!"

"Oh Wade, you did a beautiful job. This will work wonderfully! How did you find the time?" Taking out a cloth bag with a drawstring which she had made, Gabrielle gathered the chip-tiles and placed them in it. "Would you like to play?"

"Sure. I was curious, so I made time."

He stayed up late to complete it, she thought. *Amazing man.*

Gabrielle explained how to play and took out one of the children's slates for keeping score. She enjoyed their time together. It was nice to talk and take pleasure in each other's company again.

Partway through the game, Wade said, "This is amazing! How did you ever come up with it?"

"I didn't. It's a store-bought game that was popular at home. Since it's impossible to get here and we aren't selling it, I hope Milton Bradley, the makers, won't mind."

Wade caught on quickly to the strategies of the game. Gabrielle knew she had better beat him now, because with a little practice on his part she wouldn't have a chance. She was at a distinct disadvantage; many of the common words of her world weren't yet words. How could she explain car, engine, or electric to him? And those would be easy compared to computer, nuclear, or even digital.

Gabrielle won, but not by much. He was smart, and a far better speller than she. But then, that didn't take much; spelling had never been her forte. While homeschooling her children, she learned spelling rules she had never known existed. The only one she had been taught in school was "i before e..." Learning additional rules had helped her spelling immensely. Playing hundreds of games of Scrabble had also given it a boost.

As Wade stood facing the door to leave for the barn, he said, "I don't want you to leave. I hope someday you will find it in your heart to trust me enough to tell me." Before Gabrielle had a chance to reply, he was out the door.

15

In the middle of July, on a beautiful, sunny morning, Gabrielle walked into the church, surprised to see the Browns not yet there. Rose always arrived early so she could spend as much time as possible with Gabrielle.

"Wade, I'm concerned. I need to check on them."

"I'll go with you. Beth, you and the girls stay on the bench; I'll be back soon."

They stopped to tell Pastor Harris they left the girls and then hurried with Journey to the back door of the living quarters.

At the sound of their knock, Clement yanked the door open. "Gabrielle, thank goodness. It's time, and Rose wouldn't let me leave to get Mrs. Butler. Do you know what to do?"

A moan sounded from the direction of the rocker.

Gabrielle entered the room, taking charge. "Wade, go get Mrs. Butler, please. I'll miss church today, but you should attend with the children."

In the rocker, Rose struggled against the pain.

"Rose, don't fight it; work with it. Remember the breathing we practiced? It will help. Find your focal point and take a deep cleansing breath. Good, now breath in-two, three, four, out-two, three, four." Gabrielle continued repeating this until the contraction ended. "Good. Now a deep cleansing breath. Better?"

"Oh Gabrielle, I'm so glad you're here. Thank you, fear overcame me, and I forgot the breathing. It helped."

Turning to Clement, Gabrielle asked, "How far apart are the contractions?"

"I'm not sure, maybe five minutes."

"Rose, you let me know when the slow breathing doesn't help and we will change to the hee-hee method, okay."

Gabrielle put two pots of water on to boil. She always wondered what the purpose was for boiling water, but after washing her hands with the well water, not knowing how pure it was, she felt it would be a good idea. Determined that Rose would not be a victim of childbed fever, the term of the times for a childbirth infection that went systemic, Gabrielle took every precaution. Assuming this had caused Wade's wife's death, she resolved the same thing would not happen to Rose or anyone else within her reach.

"How can I help?" Clement asked while pacing.

"First, you need to relax. Babies are born every day, and relaxing makes it much easier. Next, wash your hands well with this lye soap. After the water is ready, we'll rewash. Then take your clue from Rose. Help her relax. Stroke her hand, rub her back, whatever she wants."

Mrs. Butler rushed into the room. "Well, well, so we're going to have a baby today."

As if in answer, Rose took a deep breath, prompting Gabrielle to hasten to her side. "In-two, three, four, out-two, three, four."

Mrs. Butler watched, perplexed. After the contraction ended and Rose took her cleansing breath, Mrs. Butler said, "Interesting. Well, Mr. Brown, you might as well go on to church. This is no place for a man. Rose, you need to get into bed."

"Mrs. Butler, please don't take offense, but Rose and Clement have decided they would like for him to stay with her throughout the delivery. And right now Rose feels most comfortable in the chair. We'll just let her decide whether to sit, stand, walk, or lie down." Gabrielle's gentle and quiet speech shocked the woman.

"Well, if I'm not needed, why did Mr. Mitchell come fetch me?"

"Oh my, of course, we need you, Mrs. Butler. I'm not a midwife. I've never delivered a baby for someone, only my own. I am acting as Rose's doula."

"Doula?" she asked."

"A doula, or advocate, looks after the mom's wishes and assists wherever needed. I'm here to help Rose stay calm and have as easy a birth as possible."

"Since when did birthing a baby become easy?"

"It's definitely hard work, that's why they call it labor. However, it can be made easier by not fighting it, but instead, working with it. Will you please trust me on this? Rose needs us both."

"Okay, but…" Mrs. Butler gave Gabrielle an odd look and let it drop.

With another contraction beginning, Mrs. Butler watched Rose's calm demeanor as she breathed.

When it was over, Gabrielle asked, "Mrs. Butler, could you please wash your hands well with that lye soap? We will all rewash them after the water boils."

"My hands are clean!"

"Mrs. Butler, I know you are a clean woman, but by making sure birthing conditions are as sanitary as possible, we can help assure the wellbeing of both Rose and the baby."

"I'll do as you say, but you certainly do have some mighty odd ideas."

"Thank you," Gabrielle said with an understanding smile while taking the boiling water off the stove to allow it to cool.

As labor progressed, Rose stood and swayed through each contraction while she breathed. Mrs. Butler watched in wonder, accustomed to women in this stage of labor screaming and losing control.

As the contractions grew more intense and Rose struggled to control the hee-hee breathing technique, she moved to the bed.

"Shouldn't be much longer now. I'm going to need to check you."

"Can you please rewash your hands in this sterilized water?" Gabrielle said as she finished washing her own hands.

With a lift of her eyebrows, Mrs. Butler allowed Gabrielle to pour the still warm water over her hands, lathered with the lye soap, scrubbing well as previously instructed by Gabrielle. Then Gabrielle poured rinse water. When done, Clement re-washed his hands in the same manner.

"I need to push!" Rose cried out.

"Hang on honey, give me a minute." Mrs. Butler's calm and quiet demeanor spoke of her professionalism.

Gabrielle reminded Rose about the pa-pa's. Puffing her cheeks and saying pa with each exhaled breath restored Rose's calm.

While Gabrielle and Clement helped hold Rose's legs, she pushed with everything she had. After just a few pushes, the healthy cry of the tiny baby boy, whose bright red hair left no doubt who he belonged to, made Gabrielle's heart soar. When Mrs. Butler stood to carry the baby across the room, Gabrielle stopped her. Wrapping a blanket around him, Gabrielle laid him on Rose's stomach.

As Rose and Clement exclaimed over their new son, Mrs. Butler shook her head at Gabrielle. "I don't know where you got your ideas, but they sure do seem to work. I've never seen an easier birth. I'd like to work together again. Mrs. Harris is due any time now; perhaps you could help."

Watching the new life with his parents, Gabrielle nodded. "I would love to."

After time for the family to bond, Mrs. Butler took the baby and cleaned him, returning him to his mother for his first nursing.

Gabrielle took Rose's hand. "We will leave the three of you alone. You have a beautiful son. What's his name?"

Rose beamed with tired eyes at Gabrielle. "Thank you so very much. His name is Lucas Gabriel Brown," she said, changing the short A in Gabrielle's name to a long A, and the spelling from feminine to masculine.

With an uncontained smile, Gabrielle opened the door to leave, but Rose stopped her. "Gabrielle, whatever it is, you need to tell him. He loves you."

On the ride home, Gabrielle thought about what Rose said. She argued with herself; Wade would think her insane. What would she do upon hearing such a claim? Kyle's veiled threats to commit her came to mind. If she were Wade, she would certainly consider it if told such a story. On the other hand, where in 1848 Oregon could one be committed? The marriage proposal would be forgotten in his haste to separate her from his children.

He told her to trust him. Trust works both ways. If she trusted him enough to tell him, would he trust her enough to believe her?

They arrived home in darkness. They carried the sleeping children into the cabin and tucked them into their beds. Gabrielle thought about changing and feeding Journey, but she decided against it. Kissing his forehead, she laid him in his cradle and stepped outside.

With the last child in bed, Wade led the oxen to the barn, unhitched the wagon, and put them in the corral.

By the light of the moon, Gabrielle watched as he worked. Such a good man. He deserved to know why she couldn't marry him. She sat on the bench in front of the cabin. As he released the oxen into the corral and turned toward the cabin, Gabrielle's breath caught. She took a deep breath, exhaled slowly, let down her shoulders, and focused on relaxing.

"Going to fall asleep on the bench?" Wade smiled at her. "You've had quite the day."

"Wade…" she stopped, unable to continue. Instead, she said, "Yes, it was."

16

As the summer progressed, with its added responsibility of storing foods from the garden, Gabrielle stayed busy. Every few days she and the girls went for a walk, picking berries to dry or make into pie or cobbler.

Despite Wade working from sun to sun in the fields, he still did much to ease her burden. Each morning he hauled buckets of water to the cabin as well as filling the rain barrel next to the garden. Though the frequent rains kept it full earlier in the year, they hauled buckets from the creek to maintain the water level during the drier summer months. He rose early to provide the water. After working all day, often stopping only long enough to eat the dinner carried to the field by one of the children, he would help them to bed when he arrived back at the cabin after the last of the daylight. He then chopped, stacked, and carried wood for the following day before finally sitting down to eat his supper.

Though the log walls were all up, and the roof trusses were on, work on the addition to the cabin stopped there. Gabrielle assumed it would not take long to finish, but the only way to find time would be to not sleep or to work on Sunday, which was out of the question. While the extra space would be nice, it certainly was not essential; the addition could wait.

Many evenings Wade ate while sitting on the bench outside the cabin. A round of wood placed in front of the seat provided a table. Sitting outside not only prevented the children from continuing their excited tales of the day's events when they should be sleeping, but he preferred the cool night air. Gabrielle often joined him, relaxing in the peace and tranquility of the evening sounds and scents.

The children did their share of the work. Amazed by how dependable and helpful such young children could be, Gabrielle made sure they had play time. They appeared to enjoy helping; the responsibilities seemed to make them feel like a needed, contributing part of the family. Perhaps, she thought, it was a better way than in her own time. After all, how would she feel and react if she didn't feel like a necessary part of the family?

Despite the long, hard days, Gabrielle was content. While she ached for her children and worried about their well-being, she was beginning to accept that they were gone to her. As a result, the sobbing jags came less frequently, and she found some joy in her life again. Though they could never be replaced, the delight she experienced from the five children in her care helped ease the pain.

The longing and regret when she looked at Wade did not lessen with time; rather, it increased each day. Knowing Rose was right, she should tell him the full truth, did not make it easier to risk everything by telling him. At times Gabrielle caught him looking at her. The looks conveyed different thoughts, sometimes curiosity, sometimes irritation, sometimes she thought she saw love. How she wished she could accept his proposal! But she would be forever bound to Kyle, to whom she could not return. More difficult than living with not being able to accept Wade's proposal was the effort to keep her mind clear of her ever-growing feelings for him. She was, after all, a married woman and endeavored to remain mentally and emotionally faithful to her husband.

Gabrielle gave thanks that Wade was a gentleman. He did not push, nor did he seem to resent her refusal. After the night of the Scrabble game, things returned to normal. They talked, joked, and worked together as though nothing had ever been said.

As they rode to church one Sunday in August, it occurred to Gabrielle, despite the harshness, she liked this life. She had always thought she was born a hundred years too late, but had been wrong; she was born a hundred fifty years late. While she missed aspects of modern life, none so much that she would choose to return for anything but her children. She was in her element.

Taking their seats, Gabrielle appreciated the gift of an awesome church family. Then shock reverberated through her. There, on one of the benches, sat Wanda, wearing the yellow dress. Despite no sign of Mr. Volstead, she gathered Daria closer. Wanda sat next to a young man, who was speaking to her.

When Pastor Harris welcomed the newcomers during the service, he introduced Mr. and Mrs. David Farnsworth. Gabrielle's shock when Wanda and the young man stood took her breath away. Upon seeing Wanda, Daria clung to Gabrielle and looked at her with imploring eyes.

Gabrielle leaned down and assured the frightened child. "It's okay, Daria; Papa and I are here. You are safe."

Looking first at Gabrielle and then at Wade, Daria relaxed, her trust in her new parents total, but Gabrielle's anxiety remained.

How had this come to be? Wanda was only thirteen! Volstead would never let her marry; she worked hard for him. To lose her meant the loss of a field hand. Who would cook?

After service, Wade led the family to welcome the couple. As they neared, Daria struggled to hide within Gabrielle's skirt, while keeping a tight grip on her hand. Wade, absorbed in a conversation with the young man, left Gabrielle staring at Wanda.

"Mornin', Mrs. Fallon."

At a loss for words, Gabrielle hesitated. "Wanda." While Gabrielle ached for this girl and the life she lived, the trials of her time at the Volstead's, as well as the last morning, came flooding back. Seeing Wanda again brought the trauma of that period alive.

Gabrielle asked Beth to take the little girls to play with the other children and transferred Daria's hand to hers. Beth seemed to sense Daria's anxiety. Putting her arm around the child, she led her three little sisters away.

Wanda looked Gabrielle in the eye. "He sold me." She stated this in a simple, matter-of-fact way, with no emotion involved.

The shock of seeing Wanda did not compare to what she heard. "He sold you?"

"Fer a horse."

"Wanda, what do you mean he sold you for a horse?"

"Mr. Farnsworth came through a few days ago and wanted to work for a bit of food. He had a right nice filly that

217

Pa fairly drooled over. After a few days o' workin', Pa asked him what he wanted fer that horse. Mr. Farnsworth done tole him that the only things he cared more about havin' than that there horse was a farm and a wife, and he didn't figure Pa'd help him none with neither of um. Well, Pa up an tole him he couldn't help with the farm, but he could pervide him with a wife and pointed at me. Mr. Farnsworth there, first he looked real mad, then he looked at me fer a while, real thoughtful like, had kinda a sad look on his face, then tole Pa he had a deal. Next morning, yesterday it was, Pa tole me to get my stuff and go with Mr. Farnsworth, I belongs to him now. Was kinda odd though, on the way to town, when we come to a creek, Mr. Farnsworth handed me a bar of soap an had me go to the creek and bathe an wash my hair, an put my dress on afore we left. Kinda reminded me o' you an your ways."

"He watched?"

"No, he sat leaned agin a tree facin' away from the creek."

Wanda's story overwhelmed Gabrielle. He sold his daughter for a horse! "Wanda, when were you married?"

"After arrivin' in town yesterday afernoon. Funny thang was, he got us a room at the boardin' house last night, but didn't stay there with me. I spose I spected him to start gruntin' on top o' me like Pa did to Daria's ma soon as he married up with her."

Gabrielle thought the revulsion that man produced within her could not grow worse until today. *Poor Emma, her husband barely dead, forced to marry such a vile creature, and then...* Gabrielle ached for the mother of her sweet little Daria. Poor Wanda had been exposed to far too much, developing a hardness no thirteen-year-old should possess. Gabrielle's mothering instinct demanded she gather the girl in her arms and protect her, but there was little chance Wanda would allow such a thing.

"Gabrielle, may I have a word with you?" Wade said as Mr. Farnsworth ushered Wanda aside. "I've been talking to Mr. Farnsworth. Lost his wagon and oxen team coming down a mountain. While he has a bit of cash remaining, it's not enough to buy a team, and he traded the horse he had bought from a family on the wagon train. With no team, it'll be impossible to get a farm going.

"I planted way more than I can harvest by myself. Perhaps the Farnsworths could stay with us until the crops are in. It would give us both help, and we could pay them with a portion of the remaining crops."

His desire for her blessing before proceeding with the plan honored Gabrielle. "Wade, you need to know something first." She filled him in on Wanda, how she came to be with Mr. Farnsworth, and Daria's response to seeing Wanda. "What kind of man would trade his horse for a thirteen-year-old girl?"

"I believe he is a kind, Christian man." Wade's words surprised her. "He told me about trading his horse for Wanda. When Volstead suggested it, Farnsworth's first instinct was to give the man the thrashing he deserved. But then the life Wanda led occurred to him. With the sort of man he figured Volstead to be, he feared for Wanda's safety if she remained there. She's beginning to look like a woman instead of a girl.

"I'm sorry, Gabrielle, I don't mean to be crude, but you need to know the full story. Farnsworth realized the only answer would be to do as Volstead suggested. He left her at the boarding house last night because he has no intention of sharing a bed with her until they get to know one another and care for one another. He also wants to give her a chance to mature."

Gabrielle's relief came out in a breath.

"I know seeing Wanda was quite a shock for both you and Daria. I will not have either of you uncomfortable at our home. If you have any reservations, please tell me."

Gabrielle considered for a moment before speaking. "You know I despised leaving Wanda and Earl in Volstead's hands. I have felt as though I abandoned them. While I may not be able to help Earl, this could be my opportunity to reach Wanda. My concern is Daria and the other children. What if she mistreats them or her attitude affects them?"

"Shall we speak to Wanda? Would that help you?"

"Yes, I think we need to."

Locating the Farnsworths, Wade expressed their concerns.

Wanda spoke to Gabrielle. "Mrs. Fallon, I don't blame you none for bein' worried. I was so angry at ma dyin' and havin' to work harder than even before, I got more and more like Pa ever day. But when you came, I saw the differ'nce you made. I saw your kindness and gentleness. I's partial to ya, but figur'd I didn't have no chance of ever bein' like you. It just made me madder. I'm sorry for the way I treated both you and Daria. If you'd give me a chance, I'd like to learn how to be like you."

With a shine of tears, Gabrielle looked at Wade and nodded.

"Farnsworth, looks like you have yourself a job." Wade stuck out his hand and shook David Farnsworth's hand.

Gabrielle addressed Wanda. "Daria was quite traumatized by all that occurred. I will try to make this as easy as possible for her, but you need to fix it."

"I will."

"Wade, how will we fit two more people?"

"Already got that figured out. Farnsworth here will bed down in the barn room with me, and Wanda will sleep in the cabin with you. Think you can squeeze her in?"

With a moment's thought, Gabrielle replied, "I think we should be able to move Beth in the bed with the little girls, and Wanda can sleep with me."

"Good! Now let's see how the Brown family is getting on."

Gabrielle noted the concern on Rose's face at the news of Wanda coming to stay with them, but she knew her friend's kind heart agreed with the decision. Though she still had reservations, she could not turn the child away.

As the three families enjoyed a picnic in the shade of the oak tree next to the church, Gabrielle noticed Daria kept her distance from Wanda. She had observed that while she could see the child speaking when off playing with the other girls, during dinner, while she was in the proximity of Wanda, she was back to nodding and other non-verbal communication. *For Daria's sake, I hope this isn't a mistake. The poor child suffered enough at that family's hands; I can't allow this to traumatize her further.*

Wanda surprised Gabrielle by speaking. "Daria, you lookin' so perty in yer new dress. I have a new dress too. Yer life is really different since ya got yer new dress. Mine will be now too. I'm so sorry I was so hateful-mean to you. I sure hope you'll forgive me. I want to learn from and be like Mrs. Fallon here. Maybe ya can give me 'nother chance."

Daria stared wide-eyed at Wanda. She looked at Gabrielle, then let her gaze wander to all present before looking back at Gabrielle, who nodded slightly, then looked back at Wanda. "Thank you, you look pretty, too." Daria then grabbed Catherine's hand, and said, "Mama, we're going swinging." The girls ran to the swing hanging from another oak tree nearby.

At the farm, David surprised his new bride with material for a nightgown and a work dress. Then he told her that while he understood the practicality of wearing britches while working in the fields, he hoped not to see his wife in them again.

Gabrielle wished they had a dress pattern. Though she had helped Rose sew for Daria, she had no knowledge of how to make things without a pattern. Then an idea came to her. They could use her nightgown, skirt, and bodice as a pattern. While they may be large in the beginning, Wanda had already grown a great deal since she last saw her and Gabrielle had a feeling Wanda would soon develop the shape of a woman rather than a girl; the beginnings were already there.

On Monday, with two of them working, Gabrielle and Wanda hurried through the laundry. After the last of the laundry hung on the line, they cut pieces for the nightgown. Gabrielle tried her best, matching the line and grain of the material. Since Wanda was proficient with a needle, she stitched while Gabrielle cut the skirt and bodice.

"Wanda, how did you learn to sew so well?"

"My ma taught me. She insisted I spend a bit with my sampler each day afore we left home. Course, on the trail, there weren't no time. After we got here, there was even less."

"What was your ma like?"

"She was a hard worker and the only person I ever seed who could stand up to Pa and get away with it. When we was startin' out here, I was mad cause I didn't want to come. Pa just said we was goin'. That was that. But Ma 'splained to me, our land there was too small, rocky, and all used up. We'd never get nowhere there. Here we could make something of ourselves. After that, I was excited about gettin' ta Oregon. Til Ma died. Then to see Pa up and marry and carry on with the widow was more than I could take."

"Your pa loved your ma?"

"He was crazy fer her. He's never been easy. Never one to cuddle me an Earl, but he would do pert near anything fer Ma. He got real hard after she died. If'n I weren't so mad about him marryin' up and carryin' on with Daria's ma, I'da felt bad for her. He was mean to her. I think he hated her for not bein' Ma."

"Did she die in childbirth?"

"Yah. Pa shoved her and she fell. After that she started bleedin' real heavy like and died before the baby came."

Gabrielle felt sickened by what she heard. "Daria mentioned a baby doll that got burned. Do you know anything about it?"

"She had a plain rag doll her ma made her, called her Sally. When her ma died, and she saw Pa put her ma in the ground and start throwin' dirt on her, Daria commenced cryin' and screamin' somin' awful. I took her back to the cabin; it hurt rememberin' how it felt watchin' my ma buried. She was still carryin' on and cryin' when Pa came back to the cabin after fillin' in the grave. He tole her to shut up and when she didn't he grabbed Sally out of her hand and threw the doll in the fire. Daria stopped carryin' on then and I never heard another sound out of her til she tole me thank you at the church yesterday. Kinda figured it was good she didn't make no noise cause I wondered what it would take fer Pa to throw Daria in the fire after the doll."

Gabrielle absorbed the information. No wonder Daria resorted to silence whenever she felt insecure. The inhumanity of that man!

"Wanda," Gabrielle said gently, "what do you want out of life? What *kind* of life do you want?"

"Not the life I had with Pa, that's fer sure!" Wanda looked at Gabrielle, giving the question serious consideration. "I want what you have. I want to be like you. To be good and kind." She looked around. "To have happy young uns and take good care of my home and husband." She furrowed her brow. "That reminds me, how come you an Mr. Mitchell ain't married? He sure seems like a fine and kind man, hard worker too."

Gabrielle hadn't expected the question. But then, she hadn't expected Wanda to open up with her the way she did either. "It's complicated, but I just can't. As for your ambitions, thank you for the compliment. Together you and I can work to see that you have the knowledge and tools necessary to attain your goals. Which reminds me, while you are here, would you like to learn to read and write?"

"You put great store in doin' that, don't ya?"

"Yes, I do. It could make a great difference in your life and the lives of your children."

"Then," she paused, "yes, I would."

Gabrielle noticed in her reply, Wanda used the full word, yes, rather than shortening it as she usually did.

After church a few weeks later, when they managed a few moments alone, Rose asked how the arrangement was working.

Gabrielle explained that while it took time before Daria could relax around Wanda, the child's progress amazed her. Within a week, Daria talked to others in Wanda's presence and no longer clung to someone when she was around. Two weeks later, she spoke to Wanda.

"David has been a blessing for Wade. Wade says he has a lot to learn before he can run a farm on his own, but he's a willing worker and a quick learner. He's never farmed but wanted to come West, and farming attracted him more than trapping or anything else he could think of. He naively thought he would figure it out as he went along. He seems thankful to have Wade as a mentor."

"What about Wanda?" Rose inquired.

"She's like a different girl! She's helpful, eager to learn, respectful, and I enjoy having her with me. Though shocked and appalled when I heard how Volstead traded her for a horse, and very anxious regarding the outcome of such a transaction, I now understand this is the best thing for Wanda. She is well away from Volstead; David's patience and respect demonstrate both his character and upbringing. He sleeps in the barn room with Wade and insists he will wait to claim his bride until she is ready to be a wife."

"What a relief! It's troublesome to see how young some brides marry. I know by Wanda's age they are usually putting in as full a day as any woman, and the single men need a helpmate, but it is still distressing."

"I agree. It was quite a shock. Where I come from, it would be a criminal offense to marry one so young."

Gabrielle continued. "I'm teaching her to read."

"How wonderful! Do you have any books available?"

"McGuffey Readers, the Bible, and two Jane Austin books Wade's wife brought with her."

"That's wonderful! Few books made the full trip. They are heavy and one of the first things unloaded along the trail to lighten the weight in the wagon. Of course, you would know that."

Eager to change the subject, so as not to necessitate a lie, Gabrielle asked about Lucas, "Have you heard from your family since Lucas's birth? Do they know about him?"

"No, I don't expect they've even received my letter telling them the news yet. It's amazing how fast he's growing! He'll be into everything before we know it. It's wonderful

Lucas and Journey will be so close in age. While it may seem like a lot right now, in a few years, they'll be into everything together. Don't you just love being a mom?"

At the stricken look on Gabrielle's face, Rose realized her blunder, but Gabrielle gathered herself. "It's one of the greatest things that can happen to a woman. I am more thankful than I can say for the five children in my care, as well as the three who are lost to me. All eight of them have brought more joy and contentment to my life than I deserve or expected."

With a sigh, she continued, "I suppose you could say I have six now. While Wanda may be married, she's still a child, though she works as hard as any grown woman." After a thoughtful pause, she said, "You know, I'm thrilled to have Wanda and David there. Besides being an immense help to both Wade and me, there is the selfish reason that now I can make up for part of what I wasn't able to achieve while at the Volstead's."

After the families enjoyed their dinner together, Gabrielle gathered their things for the trip home when Rose whispered, "Did you ever explain things to Wade?"

"Oh, Rose, I started to, but I just couldn't bring myself to do it. I know I need to, but, honestly, I'm afraid."

"Gabrielle, my sweet friend, while I have no idea what is stopping you from marrying that dear man, I do know there will never be a reason for you to fear him or his reaction to anything. Please, think it over."

17

The pulse of the hot water showering down upon her body felt heavenly to Gabrielle. She couldn't remember a shower ever feeling this good. As she rinsed the shampoo from her hair, she let the hot water flow over her body in what felt like a decadent waste of water and time, but she could not resist. The warmth of the showering water enveloped her, hugged her. She felt so clean, so refreshed, relaxed, and rejuvenated. Spreading the conditioner through her hair, she reveled in the silky feel. For once, shaving was a delight instead of a chore, as she let the conditioner do its job on her hair. When she finished shaving, she rinsed off, still lingering under the heavenly spray, breathing in the aromas of water, shampoo, conditioner, and soap, delighting in the feel of the water pulsating against her body. Reluctantly, she turned off the water, reached for her oversized, fluffy towel, and dried herself, cuddling the soft, fluffy towel as though it were a long-lost friend.

After brushing her teeth and putting on deodorant, she moved to the bedroom to dress. She ran her hand along the bedspread, enjoying the feel of the soft chenille. She breathed in the aroma of the vanilla candles on the dresser. Taking out her favorite sweater, she nuzzled against the soft feel, breathing in the wonderful smell before pulling it over her head. Everything was so beautiful, smelled so good, and felt so nice this morning. When she finished dressing, she opened the bedroom door to see the children in the kitchen, fixing bowls of cereal.

"I hope it's okay for us to have cereal this morning?" Francis asked her mother.

The sight of Francis, Nicholas, and Alyson brought unspeakable joy to Gabrielle. "Of course it is. Good morning, children!" She gave each of them a hug and a kiss. She thought her heart might explode as she held each of them. While she had always adored and appreciated these children, the love she felt for them at this moment seemed unable to be contained. "You know, you are the most wonderful children any mother could ask for. I love all of you so very, very much."

At this, all three came to Gabrielle, smiles on their faces, for a group hug that seemed to be the best thing she had ever felt. Feeling that hug made the day light up even brighter than the rays of sun shining brightly through the many windows of their home. The touch, the feel, the smells of her children, awarded intense feelings of fulfillment and relief. She relaxed fully into the sensations of this gathering of love in her arms.

The distant sound of a baby's cry tickled at Gabrielle. She struggled to ignore it, to continue holding her children, but the cry persisted. As she inched into consciousness, straining to keep the feeling of all those small arms around her, the reality of the cabin crashed in on her as the dream faded.

Wanda climbed over Gabrielle and picked up Journey. Overcome with the suddenness of being forced away from her children, Gabrielle cried, "Oh God! Help me!" Her whispered plea went unnoticed among Journey's cries. Seeing Wanda caring for Journey's needs, Gabrielle leaped from the bed and dashed out the cabin door, closing it behind her.

Stumbling, unaware of a destination, she headed toward the creek, blinded by the tears and the never-world between the dream and the truth of the cabin. As she ran, she cried out, a plaintive, wail of a cry, "No-o-o-o. No-o-o-o. Oh no-o-o."

At the creek, she collapsed at the edge of the water; sobs burst forth, stronger than since first realizing she could not return to her children. More so, since she was alone and subconsciously aware of the lack of need to hold in anything. Unaware how long she lay on the creek bank crying, she only knew her loss. The sounds of the creek, usually soothing to her ears, didn't penetrate, as the racking cries seemed to have no end. She wept as she had never wept before, oblivious to all but the pain of her loss, which held her prisoner, as though shackled and bound.

Then, gentle hands lifted her shoulders from the ground. The arms which encircled her were soothing as hands stroked her back and loose flowing hair. Instinctively, they rocked together, finding comfort in the motion. As the sobs lessened, small cries and catches of breath continued. Whether threatening another onslaught or announcing the beginning of the end, was not known for some time.

The crying stopped. Gabrielle slowly became aware of Wade, as, sitting on the creek bank, he continued to hold her against him. His embrace was comforting. She felt she could remain in those strong and gentle arms forever. With the gradual stirring of her senses, Gabrielle became conscious of the bare chest her head rested upon.

The hairs were soft, creating a cushion for her cheek. The muscles, hardened from field work since he was a young boy, were tender and perfect. As much as she wished to remain there through eternity, Gabrielle pulled away, reminding herself she was a married woman and should not be in such an intimate position with another man.

Wade pulled a handkerchief from his back pocket and handed it to her. After she blew her nose, he took the hanky and wiped the tears from her face with a gentleness such a strong man ought not to possess.

"How can I help?" he asked.

"You just did. Thank you." Gabrielle didn't know what to say. "I'm sorry if I woke you."

He continued to stroke her face, and then he ran his hand under her hair to cradle the back of her head. "I'm not. Gabrielle, I want to be here for you. Always. Can you tell me what happened?"

"I had a dream. An amazing dream. I was with my children. It was so wonderful to see them and hold them. It's the first time I've dreamt about them since…" She hesitated before continuing, "At first I feared going to sleep at night, thinking the dreams would be too painful, but when I didn't dream about them at all, I felt guilty."

"I know. When my wife died, I wanted nothing more than to dream about her. When I didn't, I wondered what was wrong with me. Then, after about three months, I had the dream. It was as if she was telling me all would work out and that I would be okay. She told me she loved me and missed me. It was a small dream, but a major blessing. After that, I found something resembling peace. Not having Anna and Journey here was the most difficult part, but creating a schedule to see them helped. Then you came, and I found a serenity I hadn't thought possible." Wade looked at Gabrielle and ran the edge of his thumb down the side of her face. "I love you, Gabrielle. I never thought it possible to love again, but I do, more than I can say. Whatever prevents you from marrying me, I hope you will eventually trust me enough to tell me. Maybe we can work something out."

"Oh Wade..." Gabrielle's fingers brushed through the hairs on his chest as she rose. He stood, and she gazed at him with a longing she knew was wrong. "Thank you," she said and walked back to the cabin as the first hint of light filled the horizon.

She knew she had to tell him. He deserved better than to be kept in the dark about her origin. But how? How could you tell someone you had mysteriously arrived from far in the future without sounding crazy? How do you tell the man who loves you that you're not a widow, but still married?

Gabrielle did the only thing she knew to do, the only thing which came automatically in times of trouble or times of joy. Seeing Wade go into the barn, she headed back to the creek. There, she fell to her knees. "Oh Lord God, you know my situation. You know the burdens I carry. While I understand and accept you have a plan here, I feel lost and tempted. Please Lord, forgive the sinful feelings I have for Wade. Please, oh please, let me love my husband and only my husband. Heavenly Father, show me what to do about Wade. If you would have me tell him of my origin, then through your divine wisdom, give me the right words. Holy and righteous

Father, I will trust in you. All praise and glory to you. In Jesus name, Amen."

She remained kneeling next to the creek for several minutes. Though she would love to hear the voice of God giving her a verbal answer, she accepted that she may need to wait for a more subtle reply.

As the weeks progressed, Gabrielle came no closer to a solution. Although nothing seemed to change in their lives, she felt an urgency press upon her. Wade and David were nearly done with the harvest. She and Wanda had enough stored away to feed three families through the winter and still the garden put forth produce. Seed packets were carefully tucked away in the steamer trunk. The children were learning at an astonishing rate. Beth, who seemed to inhale learning, was already in the second reader. Journey, now a year old, had begun to walk. Daria, while still timid around strangers, seemed to have almost forgotten the traumas she had suffered.

Even the animals of the farm were thriving. They had traded a hen for one of a neighbor's roosters in August and now had baby chicks. The remaining hens continued to lay steadily. Lilly produced plenty of milk for the family, though there was no extra. In the spring, Wade had traded a wagon of firewood for a piglet, who was now a nice, fat hog.

In September, when a settler with a wagon load of fruit trees came through, they traded some of their store of vegetables, dried foods, and pickled eggs for two of each type. They were sad little trees, having traveled overland through hard territory, with little water, but in a few years, with care, they would produce a nice crop of fruit.

Through it all, Gabrielle prayed for an answer to the question of how to tell Wade. She knew she must, but how?

18

As with the settler with the trees, wagons continued to roll by. Often, the settlers stopped to confer with Wade, buy or trade for food, or find company for an evening.

Gabrielle enjoyed meeting these pioneers. She experienced a history lesson beyond imagination. Those who passed varied in personality, looks, race, religion, cleanliness, and ambition. Her passion for history insisted she meet them, speak with them, partake in the feast of diversity these pioneers offered. Their common denominators were courage and determination.

One afternoon Gabrielle spotted a wagon stopping farther from the house than usual. Leaving Wanda to watch the children, Gabrielle lifted one of the pies she made that morning and headed out to greet the family. Wade also walked from the fields toward the wagon. He smiled as they met and continued walking.

Before reaching it, the man hollered. "Is there a doctor around here?"

"Not one for at least fifty miles. Somebody hurt?" Wade replied as they continued advancing toward the wagon.

"Mister, my son's burning with a fever, so you may not want to get any closer. My wife's been trying to burn it out o' him, but he just seems to get worse. We hoped a doctor might bleed him."

Gabrielle's shock at the idea of bleeding the child sparked her curiosity. She looked at Wade, "Burn it out of him?" she questioned.

"Theory is, if the patient gets hot enough, it will burn the fever out."

"Oh, my heavens!" Her disgust and revulsion at such a practice evident as she continued her trek to the wagon.

Wade held her back. "Gabrielle, you have no idea how contagious it may be. It could be typhus, or scarlet fever, or smallpox."

Knowing she had immunizations for most of the fearsome fevers of the day, she assured Wade that it would be okay. "I have to help."

Wade watched as she proceeded to the wagon.

"May I see your son?"

"Ma'am, are you a doctor? Are you sure you want to chance getting sick?"

"No, I'm not a doctor, nor even a nurse, but I know about caring for the sick." Anything she did would be better than burning the fever from him or bleeding him. "Perhaps the Lord brought you here. Please let me help."

The man escorted her to the back of the wagon and assisted her up so she could see into it. Six girls stood on the far side of the wagon. His wife sat next to what appeared to be nothing but a pile of quilts amongst the many supplies. In the wagon, a face showed amongst all the bedding.

"Ma'am, I'm so sorry about your boy. I've come to offer whatever assistance I can."

The teary-eyed woman looked as though she had not slept for days. "While we appreciate whatever help you can offer, aren't you afraid of catching the fever?"

"If you will trust me to help, I'll trust the good Lord to keep me well. May I look at him?"

The woman moved, allowing Gabrielle access to the child. The back of his neck, forehead, and cheeks burned with fever. She pulled quilts off of him, tossing them aside.

"What are you doing? He shakes with the fever unless we keep him heavily covered!" The mother shrieked, frantic with fear.

Gabrielle grasped the woman's hands in her own. With a soothing voice, she explained to the overwrought woman what she was doing and why. Claiming knowledge of the most advanced and modern methods of dealing with fevers, Gabrielle urged the woman to trust her. At the woman's hesitation, she again explained how the covers kept the heat in and if her son were to get much hotter, he would not survive.

Despite the mother's reluctance to respond, Gabrielle continued removing quilts. Seeing the father, she asked him to get a bucket of cold water from the creek. With a peek out of the wagon, she shouted for Wade to bring some of the drinking water she had boiled. If pathogens existed in the creek water, this was not the time for the child to drink it.

Upon discarding the last of the quilts, she shuddered to see the small boy wearing what appeared to be his father's woolen thermal underwear. Removing it, she ached at the site of the heat rash covering his body. At least she hoped it was heat rash.

"I'll need rags," Gabrielle told the woman, who reached into a basket to retrieve a handful of the requested cloths.

"This water's awful cold." The boy's father sounded concerned upon his return.

"Good, that's what we need." Gabrielle took the bucket and dipped a rag into it.

She placed a cloth under the boy's neck, another on his forehead, and with a third, she bathed his small body. Each time she dipped the cloth into the bucket to cool it, she wiped him from face to foot. As she worked, she told the woman to wet another cloth, and replace the one under his neck, re-wetting that one to replace the cloth on his forehead.

When Wade brought the requested drinking water, he placed it near the wagon. After Gabrielle's assurances, he returned to the cabin.

Gabrielle dipped another rag into the drinking water and placed a corner into the child's mouth to hydrate him. A slight pinch of the skin on the back his hand indicated severe dehydration. By dripping water from the cloth, she hoped to both hydrate and cool him. She feared the small amounts would do little, but worried about choking the unconscious boy with larger amounts.

The sun beating down on the covered wagon created stifling heat. Gabrielle wiped the sweat dripping from her. The bucket needed filled again. As she handed the bucket to the boy's father, common sense emerged. "Ma'am, grab one of your quilts to lie on the ground. Sir, please carry your son to the creek. Lay him on top of the quilt your wife will place in the shade of the tree." At their bewildered looks, Gabrielle explained about the heat in the wagon and how the boy needed to be in a cooler place to reduce the fever.

The small boy looked even smaller in his father's arms. As he laid him on the quilt the mother had spread under a large oak tree, Gabrielle took a deep breath, enjoying the feel of the coolness. Filling the bucket, which she had carried from the wagon, with water, Gabrielle continued bathing the small child. She wished for ice to pack around his still hot body.

Then she saw the man cool himself by splashing his face and hair in the creek.

The halleluiah moment made her wonder why the idea had taken so long. "Sir, pick up your son again and carry him into the creek. Hold him in the water, with only his face out," she said, with some relief.

"But that waters cold! He'll catch his death." The father's harsh objection rang loud.

Gabrielle explained with a steady, composed voice why she made the request. Despite clear misgivings, the man picked up his son and carried him into the water. *Please Lord, let this work,* she prayed, over and over. She knew she should pray for God's will, and not try to impose her own will upon Him, but it was her only thought.

When the boy shivered, Gabrielle had his father lay him back on the quilt. Hoping his fever was gone, she felt the back of his neck again. Though cooler than before, his fever still raged. She once again bathed him with cold cloths. Her fears increased as the child again grew warmer. Would this cold help to break the fever? Or just keep it from going high enough to kill him?

As the day wore on, the boy's father continued to take his son into the creek until he shivered, then his mother bathed him on the quilt until he again grew warmer. When on the quilt, Gabrielle attempted to get as much of the drinking water as possible into him. It seemed a never-ending cycle.

"Gabrielle?" Wade stood away from them. "I thought you might be hungry, so I brought venison and dumplings for all of you. I will leave it here with the bowls and utensils. Are you okay?"

"Thank you, Wade. Yes, I'm fine. This is helping to keep his body temperature down. We can only hope it will help fight whatever he has."

After eating, Gabrielle encouraged Mrs. Hobbs to see to her girls. She also cautioned her against using any of the bedding which little Franklin had used. It needed to be washed with soap and boiling water first, just in case.

As they worked together through the afternoon, they introduced themselves. Joseph and Emma Hobbs came from Pennsylvania in search of available land. Franklin, at three, and the youngest child, had six sisters, who ranged in age from five to ten, including two sets of twins. Emma expected another child in the spring.

With the girls bedded down, Emma returned to her son, but Gabrielle suggested the exhausted woman take this opportunity to sleep. Then when she awoke, Gabrielle would rest. Joseph napped between dips in the creek.

Without Emma or Joseph to chat with, Gabrielle's mind wandered. It occurred to her they may save little Franklin's life, only to discover the fever had left him with brain damage. For a moment, fear gripped her. But perhaps they had been brought here for just this purpose, and she needed to trust. She wished she could remember to trust God in all things first, rather than as an afterthought.

Emma slept through the long night. Gabrielle dozed during the minutes Joseph held Franklin in the creek. At one point, she awoke to find Joseph sponging the boy.

About dawn, Gabrielle detected a difference in the child. Though still unconscious, there seemed to be more to him, as if he were sleeping. Once again she placed her hand on the back of his neck. It seemed cooler. She felt his forehead and cheeks; they also seemed normal. The quilt he lay on was quite wet, so she retrieved a dry quilt from the wagon. With the child peaceful on the dry quilt and a corner of it covering him against the cool morning air, Gabrielle leaned back against the tree trunk and closed her eyes.

"Mrs. Fallon?" Gabrielle awoke with a start at the sound of Joseph's voice. "Is my boy gone?" He kneeled several feet from them, fear and pain chiseled his tired features.

Feeling Franklin's forehead once again, Gabrielle breathed a sigh of relief. "No, Mr. Hobbs, your son is sleeping. His fever has broken."

At this, the burly man broke down and sobbed. Unsure of what to do, Gabrielle went to give Mrs. Hobbs the good news.

Later that morning, Franklin woke, crying that he was thirsty. The child's cries brought joy to Gabrielle's heart. By evening, Franklin ate a light supper and caused his mother to fret because he wanted to play.

The Hobbs set up camp where their wagon stood. Not knowing what caused the fever, they stayed for at least a week to ensure no one else would come down with it. Gabrielle remained at the camp with the family, helping wash bedding and care for the tired family while she confirmed she would not take illness back to her own family.

A week later, when they prepared to depart, Gabrielle was sorry to see them go. She had found a friend in Emma, and her heart gladdened when Wade suggested a parcel of land nearby.

The wagons kept coming. Gabrielle and the children enjoyed greeting the various families, groups, and singles who passed by the cabin. Some waved as they passed, others stopped for a meal, and sometimes a family stayed for the night. These folks often asked for advice, or assistance, or lent a hand.

Gabrielle enjoyed visiting with those who stopped. Good, hard-working people, looking for a better life, more space, or for some, adventure. Then there were others.

The four boys walking alongside the wagon that stopped by the creek looked tired. When the wagon stopped, they gathered wood. The youngest boy, whom Gabrielle guessed to be about four, kept gathering when the others stopped. Though she heard the man yelling at him to come back, he kept gathering small sticks, ignoring his father.

Though not wishing to eavesdrop, Gabrielle continued to watch, transfixed.

An older boy jerked the little boy toward the wagon. The father grabbed the front of the small boy's shirt and screamed at him. Gabrielle heard the word "dummy" used, but not all of what he had said. Her heart wrenched at the abuse. She must do something.

Retrieving a fresh loaf of bread from the cabin, Gabrielle headed for the wagon. "Good evening! It's so nice to see other folks. I'm Gabrielle Fallon. I imagine after all your journeys you would enjoy a loaf of fresh bread."

The man glanced at Gabrielle before turning away. "Caroline, someone's here to talk to you," he shouted.

A thin, tired looking young woman came around the corner of the wagon. On her hip was a babe of about six months and next to her was a girl who might have been two. She just looked at Gabrielle, saying nothing.

"Hi." Gabrielle smiled at her. "I'm Gabrielle Fallon. I thought you might enjoy a loaf of fresh bread after all your time on the trail." Still not receiving any response, she continued, "We live in the cabin over there, this is part of our land, and you're welcome to stay the night. It's so nice to meet the folks passing through."

Still no response. Then Wade arrived and introduced himself to the man, extending his hand to shake. Gabrielle held her breath to see what would happen until the man shook Wade's hand and the two men continued conversing.

With a cautious glance toward her husband, the young woman came forward. "Thank you, ma'am. Fresh bread sounds good." Taking the loaf from Gabrielle, her face brightened. "It's still warm!"

Gabrielle smiled. "Yes, I just finished baking when I came outside to feel the cool evening air and saw your wagon and sons."

The timid woman kept glancing at her husband; she seemed worried.

"You have lovely children. They must be quite a help on the trail."

The woman smiled, looked about at her children and then the smile left. Gabrielle followed her eyes and saw they had rested on the small boy who had not returned upon hearing his father called him back.

"It's difficult, with the children and all. Such a long trip. We left just after Theodore here was born," she said, looking at the babe on her hip.

"Oh my, that must have been trying with a newborn." The young woman perplexed Gabrielle.

"He's a good baby, all the kids are good. Well, Travis is a problem, he just won't listen or talk to us, but the rest of the kids are good as gold." The woman talked as though she were in a trance. Gabrielle assumed it was due to exhaustion. Then the woman continued. "Ethan did so much better with the boys before Travis came along. Since Travis has shown himself to be so dumb, Ethan just hasn't been the same."

Shocked, Gabrielle asked, "Ethan is your husband?"

"Yes."

Feeling uncomfortable and hoping to change the subject, Gabrielle said, "I don't think I caught your name."

"Velda, my name is Velda. Velda Plune."

Despite her desire to be off the subject, Gabrielle couldn't restrain herself. "Why do you say Travis is dumb?"

"Well, he won't talk. He ignores us when we talk to him or call him. I wish we hadn't had him; maybe Ethan would be his wonderful self again."

The woman's wistful reply left Gabrielle unable to hide her shock. How could anyone not want one of their children? "Has he ever spoken?"

"Not a word. Oh, I see him talking to himself sometimes. No sound comes out, but his lips move."

After thinking, Gabrielle asked, "Have you tested his hearing?"

"Goodness no, how could we do that? Why? He'd just ignore it, anyway."

Seeing the child with his back to her, watching Wade and Mr. Plune talk, Gabrielle slipped up behind the child. Right behind his ear, she clapped. Nothing. No startle reflex, he did not turn around, he gave no response at all. She tapped him on the shoulder. He turned around and looked at her with questioning eyes. Squatting, Gabrielle smiled and extended her hand. He responded by reaching out and shaking it.

"Can you hear me?" she asked him.

Though he said nothing, the child moved his lips as though he were speaking.

Standing, Gabrielle took his hand and returned to his mother. "Mrs. Plune, I think your son is deaf. He doesn't mean to ignore you; he just can't hear. He moves his lips because that is what he sees others do, but doesn't know there is sound when they speak."

"Oh no. He can make sounds. I've heard him scream when Ethan disciplines him. He carries on something awful and makes noises like an animal."

Gabrielle's repulsion at this mother's description of both her husband's discipline and her son's noises caused her to take a deep breath. Gathering her patience and uttering a silent prayer for guidance, she said, "He can make sounds, that's good! That means he's not mute, just deaf."

"Just deaf! How can you say just? That means he'll always be stupid and an embarrassment to our family."

"Mrs. Plune, please don't assume your child lacks intelligence because he cannot hear. He may be the smartest child you have."

"If he can't hear and he can't speak, he can't learn, so how's he supposed to be smart?

"Teach him to speak with his hands. It's called sign language."

Gabrielle bent down to the boy's level, pointed at him, and fingerspelled T-R-A-V-I-S. She then pointed at his mother and fingerspelled M-O-M. She repeated this several times until the little boy copied her. He pointed at the baby. Gabrielle spelled B-A-B-Y. The child copied it, pointed at his mother, and spelled M-O-M, then himself, and spelled his name.

Gabrielle hugged the boy and smiled at him. His return smile glowed.

"Ma'am, your son is quite bright. With only a few repeats, he understood that I spelled his name, mom, and baby. He even spelled them."

"Ethan says if he were smart he'd talk."

"But he can't hear to learn to speak. He can, however, learn to speak with his hands."

"It would have been so much easier if he'd just gotten sick on the way here like some of the other children on the wagon train did."

Gabrielle's shock at the implication of the mother's statement left her speechless. Finally, she asked, "You don't want your son?"

"We love our other children, but not him. He's defective."

Not sure whether she wanted to slap her, throw up, or cry, Gabrielle did the only acceptable thing. "Wade, can you come here, please."

Wade hurried to her side. "What is it?"

Tears formed in her eyes as she explained the situation to Wade.

Mr. Plune spoke. "Deaf! You mean the dummy can't hear? How did I get saddled with this?" Looking at his wife, he said, "You gave me a defective boy!" His wife reacted to the accusation as though slapped.

"I'm sorry, Ethan, I didn't mean to."

Gabrielle couldn't believe her ears. "He's not defective! He just can't hear. He's smart and can do anything anyone else can do, except hear."

"Yeah, well how am I supposed to talk to him? How do I teach him to work the farm? Who would ever want to marry him?"

"He can speak and hear with his hands. I have already taught him his name, mom, and baby through fingerspelling. There are signs for whole words. For instance, book is…" Gabrielle put her hands together and opened them as a book. "There are schools for deaf people so they can learn. You can learn sign language also. There's no reason he needs to be any different than your other children." Though she felt as though she were pleading, the urgency of getting through to these ignorant people spurred her onward. "Don't you understand? Travis is ordinary in every way except his hearing."

The couple did not respond; they stared at her.

Wade took her arm and turned her to the cabin, "Perhaps we should go home and let the Plunes think on this. We can talk again in the morning."

Gabrielle looked at Wade with a desperate, pleading look, but he continued guiding her toward the cabin.

Upon reaching it, Wade guided them to the bench outside the door. "Gabrielle, I know you want to help, but he is their son. You can't fix ignorance, especially in one evening."

Tears coursed down her cheeks as Gabrielle tried to resign herself to someone not wanting their own child. Thinking back to Volstead, she realized this should not have been a shock, but it was. They had a beautiful family. Though quiet, they appeared to treat their other children well. Why couldn't they love all of them?

"What kind of life will that poor child have, being raised in a family that doesn't want him? He's so sweet, and smart, and... Oh Wade, isn't there some way we can get through to them?"

"Perhaps a night will make a difference."

Tears continued to flow as Gabrielle agonized over the plight of the child. Her frustration with the ignorance of the parents had no outlet. Instead, her tears turned to sobs. How could anyone not want their own child? She would have given anything to hold her own three children again.

After breakfast the next morning, Wade and Gabrielle headed for the wagon. Astonished to see it loaded and the oxen almost hitched, Gabrielle grabbed Wade's arm.

"Plune, leaving already?" Wade greeted the man.

"Gotta find a place to settle. Thought we'd head south a bit more."

Mrs. Plune told her husband everything was loaded, and the children were ready.

"We hoped to speak with you about your son. Gabrielle is sure he is a bright boy. She knows some sign language would be happy to teach you."

"We don't have time to learn to talk to a useless kid."

"But he's not useless." Gabrielle couldn't stop herself.

With a slight squeeze of her arm, Wade hushed her. Mr. Plune was a man who felt women should keep their place. *There are far too many men who feel that same way in this time.*

"Mr. Plune, I realize Travis is your son, but if you and your wife feel he is a problem, a burden, why don't you leave him with someone who feels differently?"

"Sounds good, Mister, but who wants to take on a defective kid?"

"We do."

At these words, Gabrielle's breath caught. She looked at Wade, tears in her eyes, then faced the Plunes again. With a determined look on her face, she nodded.

"Now why would you take on somebody else's defective kid?"

"We don't view him as defective. He's a child. A child, who, like any other, needs love, affection, teaching, training, encouragement, and parents who love him."

Mr. Plune looked at his wife; she nodded once.

"Take the kid, but don't ask us to take him back. You'll have to clothe him; we'll need his for the younger one."

With that, he grabbed Travis by the arm, yanking him over to Wade and Gabrielle, then climbed on his wagon and drove off, leaving his son with total strangers.

Wade and Gabrielle stood holding Travis's hands as the three watched the wagon roll away, with Travis's three brothers, one sister, and mother walking beside it, the baby on Mrs. Plune's hip. Neither parent bothered looking back.

Gabrielle had never seen or heard anything so astonishing. Even her trip through the whirlpool into 1847 seemed more believable in her mind than parents giving away a wonderful child to complete strangers. It occurred to her what Wade had just done. Looking at him, she croaked the words, "Thank you."

"I thought about it all night, barely slept at all, and it was the only sensible solution. From the way they spoke of him yesterday, I didn't figure it would be a problem to get them to leave him. I prayed for a good way to make it happen and maybe seem like his idea."

They looked at the small boy between them: bare feet, ragged nightdress, none-too-clean, and feeling so alone in the world.

Wade picked him up before heading back to the cabin.

"Wade Mitchell, you are an amazing man."

He grinned. "Then I guess that makes us two amazing people."

Walking back to the cabin, Gabrielle knew her love for this wonderful man grew by the day. What was she to do? She gave thanks for Travis. She prayed for a solution to her problem. They were becoming quite the family, but they weren't a family, and could never be.

Wade opened the door to the cabin and greeted the girls. "Girls, say hello to your new brother!"

Six sets of eyes stared in wonder at Wade. The four girls, Wanda, and even Journey, stared at Wade in stunned silence, with wide, questioning eyes.

"This is Travis. Gabrielle, can you tell the children how to say hello to Travis?"

Gabrielle placed her open hand against her the side of her forehead and then pushed it outward, much like a salute.

"Travis is deaf, meaning he can't hear. He will learn to speak with signs, just as we all will."

Gabrielle repeated the sign for the children. They all copied it. Watching, Travis copied it right back, much to the delight of the girls.

With a look at Travis, Wade told Gabrielle he would bring in water to heat for a bath. As the water heated, Gabrielle gave him a breakfast of cornbread in milk while she and Wade answered a slew of questions. Then, shooing the girls out of the cabin to play, as Gabrielle undressed Travis and placed him in the washtub, she wondered what clothes she could put on him.

"Gabrielle, I thought perhaps we could sew a new nightdress with the extra material we had from my nightgown and use my old shirt to make clothes for Travis. David doesn't like me in pants."

"Brilliant idea, Wanda!"

As they watched Travis play in the water, Wanda and Gabrielle got busy, once again using Travis's old nightdress as a pattern. Wanda busied herself sewing as Gabrielle cut small boy-sized clothing from the man's shirt Wanda no longer needed.

The following Sunday at church they received many positive responses to the addition to their family, as well as a few whispers.

"Gabrielle, what the two of you have done is amazing!" Rose said as they met after service. "But when are you going to make this family official?" Her whispered question audible only to Gabrielle.

"Rose, I wish I could, but as I told you, I can't marry Wade."

"But why? Gabrielle, I don't wish to invade your privacy, but it makes no sense. You are both widowed, that means you are both free to marry. Don't you love Wade?"

Torn between confiding in her friend and the fear of rejection, Gabrielle said, "Rose, to explain this would take far more time and privacy than we have."

"Let me feed the baby, and then we'll take a walk, just the two of us." She giggled. "Think those men can handle the children?"

Laughing, Gabrielle said, "I think those three men can handle anything they set their minds to. Besides, Wanda is a wonderful helper."

Later, the two women walked along the river, which bordered the town. Rose pushed the issue. "Okay, my friend, you love Wade, don't you?"

"Oh Rose, this is such a mess, I don't know how to begin. Yes, as wrong as it is, I am very much in love with Wade. He is the best person I've ever met. Kind, generous, fun, trusting. Oh, Rose, I'm not worthy of his trust!"

"Gabrielle, what is it? I've known you for some time now and have seen nothing but a loving, generous, giving, and yes, trustworthy woman. What is wrong?"

Gabrielle stayed silent for some time. She loved and respected her friend. She feared losing that friendship. She feared losing Wade. *Ridiculous!* She thought, *How can I lose what cannot ever be mine?*

"Do you remember when Mr. Hargrove first brought me to the store?"

"Of course I do, that was the day I found my best friend."

"The Hargroves came to a conclusion which I failed to correct. I didn't wish to deceive them, but I was so confused. It seemed like everything was in a fog. I still didn't believe what I was seeing."

"Of course you were overwrought; you had just lost your entire family."

"Yes, I had, but not in the manner they had assumed."

The concern on Rose's face showed as she listened to her friend.

"Rose, I know this will sound insane, but my husband and children didn't drown in a river crossing."

"What did happen? Where are they?"

"Remember how I wanted to find a telephone?"

"Yes. I thought it would be wonderful to have such a device."

"Well, the truth is, where I came from, we do have them. In fact, we have a lot of things that would astound you."

Puzzled, Rose waited for Gabrielle to continue.

As Gabrielle explained where she came from, she saw Rose's face go from astonishment, to disbelief, to amazement, to anguish. Her expression kept changing. Unsure if the facial changes were because she was losing her friend, disbelief, or empathy, Gabrielle continued with the story until the whole truth was out.

When she finished, Rose remained silent. After many tense moments, she said, "It all makes sense now!"

"What?"

"The most basic things you didn't understand. So many things."

"You believe me?

"Of course I believe you! While your story is astounding, and many would say quite far-fetched, I have often wondered about you. Your lack of knowledge about basics, coupled with your seeming expertise in things we have never heard of. Then there is your manner of speech. While not significant, it is still different. I assumed it had to do with our places of origin. I was partially correct. However, it was time origin, not place origin. Plus, I know you well. You are an honest person who could have no possible purpose for creating such a story. Such a fabrication could only bring a multitude of problems. It seems to me if it were to circulate, you would more than likely be ostracized as crazy or bewitched. People are odd that way. They fear and reject what they do not understand."

Though she despised herself for once again crying, the tears of relief flowed unrestrained. Grasping her friend's hands, Gabrielle said, "Thank you. Thank you."

The palpable warmth between the two friends continued until a look of puzzlement came over Rose's face. "But this doesn't explain why you can't marry Wade."

"Don't you see? Kyle is not dead. There was no failed river crossing. He and my children are alive and well in the twenty-first century, meaning I'm already married."

"Oh my," was all the astonished Rose could say.

As they headed back, Rose said, "Now, you must tell me about life in the twenty-first century!"

19

The second week of October, on the evening they harvested the last of the crops, Wade announced at supper that the next day he and David would cut a door and build a wall to create two rooms in the expansion on the cabin. Due to the difficulty of cutting through the log siding of the cabin, the second bedroom would, for now, be accessed through a door in the new wall. They split the remaining logs in half to form a wood floor for the cabin. He hoped to complete them by Saturday, at which time he and David would make a trip to town to pick up the window glass.

Real glass windows! The oilcloth on the window opening in the cabin served as a poor substitute for a window. While it allowed some light in, Gabrielle welcomed increased light and visibility. Now they would have three windows, one in the main room and one in each bedroom. Who knew she could get so excited over the prospect of a few panes of glass?

Wade and David moved the beds and table outside as they prepared to create the door through to the first bedroom. As the men cut away at the logs, Gabrielle, Wanda, and the children filled the cracks between the logs on the addition with the chinking material Wade had shown them how to make. While the mix she had created at Volstead's had been close, it wasn't quite right. Wade built a solid addition, but the chinking would assure the seal between the logs prevented drafts.

While working, Wanda assured Gabrielle the chinking added to the Volstead's cabin had made an enormous difference.

As she mixed yet another batch, a notion occurred to Gabrielle. "Wanda, I have an idea for something different to serve for dinner. Would you help me by supervising the chinking?"

After washing her hands, she pulled large pieces of venison from the brine barrel and washed the extra salt from it. Using the sharp knife and the cutting board outside the cabin, to avoid the mess created by Wade and David, Gabrielle cut the meat into strips. The strips she cut into chunks, which she then cut smaller. Gabrielle continued cutting the meat until it was finely diced. Then she chopped it, using the full blade. Hoping her idea would work, she tried to form it into a patty. It fell apart. Not enough fat. She knit her brow and glared at the offending meat, then smiled, nodding her head. She mixed a bit of her stored fat drippings with the minced venison, then formed a successful patty. Yes! Venison burgers for dinner.

Gabrielle formed all the meat into patties. After rewashing her hands, she picked fresh tomatoes, lettuce, and onions from the garden. In the barn, she fished pickles from the pickle barrel. What to do for a condiment? Though she had made mayonnaise as a homeschool project with her children, she wasn't sure how to do it without oil, which she lacked. As wrong as it sounded, she mashed a tomato and mixed it with butter.

With the burger fixings ready, they needed a side dish. Back at the barn, she took potatoes from the straw in which they were packed. These she cut for small French fries. After building a fire in the pit they used for cooking on hot, summer days, Gabrielle placed a large amount of the stored fat in the skillet. When heated, she dropped some fries into it. In the second skillet, she added part of the burger patties.

When she called the family to get washed for dinner, she put the burgers together with French fries on the side and set out the berry cobbler from the previous day. Reactions were interesting as the family sat at the table.

After prayers, Beth said, "You forgot the utensils, I'll go get them."

Gabrielle stopped her and demonstrated how to eat the burger by picking it up with her hands and taking a bite. The fat drippings added a wonderful flavor to the burger which she hadn't anticipated. After that, she picked up a fry and ate it. "We will, of course, need utensils for the cobbler, thank you, Beth."

"Looks good!" Wade encouraged everyone, as he picked up his burger and took a bite.

The burgers were a resounding success. It occurred to Gabrielle that the hamburger had not yet been invented, so of course, they had never seen them. If memory served her, it was a twentieth-century invention.

As much as she enjoyed the treat, she knew she would not make it often. It took too much time and work, plus two loaves of bread. Maybe if they could get a meat grinder someday.

With the door cut into the new addition, the men laid the split logs, split side up, for the floor. The next morning they finished the new floor and moved the beds into the new addition. The wall and doors between the two bedrooms would still need to be built, but that could wait. That evening Gabrielle walked through the cabin with its new wood floors, astounded how bare and large the living space seemed without the two beds. *What will we do with all this space?*

The next morning, when Wade and David worked on the wall between the two rooms, Gabrielle pondered the need for the wall but kept quiet. As the men worked in the bedrooms, she and the children resumed their normal routine.

That evening at supper, Wade said the doors would take time, so would wait. Tomorrow he and David planned to take the wagon to town. Did she need anything?

Boy, that's an understatement, Gabrielle thought to herself, with a quiet chuckle. To Wade, she said, "Not that I can think of, though if you don't mind, I may pack some items for trade."

"Sounds good," Wade replied.

Wade acted like the proverbial cat that swallowed the canary. Maybe he was excited about getting the addition done and picking up the windows. She couldn't blame him; the idea of real windows thrilled her.

With the men gone and the children working on their studies outside, Gabrielle cleaned the cabin. She swept the log walls in all three rooms; then she dusted everything before sweeping the new wood floor. As she swept, so thrilled to have a real floor again, she suspected sweeping would now be her favorite chore.

Then she listened to each of the children read before suggesting a game of knots on a log. Pleased with their progress, she wished they had more books. Daria was reading, and Anna could identify most of the sounds. Since there were now five girls and only four game boards, Gabrielle had Wanda pair with Anna. After Anna identified the letter and the sound it made, Wanda helped her think of a word beginning with the letter. Gabrielle held one-year-old Journey as the girls played. As they identified each letter, they showed it to him. He seemed to enjoy his part and Gabrielle wouldn't be surprised to see him playing within the year.

Gabrielle missed Wade's presence. Odd. He had spent virtually every hour through planting and harvesting seasons in the fields. But she had watched him as he worked, looking so very good. She shook the thoughts away and suggested they play a game. After several ripping games of duck, duck, goose, they walked to the creek. Conscious of wasted trips, Gabrielle and Wanda grabbed buckets to bring back water.

Though too cool for swimming, they lifted their skirts and waded in the water. None of them wore shoes, the ease of it encouraged them. Gabrielle wished for the warmth of summer so they could float. Kicks, splashes, and squeals erupted as she and Wanda each held one of Journey's hands, preventing him from diving headlong into the water. The boy could turn a hardpack floor around a bath in the washtub into a mud puddle if they didn't tone him down. Gabrielle felt giddy as she again thought of the new floor.

When it was time to prepare dinner, they walked back to the cabin. Gabrielle's breath caught as she saw the wagon in front of the barn. Wade and David had returned. She attempted to convince herself it was the windows that made her feel excited.

Entering the cabin, she gasped. There was Wade, standing before the most beautiful wood cookstove she had ever seen. It was larger than the one she saw at the Hargrove's and even larger than Rose's. Although not ornate, it was a full-size stove with a warming compartment above.

"Do you like it?" Wade asked.

"Like it? Oh, Wade! But, how?"

"We had a productive year. Even after paying David we did well. Though I must confess, I had Clement order the stove back in February."

"It's beautiful! Oh, Wade, I love it. It will make it so much easier to cook. Oh, and it will be so much easier to keep the cabin warm this winter. But Wade, you ordered it before you even planted. How did you know the crop would be so good?"

"I planned to plant extra and hoped for the best. It wasn't the wisest, most responsible thing I've ever done, but in this case, I'm glad I did. How about you?"

With a big smile, she nodded and replied, "Very glad!"

With the new stove and windows, it felt like Christmas, but Wade didn't stop there. While he was in town, he added a few children's books to the box of goods: *The Children's Friend*; *The Pearl*; and three from the Children's Chapbook Collection, *Mary and Her Neighbors*, *Lost in a Storm*, and *Mary Caught in the Rain*. *Lost in a Storm* was the perfect book for Daria and Anna, with only one-syllable words.

Gabrielle realized how amazing this day was, but how, in the twenty-first century it would not have been a big deal. She thought of the electric range and large library of books she had at her home in the future. What an incredible time she now lived in, small things were appreciated; big things were amazing. They had little, but used everything, wasting nothing. Shaking her head when she thought of all the storage units in her time, full of things people never used, but couldn't part with. She thought of the bill they paid to have the trash taken away, a full container every week! The phrase, reduce, reuse, and recycle wasn't yet coined, but through necessity, it was a way of life.

20

With the crops in and the addition to the cabin complete, David suggested he and Wanda move on and find a place of their own.

At this, Gabrielle's breath caught. She wasn't ready for Wanda to leave! She enjoyed her company, and the girl was learning so much, as well as growing into a lovely young woman. While a selfish thought on Gabrielle's part, she also knew Wanda did not yet feel ready to live as David's wife. Gabrielle hoped to continue her studies with Wanda; who had made rapid progress. When the girl set her mind to something, she got it done.

With only a moment's hesitation, Wade spoke. "David, you have been more help than I can say. Please, stay. Excellent land exists to the west of us. Let's look it over, and if you like it, we'll work out the best place for a cabin, and together we can build it. Though I paid you in crops and food, we owe you far more."

"Sounds good." David appeared stoic, but the corner of his mouth kept twitching.

Wanda's eyes brightened. For a child who learned the hard way not to show emotion, listening to the conversation filled her face with feelings. First, there was fear, then resignation, then hope, and then, with David's agreement, sheer happiness.

When the men returned the next evening, they shared an abundance of news. The perfect location for a cabin lay on some of the best farmland west of the Mississippi. In David's excitement, the neighboring land became the best in the West.

Despite the need to build a cabin and a barn, make furniture, and purchase a few farm animals by selling or trading some of his share of the crops, a move for the Farnsworths was in the future. With this knowledge, Wanda's desire to learn became even more intense. In addition to reading, writing, and arithmetic, Wanda constantly questioned Gabrielle regarding appropriate behavior. In this, Gabrielle felt woefully inadequate. To this end, she enlisted Rose's assistance. On Sundays, after church, they had deportment lessons. Manners, posture, carriage, behavior, and speech.

Gabrielle listened and participated with rapt attention. Though in her own time, her manners were considered old-fashioned and her posture perfect, she had a lot to learn in this time. Despite living in the wilderness, she hoped to conduct herself as a lady. This created a challenge when much of life included such hard work, but with several little ladies to teach, she must first learn herself.

Wade and David worked hard cutting trees and hauling them to the cabin sight. Between working on the cabin and the chores at Wade's place, their workday did not shorten although the days grew shorter. The scrap from the logs used on the cabin reminded David they would need wood to get them through the winter. He liked the raised hearth in the Mitchell cabin and determined it a necessity after hearing of the baby who had been burned, so they also spent many hours hauling river rock for the fireplace.

When a late arriving family came through, David traded some of the firewood he had cut, together with a bit of his share of the crop, for a pair of their oxen, thus necessitating the building of a corral. When Wade said he would send two of their hens and a cockerel with them, Wanda fairly jumped for joy.

Then, two men traveling south stopped to spread the word, gold. Gold had been discovered on the American River at Sutter's Mill in California. The excited men expected grand success. They left their families to work their new farms and would soon return with more riches than imaginable. Gabrielle ached to tell them to go home. Though aware many of the early prospectors would find great wealth, she also knew they would find disease, inflation, accidents, and deadly disputes. Even if these men found riches, how much would be enough? When would they return to their families? Or would they? Eager to find their fortunes, the men hurried on their way but left behind a wake of confusion and change.

That night at supper, Wade and David discussed the idea of prospecting. Tempted with the thought of easy money, they toyed with the idea. Gabrielle hoped they would come to a sensible conclusion on their own.

Finally, Wade said, "Well, it's fun to dream, but we have farms to work and families to care for. We can't go running off after some pipe dream."

David seemed surprised. "You mean you weren't serious about going? But think of what we could do with the money. Think of how much we could give our families. It would take years of hard work to make what we could in a few months in the gold fields."

David gave the impression he thought the gold would be lying there, just waiting to be taken, much like harvesting the golden corn. Gabrielle's insides churned at the thought of him going to California. What about Wanda? Would she stay here? Or go with her husband? A quick glance at Wanda told Gabrielle what she thought of the idea. She was terrified.

Wade remained silent before suggesting they head for the barn. He wanted to speak man-to-man. David was a good man but young and impressionable. Hopefully, Wade could bring him to his senses.

As soon as the men walked out the door, Wanda grasped Gabrielle's arm. "I don't want to go to California! I like it here. I want to stay with you, or at least near you. What about the cabin? All the work they've done? He's not going to walk away from it is he?"

Gabrielle held Wanda's hands. "Wanda, David is a good man, a sensible, God-fearing man. I'm sure once he thinks this through and listens to Wade's wise counsel, he will realize this is where he belongs."

"But what if he doesn't?"

Gabrielle felt for Wanda. Though married, with the responsibilities of a grown woman, she was still very much a child. "You know, you can talk to David about this. You do have a voice in the decision."

Wanda's eyes grew big, obviously shocked and mortified by the idea of questioning any decision made by a man.

"Wanda, I know you would have never dared question anything your father decided. It would not have been tolerated. But David is not your father by relation or temperament. He wants what is best for you, which is why he traded his horse for you. He has shown himself to be a reasonable and gentle person. You need to trust he will listen to your opinion. You need to trust he will respect your opinion."

Deep in thought, Wanda remained silent. Finally, she asked, "Gabrielle, if we are supposed to have so much faith and trust in our men, why won't you marry Mr. Mitchell?"

The question shocked Gabrielle. "It's very complicated. I do trust Wade, but..." She didn't know what else to say. "Let's wait and see if Wade can convince David to stay. But, in the meantime, think about what I said."

The next morning when Wade and David entered the cabin, bags under their eyes spoke of little sleep. When Gabrielle looked at Wade, he raised one eyebrow with a slight shrug, as if to indicate there had been no decision made.

Then David surprised them by taking Wanda's hands and asking her what she thought. Shocked, Wanda looked at Gabrielle, who nodded.

"David, while I respect the final decision is yours to make, I like it here. I like the idea of being neighbors with the Mitchells. I don't want to go to California. We have both learned so much from Mr. Mitchell and Mrs. Fallon. To go in search of gold just when we're about ready to move into our own place, well, I just don't think it would be a good way to show our gratitude."

Pride in Wanda swelled Gabrielle's chest. She had come so far. To speak out as she did, despite the fears instilled by her upbringing, took true courage. To phrase her wishes in the manner she had, spoke of her determination and hard work to learn to speak correctly. Wanda was smart and brave; Gabrielle could not have been more proud of her.

David gazed at Wanda. Then he looked at Wade. Those watching could see the turmoil and indecision. Then he took Wanda's hand and headed for the door. "Let's go for a walk."

After they left, Gabrielle looked at Wade. Wade looked back at Gabrielle. Though neither said anything, they both went to work. Gabrielle woke the girls while Wade built a fire in the stove. As she prepared breakfast, Wade picked up Journey, who had been playing with his feet and making babbling noises, and changed and dressed him.

Still, not a word was said, as if by remaining silent, they could assist David in his decision. They cared about this young couple. They had become family. While they could not tell David it would be a mistake to go—wealth could be a possibility—they wanted them to stay.

Finally, as the family sat down to breakfast, Wade said, "David will make an excellent farmer. He's not afraid of hard work and long days."

Did the statement come from premonition or wishful thinking? Gabrielle only hoped it was accurate. David *will* make a good farmer.

Not wanting to waste a day, Wade headed outside to chop wood. He told Gabrielle he had hoped they could finish the cabin door today, but if David decided to go, it might never be completed.

When Catherine and Daria returned from gathering eggs, the number of them amazed Gabrielle. The hens were laying well, producing more than needed. She had the sudden idea to make quiche. She didn't need a recipe to make the simple dish. Why hadn't she thought of it before?

As the day wore on, Gabrielle wondered when David and Wanda would return. They left before breakfast, and she was about to set dinner on the table, yet they were still gone.

The irony of the situation struck Gabrielle. A year ago, she would have been happy to get away from Wanda; now she didn't want to imagine her being gone. She had grown to love and respect the child/woman. Wanda worked hard, she learned quickly, and she showed none of the negative traits last year's Wanda demonstrated. She had grown into an excellent helper with the children. Who knew when she had kicked Daria on the bed that first night, that now Wanda would be helping Daria with her reading and cuddling her when she fell?

Gabrielle jumped with expectation when Wade entered the cabin. He shook his head. He hadn't seen the young couple. Finally, as they were about to say grace, the door opened and in walked Wanda and then David. Wanda's face glowed, leaving Gabrielle hopeful. But when nothing was said on the subject during dinner, she worried. After eating, David said, "Shall we see if we can get that cabin door finished today?"

Wade smiled and said, "It's sure not going to hang itself," as he rose and headed for the door.

After they left, Gabrielle looked at Wanda. "Well…?"

"He held my hand while we walked," Wanda began. "We talked, discussing the options. He really did want to know what I thought! It was nice, and I liked holding his hand." She smiled dreamily. "I didn't realize it until we arrived, but he took me to see the cabin. Oh, Mrs. Fallon, it's beautiful! It's not as big as this one; it's about the size of Pa's, but it has a small, beautiful fireplace opposite the door, with a raised hearth, like this one, and a window hole on each side. Plus, there's a window on the wall with the door. It's so bright and pretty!"

Gabrielle smiled as she listened to the excited girl.

"He wishes he could put glass in the windows, but oilcloth will have to do until we have more necessities. I was so excited, I hugged him without thinking. Then you know what he did?" She had lowered her voice to a whisper. She smiled. "He kissed me!"

"Were you okay with that?"

"Oh, yes. It surprised me at first, but, oh, he's wonderful!"

"I'm glad you feel that way, seeing as you are married to him." Gabrielle laughed.

"Then he told me this is our home. We aren't going anywhere."

Gabrielle breathed a sigh of relief. After his suggestion to Wade that they finish the door today, she suspected the decision had been made, but she hadn't wanted to get ahead of herself. With a smile, she said, "Let's work on those quilts. You'll need them."

21

Leaving church on the Sunday before Thanksgiving, Rose whispered to Gabrielle, "Did you explain to Wade yet why you can't marry him?"

"No, I haven't been able to bring myself to do it. The prospect frightens me."

Rose looked her friend in the eyes and said, "Gabrielle, we are to treat others how we wish to be treated. Is this what you're doing with Wade? Would you desire for him to withhold information from you?"

Rose's words hit Gabrielle hard. She was correct. Gabrielle had to tell Wade, soon.

After supper that evening, Gabrielle asked Wanda to care for the children before inviting Wade to join her for an evening stroll. Pulling her wrap closer, Gabrielle took a steadying breath.

"I need to talk to you. This isn't easy, but it needs to come out."

"Sure, is everything okay? You sound upset."

"I've come to realize that you have a right to know why I can't marry you. I have no doubt you'll think I am mentally deranged by the time I'm done, but you still have a right to know."

Wade looked at her, waiting for whatever she would tell him.

"I don't know how to say this." She took another deep breath. "Wade, I wasn't born in this century."

Wade's head jerked around to look at her. "No, to have been born in the 1700s, you would have to be fifty, at least. There is no way. Besides, even if you were, it wouldn't change how I feel about you."

"I wasn't born in the 1700s. I was born in the 1900s."

Wade's look was uncomprehending. "I don't understand."

"Let me start at the beginning." Gabrielle told him about the picnic in Montana, the book, the rock, the fall, the whirlpool, the underwater cave, and waking up on the grass in 1847 Oregon. "I can't marry you, because I'm already married."

When she finished, he stared at her. *Please say something.* His silence stretched on and on. With no idea of what was transpiring in his mind, Gabrielle assumed the worst. Fear gripped her.

After a while, he asked, "I'm supposed to accept this tale?"

"I know. I wouldn't believe me either." She thought for a moment. "Wait here." She rushed to the cabin. Reaching deep inside the trunk, she pulled out the book, lit a lantern, and went back outside.

"This is the book I had in my pocket."

"You are saying it came from the 1900s?"

"Actually, it's the 2000s. Check inside; the copyright date will tell you the year of publication."

Wade opened the book and read the year. "2004." He stared at it for a while, not speaking.

"Wade, look at the book, the binding, the cover, have you ever seen a book like this?"

"I need to think," he said, and walked toward the barn, carrying the book with him.

"Wade," she called after him. "You asked me to trust you, and I did. Now it's your turn to trust me."

He didn't look back but continued meandering toward the barn.

Gabrielle could not sleep. She tossed and turned, disturbing Wanda. Unable to lie still, she surrendered, rose, dressed in the dark, grabbed two buckets, and headed for the creek for water. The full moon provided light as she followed the familiar path. Returning, she dumped them in the rain barrel next to the garden and headed back to the creek for more. Though rain would fill the barrel, she needed the action. Stay occupied or surrender to yet another crying jag. After several trips, her arms shook from the exertion. Depositing the last two buckets on the table in the cabin, Gabrielle headed for the garden. Though too dark to pull weeds, she picked up the hoe. Her tired arms sent ignored complaints as she vented her pain and frustration.

"You aren't married."

Shocked, she turned to see Wade and asked, "What?"

"You aren't married."

"But Wade, I explained to you, I am. Kyle is still living in the twenty-first century."

"Is he alive in 1848?"

"No, he hasn't been born yet."

"So in 1848, right now, he is not alive."

"But he is alive in…"

"Are you alive right now in his time?"

"No, I'm sure they think I'm dead, but I'm alive here."

"What year is it?"

"Wade…"

"What year is it?"

"1848," she said, exasperated.

"Okay, will you still be alive in 150 years?"

"No. What are you getting at?"

"Gabrielle, Kyle is not yet born. He is *not* living. By the time he is alive, *you* will be dead." He let that sink in for a moment. "Your wedding vows said as long as you both shall live, correct?"

"Yes."

"Will you ever *both* live at the same time again?"

"No."

"Gabrielle, you can't be married to someone who isn't even born!" In his determination, he shouted the words.

Gabrielle stood still, not saying a word, digesting Wade's words. The world spun. She couldn't breathe. Then the spinning stopped—on Wade. It all made perfect sense! Seeing his expectant face, waiting for her comprehension, brought light to her again.

Wade took her hands in his and said, "I love you, Gabrielle. Marry me."

With a silent prayer of thanks and eyes welled with tears, she said, "Yes."

His arms encircled her as he lifted her and whirled around. When he stopped, he ran his hand through her still loose hair, pulled her to him, and kissed her tenderly. Holding her as though he would never let her go, they watched the sun peak over the mountains.

The children awoke to the aroma of breakfast cooking. Eggs with veggies, bacon, potatoes, pancakes with butter covered with mashed blackberries, and fresh milk.

"Wow! This looks amazing, what's the occasion?" Beth asked when she saw the feast, which differed from their usual quick breakfast of cornbread and milk or oatmeal and milk with a bit of fruit.

Eyes questioned Wade, who looked like he might burst. Taking Gabrielle's hand, he said, "We are going to be married."

Bouncing and hugs accompanied a very joyful noise.

"Does this mean we can call you mama?" Catherine asked.

"Absolutely." Gabrielle thrilled in the hug which came with her reply.

"When are we getting married?" Beth inquired.

Wade and Gabrielle looked at each other.

"While we could go back to town today, I don't think either of us has had any sleep. How about Sunday?" Wade asked Gabrielle.

"Sunday will be perfect."

As they entered the church on Sunday, the whole family looked ready to burst. Gabrielle led the children to their bench, but Wade held back, speaking in hushed tones with Pastor Harris.

Rose and Clement, already seated, beamed as Clement held Lucas. Though Gabrielle ached to break the news, Pastor Harris walked to the front of the church, so she took her seat.

At the close of service, the congregation expected Pastor to invite everyone to attend the Christmas pageant next month, but instead, he said, "This is a very special Sunday. We have reason to rejoice. Mr. Wade Mitchell and Mrs. Gabrielle Fallon would be pleased if everyone would stay to celebrate with them as they exchange vows, becoming husband and wife."

Pastor Harris motioned them forward as cheers erupted from the gathered friends and neighbors. Tears of joy glistened in Rose's eyes as she looked at Gabrielle.

Walking out of the church after the brief ceremony, Gabrielle felt her life had begun again.

Upon arriving home, David announced that he and Wanda would spend their first night in their new cabin. He and Wade had built a rope bed on which they had placed the straw-stuffed mattress Gabrielle and Wanda had made. In anticipation of the move, the quilts and other handmade items had also been moved to the new cabin.

Though Wanda seemed excited, when they were alone, Gabrielle asked if she was ready to live as David's wife.

With a hug, Wanda smiled. "Yes. I can't thank you enough for all you've done for me, for us, but it is time. The Mitchell family is starting fresh today, and so are the

Farnsworths. I'm excited to move into our cabin and begin our lives together, and I look forward to being alone with my husband." At the look of concern on Gabrielle's face, Wanda continued, "I know you worry because of my age, but I will be okay. Please be happy for me."

"Oh Wanda, I am happy for you! Despite some very rough beginnings, you have matured into an amazing young woman. I am so very proud of you. I look upon you as a daughter, so remember, if you ever need anything, I'm here."

After giving each of the children a hug, Wanda joined David outside to walk to their very own cabin. The Mitchells watched them walk away.

"We're going to miss having them here."

"Yes, we will."

As Gabrielle lay in her husband's arms that night, she realized God truly did work in mysterious ways. For years, she had prayed to love and respect her husband as He called her to. He had answered her prayers. She not only respected her husband, she loved him completely.

Epilogue

Five Years Later

Gabrielle watched in wonder as her children played a noisy game of tag in front of the cabin. Despite her losses, God blessed her. Her hand cradled her swollen belly and the babe within. A peaceful smile touched her lips.

Though still periodically overwhelmed by a rushing wave of grief at the thought of Francis, Nicholas, and Alyson, she had found peace. Kyle raising them without her sent prickles up her spine, but she trusted God to care for them, protect them, and love them, even more than she could. Who better to watch over her children?

Her faith had grown since landing here. *It was either that or lose my mind.* The belief this had all been designed by her Heavenly Father came some time ago, but after last night's family devotions, she gave thanks for unequaled blessings.

They were reading the book of Job. While in the past, or was it future, she had read and studied Job, but application had never been impressed on her quite this strongly before. After all his trials, God blessed Job with twice what he had before. In His abundance, she had been blessed more than twice.

She and Wade looked upon Wanda and David as their own. They saw them frequently, through assisting in work and visiting in love. The Farnsworth children, three-year-old Coleman and baby Garland, called them Grandma and

Grandpa. David made a fine farmer and a loving husband and father. Wanda, despite her less than ideal beginnings, grew into a gracious and generous woman. One attribute she retained from her early years with Volstead, all agreed they had never seen a harder working woman, especially in one so young. Not only did she keep a spotless home and family, serving delicious meals from her laden pantry, but she was also enterprising, adding to the family finances through sales of eggs, produce, quilts, and anything else she could invent. Her latest venture took advantage of her artistic talent. She made drawings of families which David framed. Some of them graced the walls of the families' homes; others were sent as gifts to loved ones in the East.

Wade's four children were Gabrielle's four children. They were so much a part of her heart, it was hard to believe she hadn't given birth to them.

Beth, now thirteen, was growing to be a beautiful and graceful young lady. Her passion for everything domestic was only exceeded by her love of learning. As soon as she turned sixteen, she planned to get her teaching certificate and begin teaching school until Mr. Right came along. Always responsible, she hoped to save much of her earnings to assist in starting her home with Mr. Right.

Catherine's sweet disposition endeared her to everyone. At eleven, her giving heart wanted to fix every injured bird, farm animal, and sick person. While she spoke of becoming a nurse, Gabrielle wondered if there was a medical school in this time that would accept a woman. Only time would tell.

Daria, sweet Daria. She held a special place in Gabrielle's heart. Though Gabrielle never showed favoritism.

At nine, fragments of Daria's reluctance with strangers were still visible, though courtesy prompted her always to be open and welcoming. It was heartening to see the special relationship she had developed with Wanda, who had more than made up for past wrongs. Quiet and studious, Daria was always helpful and loved to mother the little ones.

Anna was rambunctious. She had more energy than all the children combined. Despite this, she was disciplined. The little three-year-old girl who never tired of watering the garden that first summer, was still there at eight. Continually beginning some new project, she never failed to see them through to the end. Always happy, she was a bit of a prankster and loved to laugh.

Travis, now believed to be about nine, thrived under the care and love of his new family. Gabrielle had taught him all the signs she could remember while awaiting a book on sign language. They had considered creating signs but concluded this could cause problems. They hoped to give Travis all the advantages possible. The entire family was now well-versed in sign language, and Travis was a normal, healthy boy. He loved Wade to distraction and followed him like a puppy. Many of the children at the school also learned sign, as had the teacher, allowing Travis's acceptance as any other child.

Journey, at six, was destined to become a farmer. Despite his tender age, he could tell you almost anything about farming. But, like his father, he didn't waste words, speaking only when spoken to or when he felt he could contribute. Though smart, he had a hard time understanding why he needed to "waste" his time in school when he could learn farming instead. An exhaustive explanation by

Wade convinced the boy to the point he now took his schooling as seriously as he did helping his father.

Samuel Nicholas Mitchell arrived exactly a year after their marriage. At four, he was the delight of all the Mitchells. He radiated the happiness that surrounded him. The spitting image of his father, the similarity ended there. While Wade was a quiet man, Samuel talked constantly and possessed enough energy for several children. Thankfully, every word he spoke was positive. He never had a negative thing to say.

Mary Alyson Mitchell came two years later. Her older brother must have gotten all the words; like her father, Mary was a quiet child. From her first spoken words, she spoke perfectly, never baby-babble. Gabrielle could hear her whispering a word until she got it correct. Then, and only then, did she speak it aloud. A perfectionist in the making.

The baby she carried was due any moment. She had purposely saved Francis as a middle name for another child, since it could easily be used for either a boy or a girl, without repercussions. If a boy, his name would be Joseph Francis, and if a girl, her name would be Abigail Francis.

Soon to be nine children! Wanda and David made eleven. Add to that a loving and tender husband and two grandchildren. How could she possibly ask for more? Her only regret was the pain and hurt her children in the future must have felt at her disappearance and never finding her body. She couldn't help but wonder if Kyle had convinced the children she had abandoned them. If only she could somehow let them know.

Soon after Mary's arrival, Wade and David built another addition on the cabin. This time they added to the back of the cabin, behind the children's room. This room was larger, to allow a door directly into it from the main room. Gabrielle hoped eventually to include a bathroom in the extra space. Additionally, they added a door directly into the second bedroom. Now with a three-bedroom cabin, the boys had a room, the girls had a room, and the parents had a room. The extra rooms also allowed them to regulate the temperature of the cabin in the winter. If it got too warm, they opened a bedroom door. Still too warm? Open another door.

On Sunday after church, while she and Rose watched the children play, Gabrielle voiced her struggle regarding her three oldest children.

"Too bad there's no telephone." Rose loved the idea of the future device. "Isn't there some way you could get a message to them? You told me of their century's fascination with antiques; maybe you could leave a note for them."

"I could try, but the odds of them receiving it would be minute. Too bad I can't write them a letter." Her sigh held a note of depression.

Thoughts of decades-old lost letters delivered by the post office ran through her mind. Then the "To be delivered on" notations on many advertisements came to mind.

"Rose, that's it!"

"What?"

"Don't you see? I can write them a letter."

"But, Gabrielle, there isn't a way to get the letter through time."

"No, but the letter can wait for them. I realize there's no way I can be sure they will receive it, but it's possible."

Gabrielle worked the plan through in her mind.

"I'll write two of the same letter. One to be mailed with a "deliver on" date. The other I will pass down through my family with instructions to deliver it the day after I fell into the whirlpool. Surely one of the letters will arrive."

"Gabrielle, that's brilliant!" Then after consideration, she asked, "But how will they know it's genuine? How will they know you didn't write it that day?"

Gabrielle thought for a while before saying, "They have ways to test for age, the type of paper, the ink, and so on. Plus, on the family copy, I'll leave a place for each of my descendants to list their information so it can be traced back. Lastly, if my descendant is DNA tested against the children, it will prove they are related."

"DNA?"

"It's what makes up who we are and is extremely tiny. In the late twentieth century, they will learn to isolate DNA and use it to determine if a sample of blood, skin, or such belongs to a certain person. They will also be able to tell if people are related and how closely. Oooo, I can enclose a lock of my hair! Since I would have been reported missing, law enforcement would be in on it so they would be sure to test the hair and determine it was mine."

"Wow! I never cease to be amazed by the future."

"Too bad cameras aren't yet available, I could enclose a photograph."

During previous chats, Gabrielle had told Rose about this remarkable picture-maker.

"You can." With Gabrielle's quizzical look, Rose continued, "Wanda is a wonderful artist. She can draw whatever you would like."

"Rose, you are a genius!"

That evening, Gabrielle described her plan to Wade. His concern was also believability. "We need to assure there is enough evidence to corroborate the letter. I will add carvings to furniture to substantiate your claim. Then we will impress upon our children, grandchildren, and so on, the importance of keeping our family history."

At her questioning look, Wade said, "For instance, I can carve our names into certain furniture pieces. What was your maiden name, I could include it."

"James. Gabrielle Ester James Fallon Mitchell. Brilliant! My husband is brilliant!"

That night, Gabrielle felt the familiar odd feeling that had preceded the beginning of contractions with each of her pregnancies. Wade woke to Gabrielle's movements as she put final touches on preparations for the birth.

"Is it time?" At her nod, he said, "I'll run over and ask David to fetch Mrs. Butler." In response to her concerned look, he assured her. "Don't worry; I'll hurry. I shouldn't be gone more than twenty minutes."

"Please don't hurry too much. It's still dark."

With a smile, a kiss, and a reassuring hug, Wade finished dressing and dashed outside.

At 11:26 A.M. Abigail Francis Mitchell arrived safe and sound.

During Gabrielle's recovery, Wade made arrangements for Wanda to draw the family. He requested not just one, but four copies. One to be mailed, one to be hand-delivered by their descendant, one to place in the church history, and one for their cabin wall. He wanted each to be slightly different, and each would show Abigail's growth.

On his first trip to town after Abigail's birth, Wade picked up supplies for Gabrielle's letters: paper, ink, pen, and wax for sealing.

Around caring for the children and chores, Gabrielle worked on the letter to her children. It felt good to express her love to them. She knew in her heart, with every fiber of her being that they would receive the letter. Just as she suddenly, inexplicably knew when she arrived that it truly was 1847, she knew her children would receive her letter.

My dear children:
Frances, Nicholas, and Alyson...

Gabrielle continued to revise her letter for weeks. It had to be perfect. It must speak of her love for them, how much she missed them, and how she would always be their mother, even if she couldn't be with them. It must tell of the accident and the impossible situation in which she found herself in 1847. It must tell of her trials with Volstead and saving Daria and herself from him. It must tell of her wonderful friends, the Browns. Then, of course, it must tell of Wade and his children. Of Wanda and David. Of Travis. Of their half sisters and brother.

And of course, it must urge them to be very good for their daddy, and when he at last finds someone else to love, to be good, loving, and welcoming. All of this must be told in a gentle manner, understandable by young children.

Writing, rewriting, and revising again seemed cathartic for Gabrielle. The more she perfected the letter, the calmer she felt. For the first time since arriving in 1847, she not only accepted the situation but the fact that she would never see her children again. While it wasn't okay, it simply was. After talking to Wade, she realized the letter was freeing her from the worry of her children never knowing what happened.

Four months after Abigail's birth, Gabrielle tucked a sealed letter and drawing of the Mitchell family addressed to her children into the family Bible. With it was a letter of explanation, including instructions for delivery. In case the two letters were separated, she included the date to be delivered on the outside of the letter. Next, she mailed another copy of the letter and drawing, with a note above the address stating the date to deliver. And lastly, Wade included a copy of the letter and drawing, displayed behind glass, in the dressing table he was making for Gabrielle.

She began one more project to be passed down through the generations to her children—a journal. She wrote of the picnic, followed by her fall into the whirlpool, and all the events since. Periodically, she had Wanda draw pictures of the family in it. Then, with time, she included photographs. She continued to keep this journal throughout her life, until her death in 1907.

Gabrielle's children did receive the letter. Though the mailed letter never showed, the family copy was delivered the day after the fateful picnic by Gabrielle's great-great-great grandson Wade Nicolas Mitchell. With it, he delivered a family tree, photos, the journal, and Gabrielle's wedding ring from her marriage to Kyle.

It occurred to Gabrielle after writing the letter that she could have it delivered the day before the picnic to prevent her from falling into the whirlpool, but as much as she needed her first three children, she thought of Wade, his four children, Daria, and Wanda and knew they needed her more. God in His infinite wisdom had known this. Just as she knew that God, with his immeasurable love, would care for and comfort Francis, Nicholas, and Alyson.

Author's note:

Calapooia (originally spelled Calapooya), the setting for this story is based on the original name of the town of Brownsville, Oregon. While the story and characters are completely fictional, I have borrowed a few actual historical names.

Just before arriving in Calapooia, Gabrielle saw Kirk's Ferry. This ferry actually existed and was run by early settler, Alexander Kirk. His original expanded cabin can still be seen inside Kirks Ferry Trading Post, in Brownsville.

For Mr. Brown, I have taken liberties with everything but the surname. The first store in Brownsville was opened by Hugh Brown, who settled there in 1846. Mr. Brown reportedly arrived with his nephew, James Blakely. Rose is purely a figment of my imagination, as is every other detail surrounding Clement Brown and his store.

The Ralston's name I have borrowed from founding settlers of nearby Lebanon, Oregon, Jeremiah and Jemima Ralston, whose fifth child, Charles, was born at the Platt on the wagon train in 1847. This, once again, is where history ends and my imagination began. As far as I know, Mrs. Ralston did not serve as a wet nurse to any child other than her own.

It has been my intention to honor these towns and people through the use of these historical names.

I hope you have enjoyed reading Gabrielle's story. Please take a moment and leave a review on Amazon, Goodreads, or your favorite review site. Reviews mean a lot to authors. I do read them and do my best to apply suggestions.

Continue reading the *Out of Time Series* to learn how other women handle finding themselves *Out of Time*.

Follow my author page on Facebook at:
https://www.facebook.com/groups/834896499939990/?ref=bookmarks

Follow my web page at:

http://www.rardledford.homesteadcloud.com/

Other books in the *Out of Time Series*:

Doggedly independent, adventurous, and determined, Sage thrives on "experiences." Consequently, this drug/alcohol counselor and part-time waitress leads a nomadic life, continually adding to her life's list of accomplishments, adventures, and knowledge. She finds herself in the ultimate adventure.

Young, spoiled, and immature, this party-girl's lifestyle is all about her. Self-centered, yet without self-esteem, she believes her party life will lead to happiness. Lost, confused, angry, and alone in this new world, can Emily survive?

www.ingramcontent.com/pod-product-compliance
Lightning Source LLC
Chambersburg PA
CBHW061943170626
46813CB00006B/2517